# 'Where's My Money?'

MIKE MANSON

tangent
books

*For Maggie with love.*

Published 2008 by Tangent Books. Reprinted 2016.
Unit 5.16, Paintworks, Bristol BS4 3EH. Tel: 0117 972 0645
www.tangentbooks.co.uk  email: richard@tangentbooks.co.uk

ISBN: 978-1-906477-03-5

Copyright: Mike Manson 2008

First published in Great Britain in 2008 by Tangent Books. Tangent Books is an imprint of Naked
Guides Ltd.

Cover illustration: Øivind Hovland www.oivindhovland.co.uk
Typeset by: Gillian Marles www.thisisjust.co.uk
Publisher: Richard Jones

Mike Manson has asserted his moral right under the Copyright, Designs and Patents Act of 1988 to
be identified as the author of this work.

*"I'd always start a job with a feeling that I'd quit or be fired, and this gave me a relaxed manner that was mistaken for intelligence or some secret power."*
Charles Bukowski


*"I don't like the suits and ties*
*They don't seem to harmonise"*
Blind Willie Johnson


*'Thou rewardest everyman according to his work'*
Psalm 62

## ~ AUTHOR'S NOTE ~

This is a work of fiction. I am required to say this as I signed the Official Secrets Act when I started my employment with the Ministry of Work (see page 23). All the characters are imaginary.

So if you think you recognise yourself, you are mistaken. Even you, Ken.

Max Redcliffe

# ~ GLOSSARY ~

| | |
|---|---|
| ARF1: | Training course run by the Ministry of Work. (Reputed to be an acronym for Attitude Re-Focusing: Part One.). |
| Bridewell: | Central Bristol Police Station. |
| Cabbage Patch: | Room in the Ministry of Work where out-of-date documents are kept. |
| Giro: | Cheque issued by the Ministry of Work that can be cashed at a Post Office. |
| Goldfish Bowl: | Interview room. |
| Gulag: | Government Skill Centre: where the hardcore unemployed are sent to undertake forced labour. |
| DHSS: | Department of Health and Social Security. |
| Dole: | Hard earned tax-payers money that is given to freeloaders. |
| Hounds of Hell: | Fraud Squad. |
| JAR: | Job Appraisal Review. |
| Keynsham: | A small town of near mythical status 8 miles South East of Bristol |
| MoW: | Ministry of Work. |
| MoW 459: | Blank sheet of paper. |
| NERD: | National Employment Register Database. |
| NFA: | No Fixed Abode (No Fucking Allowance). |
| PI: | Personal Issue. |
| UB40: | Buff coloured ID card presented at the dole office when making a claim for Unemployment Benefit. |
| Union Street: | Location of the dole office. In local parlance 'Going down Union Street' is a euphemism for 'signing on.' |

'E*re, I knows you.'*

*A piece of card with a rectangular torn off corner; the stain of a wine glass on a bedside table; the smell of cleaning fluid – memories are sparked by the strangest things. As I walked up the steps to the restaurant it was a beggar that pulled me back to half-forgotten times.*

*Even in the dim light he had recognised me. I certainly remembered him. His name flashed back to me: Grolier – Otto Grolier.*

*I found myself saying, 'How you doing mate?' I don't know why, but I was pleased to see him.*

*'I ain't seen you for a while.' The old man said this as if he was talking about only yesterday. I didn't think he'd have a jot of memory left in his frazzled brain.*

*'It must be twenty five years.'*

*'Twenty five years,' he said in wonder. 'Bleedin 'ell!'*

*He reached behind where he was sitting and produced a brown screw-top bottle. I noticed the ugly raised scars on his knuckles. 'Have a taste,' he said. I could see his breath in the night air.*

*I accepted the bottle and took a hefty swig of the thick cream coloured liquid. Grace looked on, horrified.*

*'God, that's powerful stuff,' I said, sucking in my breath, desperately trying to identify the ingredients. 'What is it?'*

*'B.B. we calls it – a mate, he knocks it up – it has the desired effect!'*

*'I bet it does.'*

*Grace was staring at me, wanting to move on. I guessed she wouldn't appreciate a formal introduction.*

*'Any of the others still around?' I asked. Grolier looked at me blankly as he struggled to think who the 'others' were.*

*'Dunno' he said. 'The cold winters, they gets you in the end.'*

'Let me give you something for the drink.' I fumbled in my pocket and pulled out the first bit of cash that came to hand. It was a twenty-pound note.

'I couldn't take that from you.'

'No, you must. I want you to have it.'

'No, my friend, I couldn't. It wouldn't be right.'

'You've got to, for old time's sake.'

Grolier looked at me. I could see that he didn't want to take a handout from me. But then again... but then again... twenty quid. That would take the chill out of the winter night.

'Well, okay then. But only for old time's sake.'

I passed him the note. I felt I owed him a lot more. 'You take care, mate.'

'And you.' The old man lifted his bottle in salute, and drank. 'To them good old days.'

'Cheers.' I replied, thinking that the old days weren't particularly good.

For a few seconds the shared experience of past times had created a bond. But now it was gone. We had nothing more to say to each other.

Grace and I continued up the steps without speaking. But as soon as we were through the entrance and into the glow of the foyer she turned to me and demanded, 'Dad, who was that?'

'I knew him a long time ago. I'll tell you about it in a moment. First, I need to wash out my mouth.'

As I walked to the loo I thought about Grolier and the past. I'm not particularly proud of that time. Let's just say it was an experience, a rite of passage, the sort of thing we all need to go through in our lives, sometime or other. So the pages that follow are about how I became acquainted with that old man. Some might even say it's about me growing up. Myself, I'm not so sure. And the weird thing is, I'm certain Grolier still has no recollection of kicking the shit out of me.

## ~ ONE ~

Ashley Hill was the first person I'd met when I started at Union Street. He had been waiting for me by the entrance door. He wasn't as I'd imagined him.

'Call me Ash,' he said, offering me his hand. He had a surprisingly vice-like grip. 'You're in C Section. For the next few weeks you have the pleasure of being under my tutelage.' He said this with a tight smile that could have been interpreted as a smirk.

Ash had an angular face with an ill-defined goatee beard that had merged into his three-day stubble. His shoulder length hair was thick dusty brown; he was wearing a battered blue corduroy jacket over a tatty check lumberjack shirt. I'd been expecting a dull bureaucrat but Ash looked more like a hippie. I felt a little overdressed standing next to him.

'Before we do anything else I need to get a cup of tea. Doris doesn't open the canteen until 9.30 so we'll go across the road to the café.'

Ash led the way out of the building and along the street to the Concorde Café. I noticed he moved with a slight limp – the sole of one of his desert boots was loose.

'First lesson: never leave the building by yourself.'

I didn't like the sound of this. 'Why?'

Ash turned and looked at me.

'You are now enemy number one.' He said this in a matter-of-fact sort of way. No drama about it; that's just the way it was.

'Me?'

'Yep. You. Anybody who walks out of this building is fair game. It's just a matter of time; luck of the draw, Max. It's far better than it was though. In the days before they put up the screens, claimants would swarm over the counter like it was the Battle of the Somme.'

'But I thought we were helping these people.'

'You try telling them that! They hate you. Look, there's nothing worse

13

than a do-gooder. And you're not even that. Don't get any fancy ideas about helping anybody. Just turn up in the morning, do the job and go home.'

'But Baxter said...'

'Baxter! Ignore Baxter, he's totally spaced; he's on another planet.'

'Come on, some of my best friends are claimants – they're not going to start hating me because I've got a temporary job at the dole office.'

'Forget 'em, pal.'

'What! I was signing-on last week, things aren't going to change that quickly.' I couldn't drop Boz and Ken. We went back a long way; we'd shared a squat together and eaten nothing but Essex vegetable stew for three months. Get through stuff like that and you come out friends forever.

'Well, maybe not that quickly', Ash conceded, 'but I think you'll be surprised how swiftly attitudes can change. No doubt about it, this is war. And by the way, fraternising with claimants is a disciplinary offence.'

The Concorde Cafe was directly opposite the Bridewell, Bristol's main police station. I'd once had a cup of tea at the Concorde after I'd signed on. The place felt like an extension of the dole office: same customers, same queues.

'Well at least the cop shop's handy,' I said.

'Unfortunately the Bridewell Boys don't exactly use their Rapid Response Force when there's trouble. They like to arrive ten minutes after the action has finished. They tiptoe in like a bunch of prima donnas and make their arrests – and even then, they invariably grab the wrong guy.' Ash shook his head in disbelief but then appeared to change his mind. 'The fuzz might be a useless bunch of tossers,' he continued, 'but it is advisable to keep on the right side of them. You never know when you might need to call in a favour.'

I wasn't sure what he meant by this, but nevertheless nodded wisely in agreement.

'Second lesson,' said Ash pointing at three guys in the queue ahead, 'don't worry about them, they're the anarchists.'

I thought I'd misheard what he'd said. 'What do you mean?'

'Believe it or not, they work for the Ministry.'

Hunched in their greasy black coats they were a dispiriting sight.

'Those guys work for the Ministry? You're joking!'

'Nope.'

'Did you say anarchist? Anarchist Civil Servant – isn't that a contradiction in terms?'

Ash smiled. 'You'd think so, wouldn't you. Extreme individualism doesn't sit comfortably with this job. That one,' Ash pointed at a guy whose lankiness was accentuated by his ankle length army-surplus great coat, 'he's Che. Che's real name is Jeremy – he's called Che because he comes from CHEltenham.

Basically, they're just over-privileged troublemakers. They all went to public school, apart from Bolton Bob, the one wearing the Citizen Smith beret. He's their token working class hero. Oh, and there's The Other One. I don't know his name. He drinks his Nescafe very black, very strong, no sugar. He's a bit unpredictable.

Well, they keep themselves to themselves. At least they're interesting, they add a pleasing edge to the proceeding.'

I made a mental note to get to know the anarchists better. You never know when a bit of back-up from wacko revolutionaries might come in handy.

The woman behind the counter squirted hot water into a large chipped enamel teapot, shook it about, and poured a tannin rich tea liquid into a polystyrene cup. I remembered why I'd never made a return visit to the Concorde Café.

We sat at a table. The place stank of dishcloths and cigarettes. 'Now, my role during your first couple of weeks is to show you the ropes, act as a kind of mentor. Which is lucky for you...' Ash's voice stumbled and trailed away at this point. I was aware that he was staring at my tie – 'but ... well, let's just see how it goes.'

Ash opened his tin, pulled out a Rizla and started rolling. For a few seconds he said nothing – I couldn't tell whether he was thinking deeply about what he was going to tell me next or merely giving his full attention to the construction of a flaccid stoogie. At last he looked up and spoke.

He handed me his tin. 'Help yourself.'

'Not my brand.' I looked at Ash to check if he understood. The flicker of a glance told me he did. At least there's one freak in the dole office.

'So what do you want to know?' Ash asked.

What I really wanted to know was where in this organisation did Astral park her sweet butt. But I was being a bit forward – I'd wait a while before I came round to the important stuff.

'I dunno....what's the job involve? What do I have to do?'

'Haven't you been told why you've been recruited?'

'You're the first person I've spoken to.'

'Don't worry about the job, Max. Trained chimps could do this work.'

'Uh?' I was trying to hide my surprise.

'It's all about who's messing about with who. Office politics is what you need to wise up about. So let's start at the top. The manager is Mr Eric Blunt.'

'I've heard that he's a really nice guy.'

Ash stiffened as if a surge of electricity had shot through him. I felt that I'd said something wrong.

'Nice guy! Max, you've been listening to Baxter again. He's what's called a career civil servant. Mr Blunt sucks up and pisses down.'

'What do you mean?' I said, laughing.

Ash frowned. 'He sucks up to the mandarins and pisses down on the likes of you and me. Nice guy! He's a bastard! And do you know why he joined the Department of Work? To help people. Far-fucking-out. To help people!'

I really couldn't work Ash out. I was surprised at his candour. Was he supposed to be saying this stuff? Was this part of some terrifying initiation ceremony?

Ash continued. 'Don't make me laugh. Claimants! He hates them. He's on a one-man crusade to stamp out unemployment. His aim is to make these poor sods so humiliated that they don't dare darken the doorstep of the dole office.'

As Ash was speaking he pulled his left foot up onto his right knee and in a half lotus position inspected the sole of his shoe.

'Mr Blunt lives for his work. Boring. Boring. Boring. He's so twisted he does nothing else – he's wedded to it. 'Arbeit Macht Frei' is his motto. Do you know what that means? German – work makes us free. Don't get me wrong, I don't want to cast aspersions or anything, but those words were above the entrance to Auschwitz.'

'Heavy!'

'Thankfully, he's a one off. Well, almost.'

Ash turned to look at the clock behind the counter.

'When do we need to get back?' I asked. The strip-lighting was beginning to make my head ache.

'We've got plenty of time.' Ash absent-mindedly flicked his rollie and rubbed the fag-ash into his jeans. 'The one you've really got to watch is, Kastrina Klebb – Mr Blunt's bastard daughter. Well not literally, but you get my drift. Even the claimants have a nickname for her – says it all really.

I recognised who he was describing, though I didn't like to say what I'd heard people shout at her.

'I think I know who you're talking about.'

'Did Baxter tell you about her as well?'

'No, I've seen her in action on the counter when I was signing on.'

'Have you heard what they call her?'

'No, I don't think I have.' I thought discretion would be the best approach at this stage.

'The Ball Breaker.' Ash smiled. 'Kastrina the Ball Breaker. I couldn't have put it better myself.'

'Now you mention it, I think I did hear somebody bellow something like that at her,' I admitted hesitantly.

Ash continued. 'She does tend to stir things up a bit. 'Hurt to help' is her motto. Like cruel to be kind, but not as benevolent. Well, you won't get to meet Kastrina for a couple of weeks as she's away with the Hounds of Hell who are doing a sweep in Plymouth.'

I was losing the plot. 'And the Hounds of Hell are?'

'I should explain. The Hounds of Hell are the fraud squad – Chris Bart and Steve Feltch.' Ash drew hard on his ciggie and blew out a thin stream of smoke. 'Total wankers. Although they like to pretend they're the Special Branch, they've not got the spunk for a proper police job. They're happy to pose in the uniform, though. You can't miss them. In their overlarge sleuth macs they stand out a mile; they're like cartoon gumshoes hanging around in the doorways of vacant shops. The way they dress I'm surprised they catch anybody. Be warned though, they take their work far too seriously. They treat benefit fraudsters like mass murderers. It's unhealthy; they seem to have lost their perspective. Okay, we all agree fraud ain't too clever, but it's not like poisoning a child or beating up an old lady. Let's just say they wouldn't have had any problem getting a job during the Spanish Inquisition. Comprendez? Be careful, Max. Never tell them anything confidential about yourself – if you do they'll be sniffing round your jacksy before you can shout Sam Spade. Don't trust them an inch.

And then there's Justine. She's the one you're covering for. She's on a sicky at the moment. What can I say about Justine? Well, er...' I felt Ash was choosing his words carefully, 'she's a ... she's a ... she an interesting character. She comes and goes.'

'Meaning?'

'That sometimes she just disappears. You'll see. She always returns.'

'Well I look forward to meeting her. Anything else I should know?'

'I've saved the best bit till last...' Ash sat back and laughed '...The funniest thing of all is that Kastrina is our section supervisor. The ball breaker, she's our boss.'

'Is that funny?'

'Of course it is. It's bleeding hilarious.' He said this in a manner that was bordering on hysteria.

Ash shook his head in disbelief and took another drink of tea. He leant forward and in a quiet voice said, 'Look, Max. You don't have to join if you don't want to. You can walk out of here right now. Call it quits. I'll say nothing.'

'You're having me on, right?' I couldn't suss Ash out. Why was he working in the dole office if he thought it so loathsome?

'You haven't been listening, have you?'

I'd been listening alright, I just didn't believe what I heard. Surely the mentor's role is to gently ease the new recruit into the job – not scare the shit out of him.

'But this is the civil service,' I protested.

'What do you know about the civil service,' he sneered. 'I just want you to be aware of the consequences of what you are about to do. I'm telling you the people who work here are weird. All of them – weird. Before you realise what's happening the blood has been drained out of you. For all I know Mr Blunt and Baxter were once regular guys when they first started here. Well, maybe not.'

To leave now did sound like a good idea. But I had a problem. I didn't think that I was in a position NOT to work for the dole office.

Ash continued: 'Look, what I'm saying is – be careful. Working here can do your head in. I don't mean to freak you out, but this is a fucking evil place.'

'But I can't go back and sign-on,' I said. 'This is my first day at work. If I quit now I'm disqualified from receiving benefit for the next six weeks. You know that.'

Ash shrugged his shoulders. 'Well, that's your choice.'

'Its not my choice. There's no alternative. I can't live on fresh air for six weeks. I'm stuffed.'

'I suppose you are.' Ash sighed. 'See, you're being sucked in already and you haven't even started.'

I didn't know what to say. I looked at Ash, speechless.

'Don't worry Max, you've got me to look after you. It could have been far worse, you could have had Kastrina as your mentor.'

Ash knocked back the dregs of tea and pushed the nub of his rollie into the side of his cup. He stood up. 'Okay, let's split. Time to meet the circus.'

All the time we'd sat in the café I'd been waiting for Ash to say 'only kidding.' But he never did.

As we crossed the road on our way back to the dole office I looked at my watch. I'd waited half an hour. Time for the big question. 'Where does Astral work?'

'Ah, Astral, how do you know her?'

'I don't. I've just seen her about.'

'Everybody loves Astral' said Ash wistfully. 'She's a cute chick. But she knows what she's doing. Don't underestimate her, she's in control. Which brings me nicely to lesson number three.'

Ash appeared to be ignoring my question. I braced myself for the next ogre to be wheeled on.

'Watch out for Lee' – there, I told you – 'sometimes he gets a little over-protective. He's in our section as well. I was saving him for later. But, well, Astral and Lee. Lee's part of the package.'

'Is Lee Astral's boyfriend?'

'Technically not, but he can behave irrationally about her. He's a bit of a tosser. He doesn't like anybody touching her. Thinking about it, he doesn't really like anybody looking at her. He can be very jealous; it's a kind of King Kong/Fay Wray relationship – you know, the monster obsessed by the pretty girl, an arrangement that's sure to end in disaster. He's young, he says stupid things to wind people up. Tell him to piss off if he gets on your nerves.' Ash laughed. 'Apart from that' he added as an after-thought, 'he's a nice enough kiddie.'

We were on the steps of the Dole office building; Ash looked down at his feet. 'I need some new footwear. What do you reckon – Doc Martens or Monkey Boots?'

'Monkey Boots, no contest. Dangerous things to wear Doc Martens.

'Good point Max. People can jump to the wrong conclusions about Doc Martens. Anyway, coming back to your question, Astral's in our section – you'll be sitting opposite her.'

## ~ TWO ~

But I'm rushing ahead. Before we go any further I should introduce myself. My name is Max Redcliffe. At the dole office they called me M. Redcliffe 45C. I didn't like that. Sounded like the army, or prison.

'45C – what's that all about?' I once asked.

The bureaucrat looked at me blankly. 'What?'

'45C. 45C has nothing to do with my name.'

'Those two digits and letter are part of your National Insurance coding.'

If they can change your name that easily, think what else they can do. But that was four, maybe five years ago. I was used to the two digits and a letter bit by now.

I signed-on at 9.30 on a Wednesday. It sort of messed up my time. If I was in Cornwall, or with Boz in London, it meant that I had to be back in town for the middle of the week. And 9.30, that was heavy. I'll tell you one thing; signing-on on Wednesday certainly stopped me from working.

But it wasn't all bad. When you're in the dole queue there's plenty of time to look around. There was something about the girl behind the counter. The first time I saw her I thought, yeah, she's something special. She wasn't what you would call conventionally pretty. Alright, she had a sweet face and big Twiggy eyes – but as I stood in the queue and looked at her through the Perspex there were other things. Well, great boobs, obviously. And I liked it when her long blonde hair fell in front of her face as she looked down searching for my file, and the way she scooped her tresses behind her ears, which stuck out in an endearing way. I also liked – and this sounds weird when I say it – the slight soft sheen of blonde hair on her tanned arms.

Anyway, she was three or four years younger than me; probably about nineteen, I guessed. I thought she was too young to be doing a job like that.

The funny thing was you could sense that people liked being in her queue. Not just because of the way she looked – well, that helped – but the feeling that she was doing her best. Undoubtedly, I was in the best queue. Not like the queue two along which was run by a strutting, snarling bitch everyone called the Ball Breaker.

The Ball Breaker's behaviour just bred aggro. In her queue there was a constant melee of angry people waiting at the counter. 'Stay there'... 'get to the back of queue'... 'come back later'.... 'watch it or I'll stop your benefit' she yelled. And when questioned why, the response was always the same. 'It's the rules'. That was it – 'the rules'. No other explanation was required or offered.

I'd found out my clerk's name – Astral. I'd heard one of her work mates call her that. I fantasised that one-day I'd build up courage and ask Astral to meet me for a drink.

Each week I would try to extend our conversation beyond the usual 'Card Please' – 'Thank you' – 'Have you done any work this week?' – 'Thanks' routine. It was slow progress. Even though I had now been signing-on at Union Street every week for four months she still didn't remember my name. She looked through me as if she was staring through a pane of glass. But then why should she remember me? She probably dealt with hundreds of people a week.

Over the last few weeks I'd noticed the queue had been getting longer. When it came to my turn to hand over my UB40 I remarked to Astral that she seemed busy.

'We're short of staff', she replied in exasperation as she searched for my papers. 'Do you want a job?' she asked without looking at me.

Do you want a job? It wasn't the response I was expecting. She's actually acknowledged me. I'm not just a name on a filing card. I exist. But there was a shrill little voice in the back of my mind crying 'watch out'. Is she testing me? What happens if I say no? And if I do say no, will she stop my benefit? But she couldn't – she's offered me a job. Now my mind was beginning to race ahead – she fancies me and what's more, she's near as damn asked me out.

'Urr...well... yeah,' I found myself replying.

So here I was. She was speaking to me as if I was a normal human being. 'Go to the main entrance round the side of the building and speak to Baxter on reception.' Still no eye contact though – what was so interesting about my claim, for heavensake?

'Can I tell him who sent me? What's your name?' Of course I knew, but I wanted to hear it from her; I wanted to be introduced formally.

'Sorry...' she said as she reached for the next file. And then she looked at me, not through me, but straight into my eyes. The corners of her mouth twitched upwards into a brief, but strained, smile. The sight of those perfect teeth indicated that our relationship had now moved a step forward. For four months I had been waiting for this moment. I grinned back. '...Sorry, but I'm not allowed to give my name to a claimant.'

Claimant! Oh, that hurt.

Baxter was consoling a woman with a sleeping child in a pushchair.

'If your Giro hasn't arrived you need to go to the Social Security and get an emergency payment. It's a twenty minute walk, so I'd go there straight away.'

The woman said nothing and moved off.

Baxter looked at me and sighed. 'Oh dear, I don't think she's going to have any money for the weekend. Anyhow, what can I do for you, Sir?'

Baxter had wiry hair and wore two-tone Eric Morecambe specs. Behind those glasses there was something unsettling about his eyes. Baxter had a bewildered, dilated pupils, shell-shocked, look about him.

'I'm after a job,' I said.

'The Job Centre is round the corner and up the slope on the left. You can't miss it.'

'No, I've been told there's some vacancies here... at the Department of Work.'

'Oh I see. Well yes, I believe there are.' Baxter looked at me over the top of his glasses as if he was checking for something. 'You want to work here, do you?'

This was a difficult question to answer honestly.

'I'm looking for a job.' At least that wasn't too far from the truth.

'Good. Now. Let's see. First, you need to fill out these forms.'

Baxter gave me a wad of buff coloured papers. 'Complete these now, and then I'll take them up to the manager, Mr Blunt.'

Baxter showed me into a small cold room lit by a fluorescent strip light. There was a tiny barred window on one wall and a large mirror on the other.

'I'll leave you to get on with it. Give me a shout when you've finished,' he said as he closed the solid hardwood door.

I sat down at a Formica table. I tried to pull the chair closer to the table but was surprised to find that both of them were clamped to the floor. In another room, far away, I heard someone give a muffled cough – or snigger. So, sitting uncomfortably, I completed a series of forms asking about qualifications, medical history, bank details and previous convictions. I ignored the paper headed Official Secrets Act, assuming that I had been given it by mistake. After twenty minutes I'd written all I could.

To my surprise, as I went to leave, I found the door had jammed. Baxter's desk was only the other side so I banged on it just hard enough to be heard.

'Hang on, hang on,' came Baxter's voice.

'The door's stuck.'

I heard a key turning.

'I locked it so you wouldn't be disturbed. How did you get on?'

'I think you gave me this by mistake.' I handed Baxter the Official Secrets Act questionnaire.

'Oh no, that's not a mistake, that's very important.'

'For a clerical job in the Ministry of Work! What's so secret about that?'

Baxter looked at me with concern.

'You never know. There's information in here people would pay good money to get their hands on.'

I didn't mean to be rude, but I was astounded. 'Like what, for goodness sake?'

'Well, for a start, the Russians are desperate to find out about our benefit system. They've been trying to work out how to do it for years.'

'You're kidding. They don't allow unemployment in the Soviet Union.'

'Exactly – they don't know how to do it.'

Did he really think that anybody, let alone the Soviet Union, was interested in the convoluted workings of British benefits? Details of the British dole system must surely be pretty low on the KGB's shopping list.

'I better warn you,' Baxter continued, 'you have to get permission to travel abroad for your holidays. Eastern Europe is, of course, totally out of bounds. I think Yugoslavia is just about all right, but I wouldn't advise it. Poor little Astral from C Section went to Dubrovnik last summer and had to fight off all sorts of unwelcome advances. Somebody even tried to get into her bedroom. Goodness knows what they were hoping to find.'

Certainly not the Ministry of Work's Instruction Book, I thought.

'Anyway,' continued Baxter, 'just sign the Official Secrets Act and I'll take your papers upstairs to Mr Blunt's office. He's a very nice man. Hopefully he'll be available to see you this afternoon and then you could start on Monday.'

Nice man or not, I was becoming alarmed. Everything was happening a bit too quickly. Okay I wanted a job. I think. But you have to psych yourself up for this sort of thing. I needed a couple of weeks, at least, to adjust my biological clock to a nine-to-five routine.

'Won't he want to take up a reference or something? I asked.

Baxter shook his head and smiled. 'Remember, this is the Ministry of Work – we've already got your details on file. In fact, I don't know why we bother to get you to fill out all this,' he said, waving the forms in his hand. 'It'll take us five minutes to find out your whole life story. And I'm not talking just about work. Our information systems interface with the tax office, the police, immigration, GCHQ, and if we need it, Interpol. Though that does take a bit longer – perhaps a couple of days. I suppose these forms are a way of double-checking your story.

'I've heard the rumours. I never realised this sort of thing really happened.'

'Not many people do. Think about it, 1984 is only nine years away you know.'

I felt I was being sucked into something and I didn't like it. That small but insistent voice in my head warning me to be careful was getting louder. I wanted to leave and never return. But they had my number and knew where I lived.

'I think you'll enjoy working here,' said Baxter. 'It can be very satisfying. I like to think of myself not so much as a clerical officer but more as a friend and counsellor to those less fortunate in their career transition.'

'Hmmm' I mumbled, the epithet most readily coming to mind for Ministry of Work staff being vindictive wankers.

As I turned to leave, Baxter looked around and gesticulated that he wanted to whisper something. I leant towards him.

'Careful what you say over the phone,' he said, tapping his nose.

The man was clearly round the twist.

## ~ THREE ~

'Urr...well...yeah.' One grunt and two little words had changed the course of my life.

I never did get to meet Mr Blunt that Wednesday afternoon. I was disappointed. I had at least expected the opportunity of an interview where I could demonstrate that I didn't have quite the right skills required for this type of work. The following week I received a letter saying I'd been accepted for a temporary job as a Clerical Assistant with the Ministry of Work and that I should report to Mr Ashley Hill the next Monday. There seemed to be no way of getting out of this.

On Monday morning I pulled open the curtains of my bedroom and looked over the rooftops of Redfield stretching eastwards. I'd overcome my initial panic and had come round to the idea that a spot of light work might not be a bad thing. It was the end of the summer, my finances were low and I needed the bread to get back on my feet.

The night before I had checked that I had something suitable to wear. I thought that jeans and a Grateful Dead T-shirt, even if they were clean, were not the sort of gear I should put on for my first day as a civil servant. The voice of my father echoed in my mind, 'you never get a second chance at a first impression,' he wittered. What a clichéd load of bollocks.

But as I rummaged through the boxes that I kept my clothes in I realised my choice of attire was going to be limited. Indeed the only items that were not jeans or T-shirts had been bought for my sister's wedding. At the time I had viewed them as the height of sartorial elegance. Three years later I wasn't so sure.

I put on a greying white poly-cotton shirt and a pair of black high-waisted mega-flares. I'd also found a tin of blue polish for my platform shoes. The platform was only a centimetre – not too showy – probably about right for the civil service. I brushed my hair, and with the edge of a comb carefully drew out a centre parting. Then, to create the desired effect, I messed it up again. The finishing touch was provided by a blue kipper tie adorned with a striking green snowflake motif. I looped the tie into a knot the size of a samosa and stood in front of the mirror to admire myself.

To be honest I wasn't pleased with what I saw. The clothes appeared to be wearing me rather than the other way round. I looked like an ill-fitting Oxfam shop mannequin. The billowing mega-flares were obviously ridiculous. I'd never appreciated how quickly fashions could change. I didn't feel comfortable either. It wasn't like being dressed in jeans and a tee shirt, where your clothes become part of you, like another skin. My tie was too tight and my jacket, I forgot to mention the jacket – it had sharp shoulders, large lapels and was cut, in a sort of regency style – was so constricting that I had to stand in an unnaturally upright manner. If I'd wanted to sit down I'd have to take the jacket off.

I decided when buying clothes in the future I'd stick to the design classics – loons, cheesecloth shirt and a tight little denim waistcoat – the sort of stuff that never goes out of fashion. But it was too late to change now.

By the time I'd left my room it was a few minutes past 8 o'clock. It was a flat grey morning. I was surprised at the number of people on the streets at this early hour. What were these pale and dazed zombies doing? I had never realised so many people hurried to work at such an unearthly time. As I waited at the bus stop I felt uneasy about being pushed so rapidly into a pact with the establishment. I sensed that I was at a crossroads in my life. And as sure as hell, Tina Turner wouldn't be driving by. But then I thought of the dole clerk, that sweet girl Astral, and for a moment I believed everything was going to be all right.

## ~ FOUR ~

A sh took me on a little tour. I noticed his paranoia extended even to the building. The Union Street dole office was housed in a substantial dark brick structure on the edge of the city's shopping precinct. It was a gloomy area; whatever the time of day the streets seemed to be in perpetual shadow.

'You will notice,' he said, 'that this building is constructed in the heavy Teutonic style favoured by 1930s fascist architects. Look at this,' he said, pointing up to a brick arch that towered about fifty feet over the front entrance, 'this sort of architecture stresses authority – and crushes individualism. It's typical of Albert Speer – Speer, the man who put the fear in architecture.'

The building was in a bad state of repair. The varnish on its heavy oak doors had blistered, the cream paintwork was gritty and peeling, there was buddleia sprouting in the gutters, and high up, in what I guessed was a roof valley, a small tree seemed to have taken hold.

Just across the road was the police station, the Bridewell. Clad in smoke-blackened Bath stone with no windows, it was an equally forbidding structure. 'The dole office and the Bridewell – two depressing buildings in a bleak part of town. Bad vibe,' Ash sighed.

According to Owen – who I was to meet shortly – Hitler's Luftwaffe had taken an unhealthy interest in Bristol. On the night of Good Friday 1941, waves of bombers flew over the city. The following morning, as the dust settled and the smoke cleared, Bristolians faced the cruel fact that their medieval town of secret streets and higgledy houses was no more. Yet, among the twisted rubble two buildings stood unscathed. All that remained of the city centre were Bristol's two most dreary buildings: the dole office and the police station. People said this was part of the Fuhrer's wicked plan.

Ash took me past closed doors, up and down flights of stairs and along endless corridors. An unusual feature of the building, giving it a crazy and

27

impossible geometry, was that it was constructed on a steeply sloping site. The ground floor on one side of the building was a deep cellar on the other. Inside, this topographic quirk induced a disorientating effect so that I never quite knew which floor I was on.

I was interested to see the signing-on hall from the other side of the counter. Even before I walked round the corner I was hit by the familiar bar-room stink of stale alcohol, smoke and sweat. The signing-on hall smelt like a cross between a pub and dog's home. But something else hung in the air. At the time I couldn't say what it was. Only later did I realise it was despair.

'Furniture? No point. They'll only piss on it or throw it at you,' explained Ash.

We went down a flight of concrete steps into what I was expecting to be the basement. In fact this wasn't the basement – this was the 'lower ground floor'. The basement housed an area Ash called 'the Cabbage Patch'.

Despite Ash's talk of twisted characters and unstable colleagues, my spirits had remained steady. They tumbled, however, when he showed me into a grim room where I would spend much of my time working.

'It's a busy day today,' Ash explained, 'so there's nobody down here at the moment. They're all on the counter getting ready – the doors open at 9.30.'

The room was cold and soulless with walls and fittings painted in mental institution brown and cream gloss. To the right was a row of small metal-framed frosted windows that obscured the view, as I was to find out later, of a courtyard crammed with dustbins and other damp piles of rubbish. With its tables and blackboard, the room felt like a classroom. The only feature of interest was a large station clock with Roman numerals and a tick-tock so loud I felt I had to shout over it. I'm going back to school, I thought. I'd hated school.

Before I knew what I was saying I heard myself plead, 'Do I have to work here?'

'No problem,' Ash said cheerfully 'I'll find you a lounger on the sun terrace. Let me know your favourite cocktail and I'll get Mr Blunt to bring it up to you.' Ash looked at me pityingly and added. 'I've got some Noddy books for you to read.'

'What?' I'd never liked Noddy and his freaky entourage.

'Noddy books – instruction manuals. All you need to know about the benefit system. Have a flick through, but don't worry about reading them too closely. The only way to learn this job is by doing it. Noddy books can't teach you how to shrug off abuse. You just get used to it. Overcoming fear, well, that takes a bit longer.' Ash shuffled towards the door. 'I've got to go now. Battle awaits.'

Before he left the room he hesitated and turned. 'There's one important thing I meant to say. The next time we've got a few moments I need to tell you about the X ray specs syndrome. I haven't got time now. Don't let me forget. Oh, and after lunch you're due to meet Mr Blunt.'

I opened the first page of the Noddy book and read about a civil service wonderland called Merton where the unemployed were grateful and I guessed the trains ran on time. I looked around the empty room and wondered how people spent their day in this clerical Gormenghast. What did they do? I had no idea what went on in an office – let alone an office at the Ministry of Work. I wondered about my work colleagues. What would they talk about? What would I say to them? Were they really that frightening? And where was Astral?

I stared at the windows, trying to make sense of the patterns of light coming through the frosted glass. Little in my life so far had prepared me for this. I needed a plan. If I spend any length of time here I'll drown, I thought.

~

Mr Blunt's office was on the first floor, down a long dim corridor with a highly polished brown linoleum floor.

'Good afternoon, Mr Redcliffe,' Mr Blunt said without the hint of a smile.

I had expected to shake hands, but as Mr Blunt made no sign of shifting his huge bulk from his chair, I thought better of it.

He was a large man with a big round face. He wore a dark green, shabby, baggy suit. At the elbows and knees the woollen material had stretched and bulged. It reminded me of a bulbous clown's suit. Yet there didn't seem to be anything particularly humorous about Mr Blunt.

For what seemed like a long time Mr Blunt peered at me through lenses as thick as double-glazing units. I observed Mr Blunt's smooth face. He had the sallow complexion of a light-shunning reptile. I felt caught in some sort of childish staring game, our eyes seemed to be locked, I was being hypnotised, I was being drawn into a dream.

'So...' said Mr Blunt at last, opening a file with my name on it. I'd only started work that morning, yet the file appeared to contain many sheets of paper. 'We like to think of ourselves at the Ministry of Work as guardians of the tax payer's money. How do you think of yourself, Mr Redcliffe?'

For a moment I thought he was joking, but Mr Blunt's unsmiling eyes indicated otherwise.

'Guardian of the taxpayer's money sounds fine to me.'

'Really? You surprise me. By our records I'd say that you have been a long term beneficiary of the tax payer.'

' Pardon? I don't understand what you mean?'

'What I mean is that you seem to be taking a lot out, but not putting much in.'

'Well, yes. On the work front things have been a bit quiet recently. But hopefully that's sorted out now.'

'Yes, I hope it is, I hope it is.'

Mr Blunt handed me a diagram of the civil service career structure. 'These are the opportunities that are open to you.' The gloom momentarily lifted from his face and he smiled a beatific smile.

There were about 40 grades. I was pleased to see that I was already about fifteen rungs up from the bottom of the ladder – above cleaner; porter, janitor, storeman, stationery assistant, paper wallah, tea monkey, and so on. Thank goodness for a university education.

'Think of this as a map of your life. It's all here, from youth to maturity; from clerical assistant to regional manager. Very few people are in such a privileged position to see their future charted like this.'

I shuddered. It was as if some hideous old crone had read my palm and identified the precise cause and date of my death.

'I want to tell you something very important about this job.' Mr Blunt's voice softened. 'You know, one of my earliest memories as a young lad was walking with my father past this very building. I remember seeing a queue of rough unshaven men. Of course I was too young to know what a dole office was. To my inexperienced eyes I thought those pale and thin flat-capped men looked rather sad. My father, who owned a busy hardware shop in Castle Street, knew better. Do you know what he said? I'll never forget it. He said: 'they need to get off their backsides. They're work shy; there's plenty of work to be done.' And do you know he was right. Even in those days.

'So this is my advice, Mr Redcliffe. Don't ever waste your time feeling sorry for these people.' He glanced over at the window. 'I see them arrive by taxi to sign-on. I can't afford to travel by taxi. How can they? And when they leave the building I see them laughing. Do you know why they are laughing? They are laughing at you and they are laughing at me. And worst of all they are laughing at the system. I see them. Pimps, prostitutes, pariahs.' Mr Blunt spat out these sour words as if he'd bitten on a lemon. 'We must crack down on these scroungers. The Government has high hopes for this department; for the foreseeable future unemployment is going to be increasing. We have ambitious targets that must be met. Mr Redcliffe, these targets will not be hit if staff are allowed to be too soft.'

I thought about Mr Blunt's expression guardian of the taxpayer's money. 'With all respect Mr Blunt, surely the Government is missing the point. If they want to put the squeeze on spongers they ought to crack down on tax fraud. That's where the big money is lost. As far as I'm concerned picking on the unemployed is small-minded vindictiveness.'

'You don't wear a beret, do you?' Mr Blunt snapped.

'What?'

'I hope you're not an anarchist, Mr Redcliffe? We've got enough of those misfits in this place already'.

'No I'm not. It's just that…'

I could see that Mr Blunt wasn't listening. He leant back in his chair, put his hands together behind his neck and closed his eyes. It was an alarming sight. His eyeballs, which had previously been magnified by his glasses into comic proportions, were replaced by a flesh coloured nothingness.

'Mr Redcliffe,' he said languidly with his eyes still shut, 'why didn't you tell us about your little incident with the authorities?'

A tingle of alarm shot up my backbone. This was the last thing I'd been expecting. I then remembered Baxter's conversation about MI5 when I was completing my application form. Is that what Baxter had been hinting at?

'Excuse me?'

Mr Blunt opened his eyes. 'Let's just say that I know, and leave it at that.'

'I'm sorry, but what are you are referring to?'

'I think it's best if we leave it at that, don't you?'

I was only too pleased to leave it at that seeing that I had no idea what he was on about. But then again, maybe I did.

'Now, Mr Redcliffe, I'll be seeing you again in few weeks' time for your initial Job Appraisal Review. We will talk about your long-term training needs then. Welcome to the Department of Work. My door is always open.'

He gestured with a flip of his hand for me to get out.

As I was putting on my jacket at the end of my first day Ash said: 'Max, I need to ask you something. Do you always dress like this? You don't strike me as the type of guy to be a member of the Bay City Rollers fan club. Why don't you do yourself a favour and just wear jeans and a shirt tomorrow. I think you'll feel more relaxed – and hopefully I won't have quite so many people sidling up to me asking 'who's the wanker?'

It had been a frightening day. I'd hit the crossroads and taken a wrong turn. I'd sold my soul to the establishment. All I had wanted to do was to chat up Astral; now I was caught in a nightmarish class war where I'd lose my friends and live under the constant threat of violence. And if I had understood Mr Blunt correctly, I was being blackmailed for a crime I knew nothing about. And worst of all, my colleagues, people I hardly knew, were calling me a wanker.

To think from the other side of the counter they had all looked so normal. Yet amongst all this wreckage I was still clinging to one hope. I was thinking of Astral sitting opposite me. I was dreaming about the moment we would meet. She'd smile the warmest most welcoming smile in the world and look into my eyes and see the beauty of my innermost soul. You don't achieve nirvana without a bit of suffering, I reckoned.

## ~ FIVE ~

It was just Ash and me. We were downstairs, sitting side-by-side checking files. Without looking up Ash said, 'Tell me about yourself.'

I'm sure it was an innocent enough question, but I was wary talking about my past. 'Uh? What do you mean?'

'What do you think I mean. What were you doing before you started here?'

So what had I been doing? I tried to think. Work... well, quite honestly the last thing I wanted to do was work. For me, getting a job was the first joyless step away from the wonderful disenfranchised world of being a teenager. I wanted to be a teenager for as long as possible – at least until I was thirty. Some of the people I'd been with at school already had jobs and were married – think of that, a wife and two kids at 23. I'd rather pull an electric fire into my bath than do that.

I'd once borrowed a book called Hit Me With a Flower from my old schoolmate Boz. Written by the notorious hippie Nevil Sponge, I can't fully recall what it was all about. I do remember, however, that I felt it sort of summed up my approach to life at the time. Sponge's thesis not only legitimised my idleness but also reinforced my view that the world owed me a living. Sponge turned a late morning lie-in into a political act. Yeah, I liked that. I began to view my extra three hours in bed as my contribution to the class struggle. By kipping under the blankets I was making a radical challenge to repressive bureaucratic rule. I was right there with John and Yoko on that one.

At university I'd spent a great deal of time cultivating the art of doing as little as possible. And the future? We were all so cocooned on our campus that thoughts about what we were going do after graduation didn't even feature as a topic of conversation. The Saturday night gig at the student union bar was about as far ahead as I could think.

33

No, that's not entirely true. There was one guy we talked about. Boz had a friend who had a job as an A&R man with a record company. Most of the work seemed to involve sitting in the back of a limo' with Tina Turner. That sounded like a job worth considering. I wondered if my sociology degree qualified me to do that sort of thing.

Reinforced by Nevil Sponge's incoherent ramblings I had developed a personal philosophy that would be inconceivable ten years later. It went like this: it's better to be poor and free than rich and a slave. No, really, it's true. Life's too short for work. It was only capitalist bread-head bastards or misfits that did the 9–5 wage slave thing. Earning money just wasn't that important to me. After all, I didn't need much. There was a grant cheque at the beginning of every term that took care of the basics. I was a talented corner dweller. Wherever I lay my sleeping bag was my home. And as long as I had money for beer, cornflakes and crisps – new brands like Golden Wonder or Walkers, but not Smiths – that little blue bag somehow hinted at exploitation – I was happy.

Once, when I was cashing my Giro, the woman behind the Post Office counter called me a lazy parasite and said I should be ashamed of myself, 'what with your good education an' 'at'. I was momentarily shaken by this. A parasite? Surely I wasn't a parasite – a freeloader maybe. Freeloader was fine. 'Freeloading Max'. That was cool. With a name like that I could imagine myself as a Furry Freak Brother. But parasite – heavy. And who did that old bag think she was? What right did she have to go round upsetting people, huh?

Back to Ash's question. What had I been doing? I felt I lived a busy and fulfilling life – but how had I spent my time over the last couple of years? It was a kind of a metaphysical existence that was difficult to break down into specifics...

'A bit of this and a bit of that,' I replied to Ash's question.

'A bit of this and a bit of that,' Ash repeated. 'What's that mean then?'

Although I knew he was just making conversation I wasn't sure how much I could tell him. Was this Ash my mentor speaking? Or Ash the hippie with the crappy shoes?

'Well you know – stuff.'

'Ohhh,' said Ash slowly, nodding his head as if I'd unravelled some long forgotten secret. 'Stuff, eh?'

'Yeah.' I readily agreed. 'Things.'

'Can you expand on 'things' a bit. What, exactly does 'things' entail?'

That was a question. Apart from reading the Guardian, skinning-up and making cups of tea it would be difficult to say what 'things' did entail. I spent a lot of time crashed out waiting for creative inspiration. (I've noticed an interesting law of nature at work here – namely, the amount of sleep you need expands to fill the time available.) I was preparing my mind for the next move. I didn't know what the next move was going to be. But man, I'd be ready for it when it came.

'The details would bore you,' I said.

'No, I'm interested.'

I reckoned Ash was probably okay. He was pleasantly strange – the sort of guy that was good to have around when the going got tough. I'd watched Ash in action on the counter and he gave off a wise vibe. People listened to him and trusted him. I liked that. I noticed he didn't take any shit, mind.

He'd told me that he was brought up in the countryside and knew all sorts of stuff, like how to slit open a deer and extract the musk gland. He didn't elaborate on what exactly he would do with a deer's musk glad, though the way he spoke implied that this was a useful skill to have. Ken and I could have done with his skills when we smacked into that deer on the Pacific Coast Highway.

'Well... I've been at university.'

'I guessed that. Doing what?'

'Sociology.'

The lectures had been crap. I'd been on the wrong course. Those guys, Marx, Durkheim and Weber – they all seemed so ancient, so irrelevant. The most useful things I learnt were during the vacation when I made my pilgrimage to the Unemployment Benefit Office. Now that was useful. I'd studied all the techniques. I knew what to say and how to say it. I could recite the litany in a dull beaten monotone. 'I'm looking for a job; I've had three interviews, but no luck. I'm desperate, this is my very last resort.' But more important than this, I could repeat the magical phrase. The password that opened the door to the Giro – 'Can I have a B1 please?' For the B1 was the form that got you the money. Sometimes I thought I ought to have got my 2:2 not for Sociology, but for Dole Office Studies.

The fascists at the dole office were under strict instructions not to issue a B1 without being asked. Many an innocent had patiently waited, to no avail, for their benefit. Eventually, weeks later, they'd join the queue to check the progress of their claim and be greeted with mock incredulity. 'But you haven't signed a B1. You don't get any money without a B1.'

'You didn't offer me a B1.'

'You didn't ask.'

And here's the killer – the B1 couldn't be backdated. Bastards. It was a harsh system.

The other great thing about being a student was that you didn't have to mingle with the dispossessed at the Job Centre. Graduates were required to sign-up with the Professional and Executive Register, the PER. These days the world's drowning in graduates – back then so few went to University we were an elite. The PER epitomised the duality of the world of work. Them and us. The management and the scum. The PER had carpets and 'easy chairs', the civil servants treated you with an emollient deference – after all you had a degree, you were clever – even if your hair was down to your shoulders, you stank of smoke and sweat, and had an unnaturally languid manner. And what was even more brilliant – you won't believe this – was that once you were registered with the PER you were under no obligation to accept the crap jobs. The PER was the most fabulous cushion for graduates against reality.

Once, some Uriah Creep had asked me whether I'd be interested in a clerical job at the Tax Office. I played along with his game. Although it was agreed that this wasn't social research, I'd nevertheless go and check it out to see whether this job offered any suitable opportunities commensurate with my degree in sociology. It seemed that the PER was as vague as I was with regards to what a social researcher actually did. So I went to be interviewed by a grey man in an office cluttered with wooden filing cabinets. After half an hour it was agreed that my skills would be better used elsewhere. Which was absolutely fine by me. When I reported back to the PER, the man consoled me. 'Not really your type of thing, I'm afraid,' he said.

It got even better. When I'd left university and had been signing on for six months I lodged a claim for a clothing allowance. For this I had to put up with the inconvenience of a snoop from the DHSS checking the clothes in my wardrobe. Once the appointment had been arranged I had plenty of time to move my best jacket and strides to Boz's pad. A week later I received a cheque for a massive £49.00. I could score some good shit with that.

So signing-on was all part of my life's philosophy. I didn't need money; all I needed was love. And when things got a bit too tough, and love didn't pay the bills, I could always go home to Mum and Dad.

That's not to say that my parents never hassled me. But I was ready for them. In Nevil Sponge's eyes parents were the building block of capitalism, and although he didn't go as far as to say they should be strung up from a lamppost, his diktat was they should be shunned and their old fashioned ways ridiculed. During the holidays in Ruislip Dad would invariably ask the same question. 'What are you going to do with your University education, son?' 'Change the record Dad.' Although – unlike the woman in the Post Office – they never actually used the word scrounger, this is what they seemed to hinting. I would mutter vaguely about social research. Whatever that was. But as time went by, I went home less and less. So that got rid of that little problem.

'Sociology eh? Any good?' Ash asked.

'Difficult to tell at this early stage.'

'Yeah, sure, but you left University two years ago. You must have found a use for it by now.'

'Sociology isn't the sort of thing you can rush – the benefits take a while to sink in.'

Ash stopped checking his claim and turned to face me. 'Max, what the fuck are you talking about?'

I'd risk it. Ever since our first meeting I'd guessed Ash was a freak and a kindred spirit. I might as well come clean. He'd understand.

'Look,' I said 'I'm going to be honest with you. Work isn't my scene. I'm not ready for it.'

'Yeah?' said Ash, in a manner that asked for more.

I continued, 'There's something intrinsically wrong with the situation I currently find myself in. Working here at Union Street goes against everything I've ever believed in. There's millions of people looking for work. As far as I'm concerned I'm taking somebody else's job.'

'Bit of a social conscience, then. You probably got THAT from sociology.'

'Not really... its just...' I gestured at the files and then the whole room. 'This shit is doing my head in.'

Ash gave me a comforting smile. 'That's a good sign. I'd worry if it wasn't.'

'Yeah? You understand what I mean?'

'Of course I do. How many times do I have to tell you? This is a fucking evil place.'

'Really?'

'Yeah, really. You and I are in this together.'

## ~ SIX ~

Forget work, all I really wanted to do was travel. The previous year I'd spent the summer with Ken, my best mate from University, criss-crossing the States delivering cars. It was slacker heaven. All we had to do was drive big autos across the country for rich bastards who didn't have the time to do it themselves. The driving was mind-altering – after 24 hours of non-stop travelling the 55-mile an hour speed limit gives you a spaced out slow-mo view of the countryside. It made the distances seem even bigger, the sky even wider. In the prairie-lands we felt we were moving so slowly we imagined we were the original pioneers rolling across the plains in a covered wagon.

We'd be given ten days to drive a Cadillac from coast to coast. Fuelled by slimming pills we reckoned we could do the journey from New York to LA non-stop in four. This meant that we could take time off en-route to watch the sunset at the Grand Canyon or hangout in Las Vegas. Las Vegas, with its complimentary all-day breakfasts, was another freeloader's paradise – so long as you stayed away from the slots. We didn't even have to pay for motel rooms as we could sleep comfortably stretched out across the seats. Admittedly the front seat, with the steering wheel poking in your arse wasn't quite so good, but we'd take turns at that. Over the summer we'd notched up a number of achievements that even Neil Cassidy would have been proud of. We'd freewheeled a Cadillac 12 miles down the western slope of the Rockies to Leadville; we'd cruised in an open top Pontiac up the Pacific Coast Highway to St Luis Obispo listening to Grace Slick belting out Up Against the Wall Muthafuckers, and in the middle of the night, in Oregon, we'd smacked into a deer hypnotised by our truck's headlights – causing a surprisingly large dent to the front of the pick-up. For a moment we got excited about living on 'wild meat' for the next few weeks – but Ken couldn't locate the butcher's meat cleaver on his Swiss Army knife. Beside we couldn't lift the carcass onto the back of the truck. Man, those deer are big!

By the end of our cross-continent trip the car would be a steaming, creaking wreck. We made sure we were well down the block before the owner took it for a spin.

In between jobs, when we didn't have a vehicle, we'd hitch. As I was to find out all too soon, shell-shocked 'Nam Vets, religious extremists and gun-toting rednecks were about the only people who would stop to give two English hippie guys a lift. We consoled ourselves by thinking that this was all part of the experience. The experience of meeting some real people, of meeting some really twisted real people.

Once, in the Nevada desert, when the hitching had got tough, a young Mormon pulled over to offer us a lift. Ken and I had been standing under a yellow sky on a wide flat plain for several hours. Not one single car had passed. It was now twelve noon and what little shade we sought from a signpost had all but gone. The air was thick with heat. I'd had never heard such quiet. The omens were not good. A previous hitchhiker had scratched on the post with a stone the number of hours that he'd waited – there were eight strikes.

At last, a car drew up. An amiable young man in a madras short-sleeved shirt opened the window.

'Where ya goin'?'

'Anywhere? We just need to get away from here.'

'Well, I'm heading for Vegas. That suit you?'

'Vegas would be great.'

What happened next was the last thing I was expecting. While Ken went round the back of the car to put his rucksack in the trunk the driver asked me in a quiet, tentative voice.

'Hey, can I suck your cock?'

'I beg your pardon?' I said in my best English accent, hoping that I'd misheard.

The guy repeated his request. There was a slight tremor in his voice. By this time I had recovered my composure.

'No, sorry, mate, not my scene.' I then pointed to Ken. 'Ask him.'

The young man, who obviously had his heart set on me, drove off at speed. We were left standing in a cloud of dust. Ken, who hadn't heard any of this, turned on me. 'What the hell did you say to him?' he asked accusingly, still clasping his bag.

'He wanted to give me a blow job.'

'You what? What are you talking about?'

'I said 'no'.'

'You said 'no'! That's bloody great – how are we going to get a lift now? You selfish bastard.'

'He didn't seem interested in you.'

'That's lucky, because I wasn't offering.'

'Well, neither was I.'

We stood by the roadside pissed off with each other and not saying anything. Ken picked up a pebble and threw it into the scrub. After a while he said. 'Well I suppose we ought to be grateful he didn't pull out a gun and then ask.'

'Yeah, refusal can sometimes cause offence.'

I stared into the heat haze. I screwed up my eyes trying to make sense of a contorted shape in the distance. It was a car heading towards us. 'Hey, isn't that him coming back.'

'Oh SHIT!'

There was nowhere to hide. I looked at Ken's face. His features were puckering up, as if he was imaging some intense and unspeakable pain. I waited ten seconds for the tension to rise and then added, 'No that's not him. Only kidding, Ken.'

'You bastard,' he howled.

It was too hot to be angry. I laughed and then after a moment's silence Ken laughed. Even in the heat we hugged each other with laughter.

~ SEVEN ~

My first meeting with Astral didn't go well. C Section was divided in two; the clerical staff – me, Ash, Lee, Cynthia and Astral – were clustered round five tables put together to form a rectangle, while Kastrina's empty seat was placed at a separate table a few feet away. Kastrina's position of authority was also denoted by the fact that her chair had arms.

For half an hour I'd been sitting directly opposite Astral with my back to the door. Astral was concentrating on some files and seemed oblivious to my gaze.

I looked at Astral's long eyelashes and her high, round cheekbones. She pushed a tress of blonde hair behind her ear.

I coughed. 'It's thanks to you that I've got this job,' I said. Although I had now been working at Union Street for almost a week this was the first opportunity, apart from a brief introduction on my first day, I'd had to speak to her.

Astral looked up. She appeared to have no idea what I was talking about. 'Oh?'

'Yeah, when I was signing-on, you told me there was a job going.'

'Oh yes,' she said absently while gazing intently at her black civil service ballpoint pen.

'You told me to go round the corner to speak to Baxter.'

'Oh right.' She said this in a distant manner that indicated she didn't recall this groundbreaking moment in my life.

'You wouldn't tell me your name because I was a claimant.'

Astral put down her pen and looked directly at me. She stared at me; it was the kind of interested stare that a zoologist might give a newly discovered breed of monkey. She straightened up in her seat and crossed her arms.

'I'm sorry, but I've got a dreadful memory for faces. You are...', she hesitated, 'how can I explain it? You are out of context. If I'd seen you behind the counter I might have thought, hello here's one of my claimants. But sitting here opposite me on C Section, I just didn't put two and two together.'

She still doesn't know who I am. 'Sure. That's fine. I understand.'

Astral must have guessed I was disappointed. 'Don't take it personally, I see thousands of people a week, and I tell hundreds of them to see Baxter. I'm sorry.' She changed the tone of her voice and speaking quietly said: 'Can I give you a bit of advice?'

'Go ahead.' I was pleased that she was at last taking an interest.

'I see Ash has taken you under his wing. Be careful. He's not exactly flavour of the month, round here.'

So she had noticed me.

Knowing Ash's attitude towards most of the staff I wasn't surprised by her warning. But I wanted to know more. 'What do you mean?'

Astral suddenly gave a little start. Something had happened. Her natural glow vanished and a look of alarm crossed her face.

'Maybe I shouldn't have said anything,' she added quickly.

'Why isn't he flavour of the month?'

Astral was looking anxious. 'I shouldn't have said that about Ash. Can we change the subject?'

'Excuse me, but you can't make a heavy accusation like that and then expect me to ignore it. If there's something funny about Ash I need to know. He's my mentor; I can't really avoid him, can I?'

'Just drop it, Max,' she said in quiet desperation. 'Please.'

Those pleading eyes. She was even more adorable. Before I could stop myself I was astounded to hear a voice saying: 'Any chance of buying you a drink to thank you for getting me this job?'

'Oh! I don't think so,' said Astral, now blushing violently.

Why did I do that? I'd hardly spent five minutes with her and I was asking her out. By the way she was looking at me I might as well have said 'fancy a shag?' Her rejection made me feel like a total prat.

Astral opened a new file and returned to her work. End of conversation.

It was only then that I realised Lee had quietly entered the room and was standing directly behind me.

## ~ EIGHT ~

Not everybody was as frightening as Ash had made out. For a start there was Cynthia, a no-nonsense older lady with gardener's finger-nails, who sat near me. I couldn't understand why a tweed skirted biddy like Cynthia – I guessed she must have been at least 40 – worked at Union Street. Ash said she had a husband who was 'big in frozen foods'. She obviously didn't need the money.

Sometimes Cynthia said the most ridiculous things. 'For the first time in history, we're warm, we're safe, and we have time for other things. We're lucky, Max.' She must have had a tough life if she thought this was lucky. I supposed it was the generation gap – she obviously had no idea about modern life.

Apart from being the 'fishfinger king', as Ash put it, Cynthia's husband, Doug, was also known for being accident prone. This is one of my favourite stories about him. On a holiday in County Donegal, Doug had attempted, for good luck, to climb through a doughnut shaped prehistoric stone but had got stuck halfway through. The Fire Brigade was called and despite their ingenious efforts they were unable to budge him. They pushed, they pulled, they used dry ice to cool the stone, they smeared his stomach and back with lard – but he was wedged as tight as a bung in a cask. As dusk neared, Doug was becoming dangerously distressed. There was only one thing to do. It seems that these ring shaped stones are as common as a cart of shite in this part of Ireland, so stone cutting equipment was brought into action. An hour and a half later Doug was free while the 5,000 year old menhir was in two neat halves.

'The thing is' added Cynthia, 'these stones only bring you good fortune if you climb through them towards the rising sun. Doug had attempted to go through the wrong way – which would give very bad luck indeed. It could have happened to anybody,' she sighed.

As for Cynthia's assertion that we were lucky, well, I suppose I wasn't being conscripted into the army. In fact, thinking about it I couldn't totally disagree with Cynthia's assessment of our situation. I was grudgingly grateful I didn't have to do the crap jobs if I didn't want to. I'd never had to be the tea monkey in an office, I didn't have to pick out the burnt bits in the crisp factory, sort offal in an abattoir, or do undignified stuff like the bin men's dead dog run. I didn't even, God forbid, have to work in a bank. So far, on a scale of one to ten this job rated as about 6, no 6.5 even. Not bad really. Though I hadn't yet experienced the pure fear of a PI afternoon; that would push the score down a bit.

Cynthia had two practical pieces of advice for me. First: never suck the top of your pen as you don't know where it's been. Second: never accept food from claimants. A previous member of the team, Ed Chicken, had done just that and the lemon sherbet had been laced with LSD.

'Ed now calls himself Hawkwind and is living in a tepee in North Wales with three wives,' said Cynthia. 'Poor man, his life is totally ruined.'

I thought it sounded rather appealing.

More advice. Ash waited until Friday to give me his final piece of wisdom.

'Before you leave this evening, Max, there's one thing I need to tell you. This is very important. In fact it's probably the most important thing anybody will say to you during your induction, and it's something that you must always keep at the back of your mind.'

'Oh yeah,' I said sceptically. I braced myself for the news that my reputation as a shameless and rampant onanist had spread like wildfire throughout the civil service.

'There's one moment in this job you must look out for. When you reach that moment it's decision time. Stay, and you remain with the Ministry of Work forever. Go and you might just be saved – if you're lucky.'

'And when, precisely, is that moment?' I asked.

'It's when you are standing behind the counter, there's a queue at your window so long that it's out of the door, and you are talking to a colleague about drinking Metaxa Three Star on your effing holiday in Crete. Technically it's called the X-ray specs syndrome. Max, if you ever get to the stage when those poor desperate sods in the queue have become invisible, when you see right through them, you have got to leave immediately.'

In my mind I could see Mr Blunt's alarming career structure. 'I'm outta here way before that, man,' I replied. If I ever needed to get a proper job I knew I could always chuck in the slumming at the dole office and head down the PER and get something half reasonable. Not that I would ever give

Cynthia the pleasure of saying this.

Ash looked at me quizzically. 'I hope so. I really hope so,' he said.

## ~ NINE ~

My two weeks' amnesty was up – Kastrina Klebb had returned. Since our initial discussion in the Concorde Café Ash had been infuriatingly unforthcoming about Kastrina. I was apprehensive, but also intrigued, about meeting her.

Kastrina swept into the lower ground floor with the fearsome energy of a premenstrual PE teacher. Without even acknowledging me, she strode over to Lee's files and proceeded to do a spot check. For a moment she was silent and then she yelled:

'Lee, you're doing it again.'

Lee obviously knew what Kastrina was talking about. 'It didn't seem fair,' he pleaded.

'Didn't seem fair! Fair to who? How many times do I have to tell you before you get it into your lardy head that sometimes you have to hurt to help.'

'Fair to her. She said she had to go for tests. She's pregnant.'

I was impressed. I hadn't expected there to be room for both compassion AND jealousy in Lee's under-developed emotional profile.

'Pregnant! According to this' said Kastrina, jabbing her finger at the file, 'Carmen Collins has been pregnant for 18 months. What's she expecting? An elephant? Next time she's late, cancel her claim. Got it?'

Lee muttered a broken acquiescence under his breath.

Kastrina certainly had presence. She was a good deal older than me – I guessed she was about twenty eight. Her overbearingly assertive manner was reinforced by a physique which if you were to believe Lee – admittedly, not a reliable source of information – was enhanced by what he called 'bolic steroids'. She was heavy chested and wore tight corduroy trousers that emphasised her horse-rider's thighs. No doubt about it, she lived up to her reputation. I found Kastrina frightening.

46

Over the following months I was to watch Kastrina in action. It was when she was working on the counter that her bullying was at its worst. Her attitude to claimants was legendary. She was well aware of her Ball Breaker sobriquet and appeared to revel in the title. Ash said that her stay in Plymouth with the Hounds of Hell had only served to increase her megalomania.

'That's no way to treat a customer,' a claimant complained after Kastrina had announced that his money wouldn't be sent to him until the following week.

'You're not a customer, you're a claimant.' Kastrina sneered in an ecstasy of self-importance.

'But I was expecting my money today,' the man pleaded.

Kastrina was now embarking on a routine that was to become sickeningly familiar.

'I've got just two words for you,' she continued. 'IM – possible.'

'But that's one word.'

'Well if you don't like that, here's another two words. Fuck off.'

But she wouldn't actually say it. No, she was too clever for that. She'd slowly and very clearly mouth the words. 'Fuck off.' But with no sound.

The man recoiled – shocked, as if he'd been slapped around the face. This was the last thing he was expecting from the dole office. It took him a few seconds to recover from the blow. Kastrina was waiting for this. She'd got him on the rebound and mouthed it again. This time the silent words were accompanied by a languid movement of the thumb indicating the door.

'Yeah, fuck off.'

What could the man do? He reeled out of the room like a spinning top. I could imagine the conversation when he got home to his wife. 'How did you get on at the dole office?' 'Not well. They told me to... to fuck off'. I dreaded to think what would happen next. I only hoped the Clifton Suspension Bridge suicide watch had their binoculars sharply focused.

So where do you go if you've been told to fuck off by the dole office? The DHSS of course. I quickly found out there is one good thing, just one good thing, about being employed by the Ministry of Work – and that is that I was NOT employed by the Department of Health and Social Security. In the benefits food chain the Ministry of Work is one rung up the ladder. Claimants can always be fobbed off to the DHSS office. Of course, Kastrina had a little trick for that as well. Her routine was to send sad desperados to that last chance saloon knowing full well that it would be closed by the time they got there. Her response to anyone who dared comment on her less than helpful manner would be: 'It's their fault, they should have got out of bed earlier.'

What I wasn't expecting from Kastrina was the feral odour of lust that she exuded. I felt repelled by her, but then again, and I'd never ever admit this to Ash, I was also perversely attracted to her. I had recently read in the News of the World about a Mormon who had been kidnapped by an American beauty queen, held hostage in a cottage on Dartmoor, tied to a bed and raped repeatedly. The newspaper screamed in 72 pt lettering across two pages 'She rode him like a bitch from hell'. Until I met Kastrina, I had never been quite sure how a woman could rape a man. Looking at Kastrina I now had an inkling of how it might work.

## ~ TEN ~

'Okay, Max, we've got something different to do today.' Ash was taking me down to yet another part of the basement, to a room called The Cabbage Patch. 'We're going to do a bit of weeding.'

'What's that?'

'Chucking out old files – it's a doss.'

We entered a large, gloomy room barely illuminated by several low powered light bulbs. A sweet mustiness hung in the warm air; I could taste the dust on my tongue. The Cabbage Patch reminded me of the sort of place favoured by mushroom farmers – warm, airless and dark. The heavy atmosphere had a soporific effect; indeed Ash explained that a pile of hessian rubbish bags in a far corner frequently served as a makeshift mattress for those recovering from hangovers, or unbelievably, when passion struck – usually Christmas time or Friday afternoons – a snog and a grope.

To the right of the door was a plywood cubbyhole with windows. It housed an old wooden desk, two chairs and a kettle and was lit by a bare 40-watt light bulb on a string. This was the Filing Supervisor's office.

'Let me introduce you to Owen, he's head honcho in charge of the files.'

'Owen this is Max... Max this is Owen.' Ash continued: 'Owen runs a tight ship down here. What Owen doesn't know about filing isn't worth knowing in the first place. Isn't that right Owen?' said Ash in a raised voice. I couldn't tell whether Ash was taking the piss.

'This is an important job,' said Owen with an undulating Welsh lilt in his voice. 'Mess this up and we might as well all go home.' Owen, who must have been about 60, had the opaque pallor of someone who didn't get out much.

'You have to remember the three Rs: the Right file, the Right place, at the Right time. Get that wrong and somebody is going to miss out on their money.'

I nodded my head. I was pleased to see such commitment to the welfare of the claimants.

'One bit of advice,' he continued, 'never, and I mean never, open a file and start reading it. If you do that you'll never get any work done. Contained in these files is a person's life story. They can be fascinating. But don't be tempted; resist the temptation, Max.'

I couldn't believe what I was hearing – someone being enthusiastic about filing. Well good luck to Owen, somebody had to do this soul-throttling job, and if he enjoyed it, so much the better.

'And, of course I've got some famous files. We've got a special section for celebrities over there.'

'What? Famous people signing on?' I asked.

Owen opened his desk drawer and pulled out a board with a yellowing sheet of lined foolscap paper clipped to it. 'Max, this is what we call the Roll of Honour. Even the famous have to sign-on, you know. Look, we've got actors, musicians, sportsmen, criminals, politicians even – all human life is in these files. Of course, it is said that Cary Grant's file used to be here. It's a real collector's item. Unfortunately, I don't know where it is now. It's either been misfiled, or somebody has stolen it. I reckon it's been stolen.'

'You're having me on! What was Cary Grant doing in Bristol?'

'He was born here, of course. Everybody knows that.'

'Well I didn't,' I said, not quite believing it. 'And if he was signing-on, that must have been at least... at least 100 years ago.'

'Not that long ago – 1931 to be precise. But the famous ones we don't throw away. We keep them. We do swaps. There's a network of filing clerks across the country, trading old files. I collect cricketers. Do you know, I've got the whole 1955 Gloucestershire County Cricket Team? I reckon that's quite an achievement. It's worth a lot of money.'

I was still thinking about Cary Grant signing-on at Union Street. Cary Grant, the smoothest, suavest, most debonair of all Hollywood stars, queuing to get his dole card stamped at Union Street wasn't an image that easily came to mind.

'Surely they didn't have the dole in the 1930s? Wasn't it the workhouse or something?'

'The dole's been around in one form or another for many a year. I bet you didn't know that this is one of the oldest dole offices in the country. This is a Grade 2 listed building.' Owen said this with a tone of pride in his voice.

'But Owen, Cary Grant must have left Bristol when he was very young.'

'He did, but he came back to visit his Ma. You see Cary Grant was notoriously tight with his money; and in the early days he still wasn't making that much. So he used to come in here and sign-on. It's true, I promise you.'

I was trying to think of any other famous Bristolians who might have signed-on. 'What about Russ Conway?'

'Trevor Stanford you mean. That was Conway's real name. Virtually worthless, he signed-on scores of times. After the success in 1959 of his number one hit, Side Saddle, his career went into a downwards spiral. Well, he did the occasional spot on the Billy Cotton Band Show, but the old magic had gone. He was in and out of here like a cuckoo clock. There are hundreds of Trevor Stanford files.

Of course if you want to get into some real celebrity collecting you're in the wrong place. The tax office is the department for that. Surrey Inland Revenue to be precise. There's talk of one clerical officer who handled the tax claims of Tom Jones, Engelbert Humperdinck and Gilbert O' Sullivan all in one day. Imagine that – a full cast of top notch international superstars. Oh, they're the top end of the market, for sure. The funny thing is, he said that he got a bit blasé about this sort of thing after a while.

And these celebrities wonder why it takes so long for their taxes to be settled. It's because everyone's having a gander at their paperwork. Personally I'm surprised their claims don't get lost more often. Now back in the war...'

'I don't mean to interrupt, Owen,' said Ash 'but we have got some work to do.'

'My apologies boys, I was forgetting myself. Max, we'll continue this conversation some other time.'

When we were out of Owen's hearing Ash said: 'He doesn't half go on. Being down here on your own does funny things to your mind.'

'All those famous people drawing the dole – I'm amazed!' I said.

'So am I – I've never seen anybody famous here. You get a few people from the BBC up the road in Clifton – but they're not exactly film stars. Though I did have somebody who said he was in the Pigsty Hill Light Orchestra.'

'Who?'

'My point exactly.'

'But what about Owen's cricketers?'

'Locked away in a drawer. I have never actually seen them. Probably a figment of his imagination. Yeah, well, as I said, he lives in a different world from you and I. And don't, whatever you do, ask him about the war. When he starts on about the bombing during the Second World War he's impossible to stop. Which also reminds me, whatever you do, don't accept chocolate from him.'

'Oh, he's a bit like that, is he?'

'No, he's fine, it's the chocolate that's odd.'

We were standing next to waist high stacks of old claims.

'This is what you do. First of all here's the death list.' Ash handed me a clipboard with sheets of paper headed Deceased. 'As the list says, these are all people who have died. We therefore have to get rid of their papers, right?'

'Okay.'

'However, there's a couple of things we need to do before we throw them away.' Ash went on to describe a system that was so complicated it could have been a job creation scheme in its own right.

'Now we have to find the file; right?'

'Obviously'

'We do this by checking the name in the 'dormant' card file, which will give the location number. Once you've found the relevant file, you extract a numbered digit from the file's cover, write it on another list and then put it over there – where there is a final check before it's put in the shredder.

'Why don't you just throw the files out?' I said when Ash had finished explaining the process.

'I don't understand it either. All I know is that your mistakes can come back to haunt you.'

'So bloody what!'

'It's supposed to stop people larding the books. Dead man's wages and all that. And suppose you'd set up a false file...'

'As if. '

'... it means that you can't just get rid of a dodgy claim.'

'For such a piddling amount of money, why would anybody bother?'

'It might be worth it if you hot-wired a file that automatically paid out over several months – or years.'

'You'd have to be desperate.'

'Some people get that way. Anyhow, you start on, I'll have a kip,' said Ash as he headed for the hessian bags. 'Oh Max, wake me up if you find Marilyn Monroe's claim.'

'Marilyn Monroe's claim!'

'Yeah, she's an honorary Bristolian.'

'Very funny.'

## ~ ELEVEN ~

Just one week spent in the claustrophobic atmosphere of Union Street had made me yearn for the wider world. There was so much that I wanted to see and do. Despite the occasional unwanted sexual advance, and a mishap with customs so embarrassing I really don't like to talk about it, I longed to be on the road again. And there was one place, above all others, I wanted to check out.

The cool trip was to join the freaks on the hippie trail seeking hashish and spiritual enlightenment. With its relentless crowds, thirsty bed bugs and the inevitable Raj-runs, India was the ultimate full-on experience. But then again every Tom, Dick and Hari went there. As far as I was concerned meditating in Poona, getting out of your box in Kathmandu, and crashing in Goa wasn't exactly crossing the wire.

Besides, when I'd rail-carded round Europe I'd noticed the further east you travelled the bigger and more aggressive the cockroaches got. I dreaded to think what size they'd be once I crossed into Asia Minor. By the time I'd reached the Pudding Shop in Istanbul, I'd had enough. The journey over the Bosporus to a continent with rat-sized cockroaches would be a bridge too far.

I wanted to go somewhere different. Ever since childhood I had been drawn to the Amazon jungle. It became one of my 'When I get older' phrases. As a teenager, in the summer as I lazed on the patch of thin grass in my parents' back garden in Ruislip, I could see the planes taking-off from Heathrow. I swore that one day I would be on one of those planes, and I would be heading for South America.

I could trace this dream to my eighth birthday, when my Mum took me to the cinema to see The Lost World. The sight of a mist shrouded mesa, a last refuge of dinosaurs, bursting through the rainforest, transfixed me. This vast green landscape was so mysterious and far away. Could such a place really exist?

Many years later I watched a TV documentary that pinpointed the location of this magical place. A team of explorers navigated their thin boats up a vast black river in their quest for Conan Doyle's fictitious land. After days of negotiating rapids and whirlpools they were confronted by their grail – an enormous sheer-sided table-topped mountain. Even without dinosaurs, it was a compelling sight that served only to strengthen my desire triggered all that time ago in the Odeon.

I knew nobody who had been to the Amazon rainforest. This was going to be my own adventure. The Mazaruni River in Guyana was where I had to go. And besides, I reasoned, in the rainforest I wouldn't get the runs nearly as badly as I would in India.

As I was to find out later, this hope was unfounded. But then again my attack of the gallops turned out to be lucky. Indeed, probably saved my life.

By the end of my three years at University I had no idea what I was going to do after I'd graduated. I didn't even know where I was going to live.

Don't get me wrong, Leicester was a good place; friendly, welcoming and famous for its vibrant multi-cultural dole office. My queue – P to S – was made up of a large number of refugees who had fled from Idi Amin's genocide. I remember an Afro-Asian guy pointing to a tall man clutching a UB40. 'He is a most important man in our country. He is a Government minister.' The young man said this in the present tense, as if he was still living in Uganda. It struck me that he wouldn't be seeing his homeland for quite some time. Signing on in this Midlands city could be a humbling experience.

It was time for me to move on. So I thumbed a lift down the M5 towards the South West of England. I headed in this direction for no particular reason. I didn't know anybody there – after graduation my friends had scattered far across the country but none had come to Bristol. Maybe it was instinct. My childhood holidays had always been in the West – heading towards the setting sun felt good.

Bristol, an easy day's hitch away, was a quiet place that somehow seemed to have avoided the ravages of industrialisation that had scarred so many other towns in the country. At first I couldn't make out what made the place tick. The docks in the centre of town were derelict and there were no large factories that I could see. The city seemed to be half asleep. This laid back approach was part of the attraction.

I quickly grew to appreciate the city and the people with their slow accent and their reserved charm. Bristol pretends it's laid back – in fact there's a heroic energy to the place.

Yet, for a port town Bristol was surprisingly uncosmopolitan. I hadn't anticipated the wariness of Bristolians towards outsiders. Unlike the multicultural Midlands, the dole queue in Bristol comprised ruddy faced West Country folk and a few sad Poles with unpronounceable names. Irrational animosity seemed to run deep. Welsh bashing was a centuries old tradition in Bristol. It's the universal excuse. 'They comes over 'ere (the River Severn), steals our jobs (or women) and drinks our beer,' being the justification. And, as many boyos from the Valleys who attend a gig at the Colston Hall will testify, the tradition is still much in evidence today. Invariably, there's some poor innocent leek-cruncher who wanders away from the safety of his coach and gets his fish and chips stamped into the pavement. Or worse.

Despite all this, as soon as I arrived in Bristol I knew it was where I wanted to be. We all have our dream place. For some it's the rural idyll, for others it's the heartbeat of the city. For my parents it was the discreet charms of suburbia. Okay, this theory might not be totally water-tight. Anyhow, wherever it is, it's the place you are always glad to come back to. You know the feeling; as you drive over the hill or round the corner you're craning your neck for the first sight. It could be the smoke rising above the trees from the cottage chimney, or a glimpse of a harbour surrounded by sand and blue sea. For me it was the curve on a newly laid motorway where the city appears for the first time stretching across the wide Avon valley. Beyond the high-rise flats of Barton Hill is the peerless spire of St Mary Redcliffe; over to the right the University tower and then beyond the soft rise of the Ashton Court parkland.

But the best way to arrive in Bristol is from the West. This sounds ridiculous, but after I'd been away, I would always return to the city via Brunel's miraculous suspension bridge, even if this meant a detour of several miles. There is no more spectacular way to enter a city.

The Clifton Suspension Bridge, hanging by a thread across a vertiginous gorge, is one of the world's most fabulous bridges, and it goes nowhere. There's nothing on the other side of the bridge apart from a few big houses and a wood. The bridge is an expensive conceit. And rightly so. This golden gateway frames the Avon Gorge – transforming the landscape of grey cliffs and hornbeam woods into a sublime vision of grandeur.

As I crossed the bridge I would look down to the distant river hundreds of feet below and observe the state of the tide. The ebb and flow was a constant source of interest. Maybe this is crazy but I felt it kept me in touch with nature's rhythms. Once over the bridge you are in the crumbling suburb of Clifton, with its elegant Georgian crescents dramatically stacked up the hillside like a pile of plates.

Moving to Bristol was like putting on an old pair of Wranglers – it felt good and comfortable. All in all, I reckoned it would be a good place to settle down and sign-on.

Ash, of course, had a different perspective. He said he hated the city. 'Bristolians have absolutely no scruples about how they earn their money.' I could feel one of Ash's rants coming on. 'For a start the trading of human flesh was virtually invented by Bristolians. Look at Clifton. A beautiful area is it not? It's built almost entirely on the suffering of our fellow men. Personally I'd never live there, knowing its construction was financed by the filthy money of the slave trade.'

'That's a bit extreme.'

'Call me oversensitive, but I can feel the negative vibe. I can taste the blood in the air.'

I didn't believe a word of it.

'And then there's cigarettes – half Bristol's wealth comes from the manufacture of straights. That 200 foot University tower at the top of Park Street was built as a memorial to the tobacco barons, the Wills family. I've seen people taking photographs of it – admiring its Repro-Gothic architecture. When I look at it, do you know what I see? I see a bloody great cancerous lung. I think of it as a monument to lung cancer. And here's another thing. Don't forget the arms trade; Bristol may well have manufactured Concorde, but its not the only thing that's going on at Filton. When they're not making aircraft they're knocking up all sorts of gadgetry of mass destruction. They disguise their missile making with a fancy name like dynamics or ordinance or some sort of obfuscating crap like that. They're making bombs, killing machines, pure and simple, that's all there is to it.'

'Ash, what point are you trying to make?'

'What I'm saying is, that, if like me, you're an ethical sort of guy, getting the right type of work in this town can be pretty damn difficult.'

While I didn't like Ash's self-righteous tone, I understood what he meant. He was right. If I was to embrace the work ethic, I did at least want to know that what I was doing was useful.

Ash hadn't finished: 'But what really does my head in about Bristol is that it hasn't got any good coffee shops.'

## ~ TWELVE ~

'Come and look at this.' Ash was standing by a door marked:

## NATIONAL EMPLOYMENT REGISTER DATABASE
### Entry by Unauthorised Personnel Not Allowed.

The last time I had been shown a computer was at University. Then, the computer, which was the size of a container lorry, sat in the middle of a barn-like room giving off a warm hum. There wasn't much to see – men wandered about with clipboards looking at dials and gauges, talking in hushed tones. Apparently the computer's valves were sensitive to dust particles so the technicians wore white coats, and hairnets. It was as tacky and unreal as Dr Who.

Ash was peering into a room that was unlike any other in the Ministry of Work. It was like a room within a room. It was brightly lit, there were turquoise carpet tiles on the floor and, so Ash said, a suspended ceiling – though I'd no idea what that meant. Since my last encounter with the new technology, computers had shrunk to more manageable proportions; this one was only the size of a combine-harvester. Ash and I stood eyeing up the cream coloured metal box. I was surprised by Ash's interest; he didn't seem to be the sort of guy who'd get excited by a computer. This was Unemployment Benefits, not NASA.

A man – probably in his early twenties, the cardigan made it difficult to tell – approached. The name tag on his lapel said Colin Mills.

'Can I help you?'

'Any chance of a look around?'

Colin Mills shook his head. 'I'm afraid entry for unauthorised staff is strictly forbidden.'

'That's a shame, I was just telling Max about your laboratory.'

Laboratory! I could see through Ash's little game. Computer freaks like nothing more than the opportunity to blather on about their hardware. Laboratory made it all sound a bit exciting, a bit Professor Beaker-ish.

'Well, seeing we've got a lull in the action at the moment, I reckon I can make an exception for a technical enquiry.' He pointed at the purring leviathan. 'This wonderful machine contains the National Employment Register Database – NERD for short. She's quite something, isn't she.'

What! I couldn't believe this crap. This heap of scrap is female. 'How much does this piece of technology cost?' asked Ash.

'That's a cogent question. You wouldn't get much change from a quarter of a million. But it's worth it.'

'So what's it do?' I asked.

'Well,' said Mr Mills in a tone that was almost reverential, 'it can add up.'

I was not impressed. 'So can I.'

'It can also subtract.'

'Me to.' I was beginning to suspect that computers were over-rated. 'More to the point, can it make tea?'

'It's not a bloody Teasmade,' said Ash coming to the computer's defence.

'Of course old Nerdy is still in the development stage' – by now Mr Mills was rubbing his hand along the warm grey casing of the machine in an almost familiar manner – 'soon its full processing power will be unleashed and the slide rule will be a thing of the past.'

I wasn't particularly impressed – the slide rule had never been a major feature of my life.

'Okay. But what's it good for. Apart from adding and subtracting, what do you get for your 250 grand?'

'Well, apart from being able to add up and subtract, it does a couple of other really important things. For a start it makes sure that those who have signed-on get their Giro two days later. Which is good. But what's even cleverer is that it also stops people making fraudulent claims. This machine saves the taxpayer millions.'

'How's it do that?' I asked.

'You see the dole system revolves round the National Insurance Number,' said Colin. 'Everybody over 16 has a National Insurance Number; it's unique and you have it for life...' Yeah, Yeah, Yeah. Two digits and a letter. I knew all about this '... So N.I. numbers are contained on the NERD database.' With his chest puffed up under his white coat and his biros bristling I could see Mr Mills was in his element. 'One of Nerdy's jobs is to track down multiple usage of the N.I. number. Duplicate use of a number will automatically trigger a warning message like this.' He picked up a strip of tape about six feet long that was punched with holes and, as if he was viewing photographic negatives, held up a section to the light.

'Nine times out of ten when we check the details we find that a digit has been input wrongly.'

'How does that bit of tape tell you that?' I asked.

'Good question. We insert the tape into another machine which then translates the alignment of the punch holes into a corresponding N.I. number. So in most cases we can track the alarm back to a clerical error. But every so often we find that a claimant is playing silly buggers and signing-on at two offices at once. It's at that stage we give our friends in the fraud squad a call. Mr Feltch and Mr Bart then swoop into action. And Voila! Fraud averted. Taxpayer's money saved. Job well done.'

'Why isn't everyone wearing a hairnet?'

Mr Mills laughed dismissively. 'Third generation. Dust doesn't affect this little madam.'

Ash explained: 'It was just the computer operators – they were hoping to get more money. They were trying to make the job appear a bit special.'

'You're right, the hairnets, in fact, caused extra problems. The nylon created static build-up,' added Mr Mills. 'You could throw a bucket of water over Nerdy and she'd hardly notice it.'

'I'd be interested to see that,' I said.

'I meant that as a figure of speech.' said Mr Mills with alarm. 'Anyhow she's a very clever machine. You are looking at the future. I tell you one day we'll all have one of these girls.'

'I don't think so. Not unless we're all living in enormous houses.'

'Impressive' said Ash as we walked out of the room.

'Doesn't do it for me.' I said, 'I have to say I found Mr Mills's manner unsettling. Did you notice the way he was caressing 'old nerdy'? Do you think he has many friends? I bet he goes home to a blow-up friend in the evening. Frankly, I think he needs a bucket of water chucking over him.'

## ~ THIRTEEN ~

Mr Blunt thumbed through his files, ticking this and signing that. Ash had warned me about Mr Blunt's game. 'Just sit there – don't let him get the better of you,' Ash had advised. 'It's an ego thing. The longer you delay somebody the more important you are.'

I remember witnessing a version of this at a Rolling Stones concert. After the warm-up act, the Groundhogs, had finished the audience were kept waiting for an eternity. First, we were teased by a hairy, cleavage-arsed roadie arranging Charlie Watts's drum sticks. Half an hour later Keith Richards's guitar was ceremoniously placed on a stand. Then, after two long hours' wait there was an announcement over the PA, 'Is everybody ready? Is everybody ready for the greatest rock and roll band in the world?' Of course we sodding are. We've been sitting here for two hours, you knob head. By the time Jumping Jack Flash minced onto the stage the audience was in a state of frenzy.

But this wasn't Mick Jagger, lead singer of the greatest rock and roll band in the world. This was Eric Blunt, manager of Union Street dole office. Come on. Really!

Mr Blunt was due to give me my Job Appraisal Review. I'd felt a bit edgy beforehand and had gone to the pub for a couple lunchtime pints to calm myself. Ash had been in an unusually generous mood and had insisted on topping up my glass – several times. As I climbed the stairs up to Mr Blunt's office, I wished I hadn't had those five pints. I couldn't think straight. But then again, by now, I didn't give a toss.

As I sat opposite Mr Blunt I noticed that my file had grown bigger. What was in that file?

'So Mr Redcliffe, how do you think you're doing?'

Before I had time to respond Mr Blunt repeated the question.

'So Mr Redcliffe, how do you think you're doing?'

I hated this cod-psychology stuff, all this self-analysis rigmarole. Why doesn't he just come out and say it: 'Redcliffe you're crap, you don't fit in, you're fired.'

'Mr Redcliffe, are you okay?' I realised I was experiencing some sort of time lag – I was having difficulty getting my words out.

'Well... urr ...yes, sorry. I didn't have time for a proper lunch. Low blood sugar level,' I said as I struggled to get my thoughts sorted.

'So I'll ask you again – Mr Redcliffe, how do you think you're settling in?'

I could only mutter the words 'I dunno. All right, I suppose.'

Jesus, this was harder work than I'd expected. I felt so tired, everything around me began to look fuzzy. Where was the penetrating sarcasm, and the witty one-liners with which I had planned to disarm Mr Blunt? All I wanted to do was close my eyes and drift away.

'I wonder...could you...could you open a window,' I mumbled.

Mr Blunt did not appear pleased at this request. He shifted his large frame out of his chair and walked across the room. I could sense Mr Blunt's shadow on my back. I shuddered involuntarily.

'Now is that better?'

'Yeah, thanks.' I could feel a cool draft. I pictured an ice-cold glass being pressed against my neck; I imagined feeling the condensation making my collar damp. My mouth felt dry. I was thirsty; I craved a glass of cool clear water.

'Mr Redcliffe, are you sure you're all right?' came a distant and impatient voice.

It was no good; I couldn't do this. I was now feeling sick. The swirling multi-coloured carpet was blipping like a psychedelic light show. I pushed myself up from my seat. What a low seat, what a very low seat, I thought. And I lunged for the door handle.

'Mr Blunt, could you excuse me for a moment.'

Mr Blunt was sitting bolt upright. His face was alabaster with rage.

'Mr Redcliffe,' he said in a flat voice that barely concealed his anger, 'I'll see you when you're feeling better.'

'You did that on purpose.' I said.

'What?' asked Ash.

'Got me drunk.'

'You weren't drunk.'

'Well, I certainly wasn't sober.'

Ash pointed at his feet. 'What do you think?'

Ash was blatantly trying to change the subject. 'Dunno,' I said.

'My shoes, arsehole.'

'Oh? Urr. Yeah.' I had no idea what he was blathering on about.

'My NEW shoes. Monkey Boots,' said Ash proudly.

'I didn't recognise them. I didn't know they made Monkey Boots in brown.'

'Brown! Do me a favour. These are ox blood red.'

'Nice.' I said flatly.

'Well, Che was impressed. He said they were the preferred footwear of the International Socialists. They're made in Czechoslovakia, you know.'

I wasn't going to let him get away with this. 'Ash, stop changing the fucking subject, I am seriously narked at you.'

'Well, okay. Maybe I did help you have a couple of extra pints,' Ash confessed, 'but I thought it might help you.'

'Help me? Thanks for the concern,' I snapped, 'but it didn't.'

Ash didn't seem to notice, or more likely was ignoring, how annoyed I was. This was the first time that I had been angry with him. I couldn't believe the situation he'd got me into. Being drunk at work was bad enough – being drunk at a JAR was a definite career stopper. And Ash was my mentor, my inspiration and guide through these grim corridors.

As we talked Ash absent-mindedly fiddled with a cluster of paper clips, manipulating them into shapes with all the ease of a party-magician bending balloons.

'Forget the interview, here's something far more important. I'm going to tell you about my plan,' Ash said.

'What plan?'

'My plan to get out of here.'

'Another time.' I'd had enough of Ash's diversions for the moment; I could just as usefully have asked a claimant for hot tips on the Stock Exchange.

'One day you'll thank me for getting you pissed,' he said cheerily.

'Ah! So you did get me pissed.'

'I didn't MAKE you drink those pints. You need to take a bit more responsibility for your own actions.'

'Oh, up yours.'

'Don't worry though, you won't get the sack. I can promise you that. Mr Blunt never sacks anyone – that's his one redeeming feature.'

'Can I ask you something?' I said, 'Can you just back off and stop being so fucking helpful.'

Ash showed not of glimmer of remorse. Which was making me even more annoyed. He put a mangle of paper clips on the table. 'What do you think of that?'

'What is it?'
'Can't you see, it's a dog.'
'It's rubbish.'

## ~ FOURTEEN ~

Astral was drinking a cup of tea as I took a seat opposite her. Despite our close working proximity I rarely got the chance to speak to her. On the infrequent occasions when we were alone together she invariably needed to make a phone call, hurry to the computer room or disappear somewhere on urgent business. It wasn't as if she was unpleasant to me. No, she was always polite and helpful, professional even. I hated that.

During these infrequent transient moments I loved it when our eyes met. Astral naturally projected a steady look of warmth and humour. She would momentarily hold my gaze, but then, as if she had suddenly remembered something, look away. It was at times like this that I felt there was hope.

I was pleased therefore to find myself sitting opposite Astral in the canteen. Even better was the fact that Lee didn't appear to be loitering in the vicinity.

'Hi,' I said airily.
'Hello Matt,' Astral replied.
'It's Max.'
'Of course it is. Sorry.'
'How's things?' I was determined that I was going take my time with this conversation. I would crack a couple of jokes and flirt a bit. I would ask some gently probing questions about Ash and maybe Lee. I would definitely not ask her out.

To be honest, I'd expected Astral to gulp her tea, make an excuse, and rush away on some urgent errand. But she showed no signs of impending departure and continued sipping her drink.

'Okay.' Astral replied brightly to my question.

I felt good merely sitting opposite her. I wanted to reach across the table, hold her hands and look into her eyes. But then I remembered some unasked for and unwelcome advice Boz had once given me.

Boz explained how couples match their looks. 'Max, there's no chance of you going out with a really pretty girl, unless, of course, you come into some big money, or she's in-between contact lenses.' Thanks for the life sentence, Boz.

But today I was feeling lucky.

'We never seem to get a chance to speak,' I said.

'It's been so busy. It'll get quieter at Christmas, though. But then you get other things to contend with.'

'What sort of things?'

'There'll be more drunks. It's horrible. I know they're just trying to be friendly but a festive kiss, even on the cheek, is …. just … yuk!' Astral took a drink. 'Apart from Safran. But he's not that way inclined.'

'Thank God I don't have that problem.'

'Don't be too sure. You watch out for Mrs Kolinsky. Last year, she had Ash on the floor. Lee and Dave had to pull her off. Ash was quite shaken up.'

'I can understand that,' I said. A grapple with Mrs Kolinsky, the Polish bag-babbler, rated pretty high in the nightmare stakes.

'Of course, that was before they put the screens up. It should be better this year.'

'Hopefully,' I agreed. 'Now, what were you going to tell me about Ash.'

'Tell you about Ash?' she repeated.

'Yeah, awhile back, you said he wasn't dish of the day or something.'

'Flavour of the month. It's probably too late to tell you now but I wanted to warn you that he's got a bit of an overactive imagination. He talks a load of rubbish a lot of the time. Sometimes it gets him into trouble.'

'Yeah, he's a scheming bastard.' I said enthusiastically. I thought we could be united in our disdain.

'He's not that bad.' Astral said reprovingly.

'No he isn't really,' I hastily agreed. 'It's just that he got me drunk for my JAR. His approach to mentoring is certainly imaginative.'

Astral laughed. 'Don't worry, Mr Blunt never sacks anybody.'

'So I hear. Anyway, I don't think Mr Blunt noticed.'

'Lee says Ash has a murky past.'

'I'm sure he has. What is it?' I asked.

'I don't know.'

'What's the good of having a murky past if nobody knows about it?'

She smiled. What is it about Astral that makes her so special? The walk, the sway of the hips, the look, the smell; it all adds up. She had a halo of feminine softness round her. She'd even look genuinely pretty, not yucky pretty, in pink. When she moved through the canteen you could see all eyes swivel.

'You just have to be careful about Ash,' she said.

Careful! Everywhere I go in this building somebody sidles up to me and tells me to be careful. Working in Union Street was like wading through stinging nettles. I've never been so careful in my life.

'Thanks, I'll bear that in mind.'

Astral's face brightened. 'The team's Christmas dinner will be fun though.'

'Oh?' Nobody had told me about Christmas Dinner.

'We'll all go for a meal and a bop. Lee's a great dancer. And you should have seen Ash last year.' Astral laughed.

'What was Ash doing?'

'Now there's a secret that everybody knows about.' Astral put her hand in front of her mouth as if she'd said more than she should. 'You'd better ask him.'

But I really wanted to talk about other things. I couldn't carry on with this conversation without clearing the air. I was conscious of the faux pas I'd made when I'd started working at Union Street; I needed to get that out of the way.

'Hey, I really want to apologise for being such a prat the other day.'

'What are you talking about?' I could see she was pretending she didn't remember.

'You know, when we first met.'

'Oh that – you caught me at a bad moment. It was a bit awkward. Forget it.'

'No, I was being stupid – it was inappropriate.'

'Forget it, it was nothing.'

'Are you sure its okay?'

'Quite sure.'

And what about Lee, where did he fit into the picture? To be honest, Lee was beginning to get on my nerves. With his big flat whey face and annoyingly straight clothes, he was always lurking in the shadows. He didn't say much, but just watched. Lee had a dull expressionless face, until he smiled, and then his mouth pulled right back to reveal his rear molars. His smile revealed teeth in profusion that would keep a dental hygienist busy for several appointments. While yellow is one of nature's more uplifting colours, it isn't particularly attractive when it comes to teeth.

'Tell me if I'm prying, but are you going out with Lee?' Although I knew she wasn't, I thought it would be interesting to hear her response.

'Going out with Lee Woods!' she laughed. 'God no! I can't believe you thought that.' Despite her protestation there was a softness in her voice. 'He's just a friend. When I left the hospital and started here he was very good to me. I was a bit shaken up at the time and he helped me through it. He always seems to be around when I need help.'

'You two seem to be very close,' I said.

Astral smiled.'We've known each other for ages. We were at school together. He's like a brother to me. Look, I know he acts like a wally at times. But he's young, he doesn't mean it. I think he feels threatened by you and Ash with your university education and experience of life. He's never had the benefit of all that stuff. Do you know that apart from a couple of trips to Weston super Mare, I don't think Lee has ever left Bristol. He sometimes feels a bit intimidated when he hears you talking about all the places you've been to, and the things you know.'

'What! Threatened by me and Ash. You must be kidding.' I was genuinely surprised. And a little ashamed.

'Sometimes I wish Ash would just lay off Lee. He's always being so horrid to him.'

I thought about what Astral had said. Maybe now was time to start being extra nice to Lee.


'Never accept sweets from a claimant,' said Ash.

'Yeah, Cynthia already mentioned that to me.'

Although I was still pissed off with Ash, I'd have to admit that I was beginning to appreciate his idiosyncrasies. Sure he was full of it, and full of shit. Yet he was an entertaining person to be with in the canteen. He read serious science fiction: Isacc Asimov and Arthur C Clark. Something to feed his overactive imagination, I guessed. Although it wasn't my bag, I was more into the Beats and new journalism – Kerouac, Raoul Duke, Tom Wolfe, that sort of thing.

During the break he'd pull out his tin and his pack of Drum and go through the ritual of rolling what would invariably turn out to be a pathetic stick of a cigarette. 'I don't smoke – it's a ritual,' he'd say. The tin had been lovingly customised; round the side it was embellished with matches, split and varnished, while the lid was decorated with a futuristic Roger Dean type landscape. I had the feeling that this tin was about the only material possession that Ash really cared for.

'Did Cynthia tell you about a guy who calls himself Hawkwind?' asked Ash.

'She did.'

'And his three wives?'

'Yes.'

'Living in Machynlleth?'

'Well, she said North Wales.'

'In a tepee?'

'Yes.'

'Sorry to disillusion you, Max, but that story is all total stoned guff.'

'What do you mean total stoned guff?'

'One hundred per cent total stoned guff. Well, Ed Chicken did trip-out and quit the civil service. That bit is true, but all the rest is my fantasy. I made it up. It was a joke that got out of control. I'd come back from the pub one Friday lunchtime and told Cynthia that I'd seen Ed Chicken staggering out of Zodiac, the head shop on Park Row, with all sorts of smoking paraphernalia. You know, extra large Rizlas, spiral bongs and all that. It was meant to be a joke; it was a wind-up. Well, I had seen Ed Chicken, that part was true, but he was coming out of Barclays Bank, not Zodiac. All that rubbish about how Ed had gone feral and was living the life of a wild man in Wales was a fabrication. Cynthia, however, was so taken by this that in the end I didn't have the heart to tell her I'd made it all up. I'd had a light herbal lunch and was enjoying the story. You know how she is, the more I told her the bigger her eyes got. They were like dustbin lids by the time I got to the bit about the three wives. I didn't know how to break the truth to her. In the end it was easier to leave the story as it was'

'So what is this Ed Chicken really doing?' I asked.

'A 'suits' job, working in accounts for the City Council, or some soul stifling shit like that.

'Oh, and another thing,' said Ash, 'don't ever suck the top of your pen.'

'Yeah, I know all about that, you never know whose arse it's been shoved up.'

## ~ FIFTEEN ~

So, I wasn't exactly sure what to do with my life. I was confused. Is that such a bad thing when you're 23-year-old teenager?

As I'd explained to Ash, mostly it was a political thing, a hangover from 1968, when I branded anybody who earned a living as a bread-head and a fascist. Being unemployed was my anti-capitalist statement. While protesters marched the streets and set fire to embassies I made my point by opting out of the work ethic. Sometimes, when I was feeling particularly righteous, I would support my argument with a home-grown Zen Buddhist slant that said true enlightenment was only possible through the rejection of work.

That's what I'd say. Nevil Sponge was right behind me on that one. But excavate deeper and there were other reasons for my state of suspended ennui. The world was changing – we'd got youth culture, we'd got rock and roll, there was even, so I'd heard, free love. But despite all this excitement there still seemed to be an awful lot of boring office jobs around.

School had been a non-event – little motivated me in the classroom, even less on the playing fields. As a kid my favourite phrase would be 'When I get older...'. 'When I'm older I'm going discover a stone age tribe in New Guinea; I'm going to design a building wackier than the Sydney Opera House.' Sometimes I would go to the observation deck at Heathrow and watch the planes and wonder how people got to travel. But mostly I would dream. I would dream, rather than do.

At school I'd noticed the careers adviser going to her dark little room at the back of the library. I'd once thought about talking to her but felt embarrassed to admit that I didn't know what to do. I felt it would be like to going to confession and declaring that you hadn't sinned.

I've never admitted this before, but my attitude towards employment wasn't entirely based on bed-in politics. Sure, I admired Danny Cohn-Bendit – I was impressed how a short round-faced ginger man could have so many chicks hanging on his every proclamation – but there were other, deeper, forces operating. While I'd say I wasn't temperamentally suited to work, the truth was that I had absolutely no idea what to do with my life. As a kid I'd had ambitions, sure. But all the jobs I wanted to do, I didn't know how to. At school I'd dreamed of being an anthropologist, an archaeologist, an architect. And that was just the 'A's. But how do you do it? Where do you start? I wondered how long I could bide my time – I'd seen some people make a career out of biding their time. I didn't want to make that mistake.

Sadly, I came to believe that the things I aspired to were done by other people. Not by people like me, Max Redcliffe living in Cherry Tree Avenue, Ruislip, within earshot of the A40.

My parents weren't much use either. They weren't consumptive, alcoholic or about to have an acrimonious divorce. Not only were they boring, as far as I could see they didn't have any contacts or move in the right circles. 'What does your Dad do?' It was a common question at school, and one that I didn't know how to answer. 'He's in insurance,' I would reply in a manner of finality that didn't allow further questions. But what did 'in insurance' mean? It didn't have the same ring as Architect, or Doctor or working in a shop. You knew what these people did. They had a persona. You could picture them at a drawing board, in the surgery, behind the counter. But being 'in insurance'? All I knew was that my father caught the 8.12 from Ruislip and walked five minutes from Marylebone to his office in Baker Street, but what did he spend his day doing? His clothes didn't give anything away – he didn't wear overalls, a white coat or a uniform. No, like everyone else on the 8.12 he wore a heavy pinstripe suit. And apart from a slight odour of sweat in the summer, he didn't even smell of anything. I hadn't the vaguest idea of what went on in my Dad's life. I never asked, and Dad had never told me.

As for my Mum, well, she was a housewife. I once remarked to her that it must be nice staying at home all day. I was surprised when she said no, it was boring, and that she missed out on all the fun you have at work. I never realised that you could have fun at work. Surely my Dad didn't have fun at work. The thought of Dad having fun at work was slightly unsettling – like my parents having sex.

Now I was older, there was nobody else I could blame. Studying sociology had enabled me to put plans on hold for three years. These days the get-out clause of 'When I'm older' was becoming increasingly difficult to hide behind. Starting work at Union Street didn't make things any better. My vision of the future, which had always been a bit fuzzy round the edges, was now blocked by a depressing grey fog. Time was no longer on my side. Increasingly, it seemed like it was up to me.

Alongside the Noddy books, Ash began to dispense advice of a more personal nature. One day, apropos of absolutely nothing Ash said:

'Look Max, what I'm going to say next is with your best interests at heart. Not to put it too bluntly, you are way out of her league.'

I wasn't expecting this. 'What are you on about?'

'C'mon man, it's embarrassing. The way your tongue hangs out – you're like a dog, it's pathetic.'

Was I that obvious? I couldn't help it. I found myself just staring at her. I wanted to look at her gorgeousness. I wanted to check out how it all fitted together – her mouth, her nose, her eyes, her smile – individually they were all fine, but together they were perfection. My gaze was constantly drawn to her. I'd look over her shoulder and check out what was happening in the room. But this was time wasted; I wanted to look at her.

'What's it to you, anyway?' I said.

'I don't want to see you getting hurt.'

'You think Lee's going to mash me up.'

'No, not like that. Emotionally hurt.'

'Let's be clear about this Ash – is this advice part of your mentoring duties? Or do you charge extra for the counselling service?'

'Max, just shut up and listen. This is for your own good. What I've got to say, hurts me as much as it hurts you.'

'Oh I get it. YOU'VE got the hots for her. You're warning me off.'

'Max, she's a great girl, but she's not my type – reminds me of my sister.'

'Introduce me sometime.'

'Wouldn't be a good idea. Little Sis says she's allergic to civil servants. All that dust.'

'But I'm not ...'

' 'fraid you are pal.'

I could guess where this conversation was heading, and I knew that it wouldn't be boosting my self-esteem.

'She's far too good for you. I don't mean this unkindly – but what have you got to offer?'

I shrugged.

Ash continued 'Okay, I wouldn't go as far as to say that you're conventionally ugly, but you're not exactly David Cassidy, either.'

'That's a disappointment that I can live with.'

'But most important of all, you've got no money. It's in the human psyche to breed upwards, to improve the breeding stock. A class chick like her could have the pick of the bunch. She could go for money. She could go for looks. With her body, all she has to do is go to some Bristol University ball, flash her boobs and she's picked up a chinless wonder. She's made for life. It's easy for a girl like Astral. Somebody of her physical calibre just isn't interested in the likes of you.'

'Astral's not that shallow. What about intelligence and integrity?' In my mind I wasn't thanking Ash for this lecture on human evolution.

'Yeah. What about intelligence and integrity. You haven't got those either.'

'Ash, how does this conversation hurt YOU?' I asked.

'I don't like telling you this.'

'Well, snap! I don't like hearing it.'

First Boz, now Ash. How come everybody felt it their duty to be so unhelpful about my love-life? Give me a break guys. My morale needed a boost, not a cold shower.

The following day Ash was due to tell me about the pivotal event of the week, the event that everybody dreaded, PI day. For their first few weeks new members of staff were shielded from the full trauma of this ordeal. But now it was Thursday and my time had come. I had already heard colleagues talking about PI day in nervous tones. I could sense the edginess on Thursdays – everybody hated it. Except Kastrina. But even she acknowledged it wasn't a good time to administer her hurt to help power-trip.

Unusually, Ash had asked Che to take me through the details. 'He has a different perspective on things – you might find it interesting.' In truth I felt Ash was steering clear of me after the unasked for advice he'd given about Astral.

Che explained, 'If a claimant doesn't have an address or their address is a communal letter box where a Giro could easily be nicked, we have to make them a PI – a Personal Issue – which means that they have to come in and pick their money up from Union Street.

'A straightforward sensible solution you would think? Not so, comrade. It's a recipe for disaster.'

Che got up from his chair; he seemed a bit edgy, a bit ill at ease. 'On PI day you have assembled in one place more mad, angry, and dispossessed people than is imaginable.'

He began walking back and forth with his hands behind his back as if he was delivering a lecture. I was having trouble taking Che seriously. According to Ash anarchists have to go through an initiation ceremony. Che's task was to throw a petrol bomb at the Army Recruiting Office. Unfortunately the mollie bounced off the plate glass window and set his trousers on fire. He legged it down the street with his strides glowing in the dark like a three-skinner.

'It's like they emptied the prisons, the madhouses, the dosshouses, the dope dens and the squats and assembled all the inmates in the local village hall. PI day is a social time bomb – and it's set to go off 2.00 p.m. every Thursday right here in Union Street. There's scores to be made, and there's scores to be settled.' Che spun on his heels and pointed a finger at me. 'And there you are, Max Redcliffe, Mr Civil Servant – the enemy.'

'But…' I wanted to make it clear to Che that I really didn't think of myself as a civil servant.

Che interrupted. 'No buts, Max, they hate you. You're just a state funded bully. Nobody gives a shit about you. Why should they? Because they've got more troubles than you can ever imagine. They're on the very bottom rung. Unlike you and I, they have nothing to fall back on. They are desperate. And if they don't have their cheque, they're fucked. There's only a flimsy plate of Perspex between you and this mad mob, and man, with a bit of adrenaline they can jump over that screen with the ease of a grasshopper. I tell you, one day soon a fucking riot's gonna happen here. And personally, Max, I just hope I'm not on the receiving end.'

For a few moments Che stared absently at the grey winter light coming through the window. He then turned and looked at me. 'In fact, I might just be the person who starts that riot.'

Now, that was a different perspective.

I soon learnt an important lesson. On PI afternoon the doors were always opened at 2.00 pm – sharp. It was crucial that there was no delay. The longer the wait, the more likely the detonation of Che's human time-bomb. Today, however, things were running a little late. There was a claim missing from Astral's box and she was in the main room searching for it.

The crowd outside was getting impatient. I could hear shouting and jeering, and could see shadowy faces peering through the frosted glass. By four minutes past two a young fast-track trainee manager, who was slumming it for a couple months in Union Street to see how some of the more unspeakable corners of the Civil Service were run, had had enough.

'I'm going to open the doors, whether you're ready or not,' the wet-back said.

Ash looked at Lee in alarm: 'Does he know how to do it?'

'We'll soon see.'

Because of the pressure of the crowd, the bolts had to be pulled in a specific order. We watched. It was obvious that the trainee didn't know this.

Kastrina stopped humming her song and shouted 'Stand by with the First Aid Box'. Although I knew she was joking, I visually checked the green box on the wall by the interview room.

The trainee had undone the top bolt of the right hand door. The crowd outside heard the clunk of the brass bolt and started to put pressure on the doors. The trainee undid the enormous latch than ran across in the middle of the door. It was as if some dreadful pack of wild animals was straining to get in. There were bangings and yelps. The door appeared to be bulging at the edges. The trainee then bent down to pull up the bottom bolt.

'Hey, err, don't!' cried out Lee. Nobody knew the wet-back's name.

Bent double the trainee looked over to Lee at the counter.

'What?'

And without waiting for an answer he pulled up the bolt.

THWACK! With a mighty force the door swung open, cracking the trainee on the head and sandwiching him against the wall.

Everybody looked on in silent horror. Luckily the trainee was protected from the worst of the stampede by being pinned behind the door. All that could be seen of him was a leg and an arm that twitched and then went limp.

'Stay at your posts!' commanded Mr Blunt, who had appeared as if from nowhere. 'We'll send somebody out to get him when the rush is over.'

For a second I looked at trainee's twisted limbs. Never, ever, volunteer to open the doors I thought.

But then a UB40 was being waved in front of my eyes. By now the signing on hall was noisy with the sound of yelling and expectoration.

'Evans 45B,' the man said.

'Address?' I shouted.

My first P.I. session was under way...

At least working on the counter was interesting. For three days out of five I spent my time on clerical work.

Civil service speak; it was crazy – you couldn't call anything by its name, everything had a code. Even a blank sheet of paper was M.o.W. 459 or something. The sorting and checking of papers was so mind-crushingly dull that I found it difficult. I hadn't yet learnt the art of disengaging parts of the brain. Being methodical was an important part of the job. The constant tick-tock of the clock on the wall clouded my mind. My thoughts would drift and I'd lose track of what I was doing. I would dream of a steaming tropical jungle and Astral in a moist tee-shirt.

I felt stupid – I'd got a degree in Sociology yet I couldn't do filing. More than once Astral had picked up claims from my table that should have been input on the computer. It made me wonder how people coped; how could you do this for the rest of your life? How do people survive with only this to look forward to?

'It's like Alcoholics Anonymous, you take it one day at a time,' said Ash, as he sorted through his box of claims. 'One day I'll tell you about my four point plan to success.'

Yet another of Ash's Rizla dreams. If it was that good I wondered why he hadn't put it into action.

Ash continued, 'Whoever said work was going to be fun? You do it because you have to, not for enjoyment. There are only a very few people in the world who have jobs that they really enjoy. The middle classes say that hard work never killed anybody. That's not true, real hard work is genocide. Think of all those poor sods who work down the mines. Imagine it. Underground all day, in the dark, breathing air that's so thick with dust that within a week your lungs are blackened for life. Bursting their bodies with the sort of physical labour that you and I couldn't begin to imagine. What do you reckon their wives say at the end of the day? Had a good day down the mine, dear? For most people work is shit; it's a way of paying the bills. It's something to be endured, not enjoyed.'

'Ash, you're a cynical bastard.'

'Maybe. It's just that I've got better things to do with my life than spend it shuffling buff coloured bits of paper round a grey table.'

'So Ash, what the hell are YOU doing here, then?' Ash's attitude was pissing me off.

Ash looked-up from his claim box and stared directly at me. He cleared his throat and for a moment looked as though he was going to say something profound, something personal. But then he changed his mind.

'What the hell do you think I'm doing in Union Street?' The brief moment of profundity had already passed. 'Like you, I'm trying to earn enough money to get out of here.'

## ~ SIXTEEN ~

Despite Astral's accusation that he had an over-active imagination I was beginning to realise how restrained Ash had been with his descriptions of colleagues. He was certainly right not to give me the low down on Kastrina. If he'd told me the truth I wouldn't have believed him.

Even the naivest request to Kastrina would be met with derision. One dazed man, still in a state of shock at finding himself in the intolerable position of taking a B.1 to the DHSS, innocently asked: 'What do I do? Just walk in?' This was an opportunity not to be missed. Kastrina's reply was whiplash quick. 'Walk? No. I'd crawl in, if I was you.'

I once asked Kastrina why she showed so little compassion towards the claimants.

'It may seem cruel to you, but these people need it. I know what I'm talking about Max, I grew up with them. They need kicking into action. Its all very well for you middle class nancies, brought up wrapped in cotton wool, knowing that Mummy and Daddy will bail you out if the going gets tough. Well, I didn't have that – there was never any safety net in my life. And most of the people signing-on don't have that either. It's sink or swim. My approach is to make them damn-well swim. They'll drown otherwise. Believe me I'm doing them a favour.'

For a moment I thought about this and thought 'yeah, she's right.' But then I thought some more and realised that Kastrina was talking total bollocks. She was an alpha-bitch and sadism ran through her like the lettering in a stick of rock. Her mission was to make the lives of claimants as miserable as possible.

'Bloody hell Kastrina, if that's a favour I'd hate to see what you're like when you're being unhelpful.' I couldn't work her out. Perhaps she'd been bullied at school and this was her revenge. Bullied bad. She must have had a real tough time to get like this.

Kastrina stared at me. 'Max, you ought to be a social worker,' she said sticking her neck out and lifting up her nose as if there was a turd underneath it. 'Then you can really help people fuck-up big time.'

In a way Kastrina was right. Not about the fuck–up, but if I had to work, I wanted a job that benefited or helped people. I felt that my work at Union Street could fall into that category.

I remembered a conversation I once had with Ash. 'Okay, all this paperwork is crap – but what about on the counter, don't you think you can do something worthwhile there?'

Ash had looked at me in amazement. 'What sort of fairyland do you live in, Max? Filling out these forms, filling out these forms in bloody triplicate, useful! As far as I'm concerned this is the biggest waste of time EVER. The sooner we can get Mr Mill's computer to do all this rubbish, the better. People can then be freed up to do some useful jobs. Or not work at all – which would be my choice.'

I continued. 'I couldn't do this if I didn't think it was useful. I remember reading about this guy who worked for an American oil company – his job was to look after a valve on the main pipeline. Every half hour he had to leave his wooden hut, cross the path and turn on a valve for exactly 30 seconds. It was an important part of the process; he did this for 25 years. One day the valve got stuck and a maintenance engineer was called. It turned out that the valve was connected to a pipe that had been diverted, many years before. It was empty, it connected to nothing. For the last 15 years the man had been turning on a valve that served absolutely no purpose. He went home and shot himself through the head.'

'Bummer,' said Ash. He was silent for a moment and then added, 'Well, maybe you're right, we all like to feel that we're doing something useful.' He looked at me and nodded. 'I tell you what though, it helps if you've got a job with people you like.'

'Yeah that does help.'

And,' Ash said this as he looked in the direction of Astral who was sitting on the other side of the canteen, 'if you can work with somebody who's easy on the eye, well, that's a bonus.'

'Where's Justine? asked Kayne Bender, a lugubrious character from the finance section.

The salacious grin and the knowing glint in Kayne Bender's eyes suggested that there was something about the absentee Justine. Although nothing was ever specified, it was becoming clear that she had a reputation. I got the feeling, judging by the coughing, whistling and general leeriness that mention of Justine's name aroused, that she was a bit of a goer.

So, one morning, I asked Lee about Justine. Lee was chewing a limp slice of toast from the Concorde Café.

'She's durty,' he smirked.

'She's dirty – what do you mean?'

'She's durty. She's durty' he paused, 'and she's loud. She's durty, she's loud and…. Lee took another bite of toast and thought for a moment as he constructed his less than charming cameo …she's a cider-head. Yeah…' he said with a big grin on his face, as if he was introducing an act on New Faces. '…She's DIRTY, she's LOUD and she's a CIDER HEAD.'

'Cider head? – I thought cider was for kids,' I said, thinking of the Nutcracker Cider I drank as a fourteen year old.

'Purgh!' Lee spat. 'Cider round these parts ain't for bumfluffers – it's a real man's drink.'


Seeing that we were getting on so well I thought this would be a good opportunity to start my charm offensive to win Lee over.

'What do you do when you're not at work, Lee?'

'I'm a gas head.'

'A gas head. What's that?'

'Are you stupid or summat? I support Rovers.'

I wondered if this explained Lee's strange clothes – he was always dressed in proper trousers. Trousers, not jeans. Today, he was sporting a big tie – in the same vein as the one I had worn, and quickly discarded, on my first day – and a tight fitting brown and orange patterned tank-top. His hair was short and combed – and I was sure that he splashed some less than masculine grooming products onto his pallid body.

I had no interest in football; I decided to change the subject.

'How long have you been working here?'

'Since I left school. This is my first job. I saw an advert in the Post for a clerical assistant at the Ministry of Work, and thought that sounds like a good job. With prospects too.'

Why would anybody WANT to do that? What was wrong with studying for A levels and a degree as all my friends at the Grammar school had done?

'Oh yeah. Prospects.' I'd forgotten about the prospects.

I like to think of myself as an open-minded type of guy. But just two questions had confirmed what I suppose I already knew. Lee and I really did have nothing in common. Freak and straight – those who did and those who didn't – like oil and water, we didn't mix. It was simple as that.

I found Lee effortlessly annoying. It's difficult to say why; he just was. Maybe it was his particularly daft voice (to the trained ear there are said to be seven distinct Bristol accents – his was the soft version spoken in the central-east area of the city) or even the amount of space his large frame took up. Lee was about six foot something; I'm five foot nine. It wasn't as if Lee gave off an aggressive vibe, it was just that he was there.

And another thing. What bugged me, what really bugged me, was that Astral appeared to confide in Lee. Astral genuinely seemed to like Lee. That did hurt. Why him, not me? I would console myself with the thought that sometimes it's easier to talk to a brick wall.

But I needed to keep the conversation going. 'So when do we expect Justine to return?' I asked.

'Dunno. You'll be out on your ear when she comes back, though.' This surprised me. I hadn't realised that my position depended on Justine's absence. This certainly wasn't what Mr Blunt had intimated.

'Are you sure?'

'Yeah, positive.' Lee smiled his big yellow teeth smile and gave a Sooty and Sweep wave 'Bye-bye Max. Bye-bye everybody.'

If only it could be that easy.

## ~ SEVENTEEN ~

I had been looking forward to the Christmas dinner for some time. Ash tried to put me right on this. 'It'll be crap,' he said.

I ignored Ash's comment. I'd heard that he'd had a traumatic experience the previous year and any mention of Christmas put him in a dangerous mood.

'That may be your approach. I'm going to enjoy myself.'

'You'll sit next to someone you don't like, the food'll be shit and you'll end up getting drunk and making a total arse of yourself by tonguing some hideous old bag, who in normal circumstances you would avoid shaking hands with. I can do without it, thanks.'

I had no intention of making an idiot of myself. I also knew exactly who I'd be tonguing, and she was far from hideous.

Astral raised the topic at the Wednesday staff meeting. 'I know Christmas is still ages away...' groans of 'Jesus, it seems like I've only just come back from my summer holiday' – '...but the best places get booked early. I'll phone some restaurants and get some menus sent to us. Any suggestions?'

'Yeah F. off.'

'Thank you, Ash. Any sensible suggestions?'

Not being familiar with this annual charade, I made a sensible suggestion, 'Astral, The Raj Mahal on Park Street do a shit-hot curry.'

'A shit-hot curry doesn't sound very Christmassy, Max,' said Kastrina.

'If you want Christmassy, what about the Mandarin?' suggested Lee. 'They serve a lush Peking duck.'

'Err Lee? Since when has Peking duck been Christmassy?' said Ash.

'My parents sometimes have duck at Christmas,' replied Lee.

'Duck my arse!'

'Just shut up, Ash.'

'I don't like any of this foreign muck,' said Kastrina. 'Why don't we go where we went last year? You know that place on Park Street.'

'It's just been closed down by the environmental health people.'

'For God's sake, Ash will you SHUT UP.'

'Yeah, shut it, Ash,' said Lee.

'It's called Le Hotpot, and it's crap,' retorted Ash,

'You seemed to enjoy yourself last year,' said Lee.

'I didn't,' said Ash curtly.

'Yeah, well, if I remember correctly your enjoyment had little to do with the food.'

'Lee – will you just piss off.' I could see that Ash was on the verge of losing it. 'Get a life – instead of watching me, you...you sad voyeur.'

I could sense a general uneasiness around the table. I wasn't sure what to make of it. I felt there was more to it than Ash's unfortunate incident with Mrs Kolinski.

Kastrina quickly said, 'All right, if nobody likes Le Hotpot, what about Mel's Diner. They do a good steak and chips.'

'But I'm vegetarian.'

'Cynthia, You can have omelette and chips.'

'What's so Christmassy about that?'

'For God's sake' said Kastrina, who was getting increasingly exasperated, 'you can have a sprig of holly sticking out of it.'

It was obvious that a sensible discussion about the Christmas meal was becoming increasingly unlikely. 'I tell you what we're going to do. Astral will get some menus and if next week we can't come to a mutual agreement I'm going to have to make an executive decision.'

'What's executive decision mean?' asked Lee.

'It means,' said Ash quietly, 'that Kastrina has already made up her mind and we're going to Le Hotpot.'

Kastrina got up from her chair. She seemed keen to finish the meeting. 'That's enough of that. We've got some signing-on to do.'

Lee cleared his throat and said 'Excuse me, but before you all disappear back to your work I've got one last item on the agenda. Mr Blunt has instructed me...'

'Whooo...Lee, ....Mr Blunt has instructed me...' Ash repeated in derision as he got up from the table.

'....Mr Blunt has asked you all to desist from throwing sandwich crusts, half-eaten pies and other rubbish into the yard at the back of the building. It's a health risk and is likely to attract rats.'

By the time Lee had finished his last sentence, there was only me and him left in the room.

## ~ EIGHTEEN ~

It was a gloomy December morning when Kastrina said that Mr Blunt had requested to see me at 11.30. I was surprised it had taken as long as six weeks to re-arrange my JAR. I felt an uneasy twinge in my stomach.

As I passed Baxter at his desk he surreptitiously passed me a folded piece of paper.

Ash had already told me about Baxter. It was Ash's view that Baxter's role on reception was to out-weird the weirdest. In just five minutes even psychotic street-shouters felt normal after talking to Baxter.

'He's a nice enough guy, but he's absolutely barking. In his early days Baxter was seen as a whiz kid; he saved the Department thousands of pounds by inventing the re-usable envelope. Do you know that nobody had ever thought of it until Baxter came along? He was given an incentive award for that bit of thinking. Don't get too excited, it's no big deal, the maximum award is £20. And then it's got to be a really good idea, the sort of thing that will save the Department millions. Shit, they're tight arsed bastards.'

'Unfortunately poor old Baxter was never able to top his re-usable envelope idea. After that he had a hell of a reputation to live up to – too much, too soon you could say.' I wasn't sure whether Ash meant this to be funny but I laughed anyway.

Baxter smiled and motioned with a nod of his head that I was to carry on. I walked up the stairs to the canteen and unfolded a page of paper that had been torn from an exercise book. In green ink, in a whiskery hand, were written the words:

DON'T GO TO KEYNSHAM[1]

I shouted down the stairwell 'Thanks for the advice, Baxter.'

I was already a few minutes late for my appointment. I knocked on the door and walked straight into Mr Blunt's office. Mr Blunt, who was sitting behind his grey metal desk, was concentrating on reading. Without looking up, he said. 'Take a seat Mr Radcliffe – I'll be with you in a moment.'

Radcliffe! I sat on a wobbly wooden chair in front of him. I looked at Mr Blunt. He was big and globular with taut skin – like a bag of jelly – that could so easily pop, with unspeakable consequences. He continued to ignore me.

Even though I hardly knew the man I hated him. I was annoyed with myself for spending so much time thinking about Mr Blunt. As I walked to work, or lay in the bath, I would rehearse verbal duals. In these imaginary conversations I would humiliate Mr Blunt in front of C Section with some clever witticism. With my natural charm I would disarm him and send him on his way. My reverie would always end in the same manner. Astral, who had witnessed the sparring, would hug me and coo 'I think you're marvellous.' That bit was okay.

I was puzzled why I was so deeply annoyed by Mr Blunt. Was it to do with his sneering 'so much better than thou' attitude? Or the constant innuendo that he knew something that you'd rather he didn't? Certainly, that didn't help. But there was something about his demeanour; a glum sterile cloud hung over Mr Blunt; he exuded a joie de mort. I was also disturbed by his singular dedication to the job. I could see it in his humourless features; Mr Blunt loves every minute of the day at Union Street. As he left the office I could imagine him deflating like a punctured balloon.

But what really unnerved me about Mr Blunt was his constant presence. It was as if the man had a sixth sense. If I was messing around, you could bet your Giro that Mr Blunt would come sailing round the corner; if I was slagging him off, sure enough, he'd be standing, unnoticed, right by my shoulder; think an evil thought and he'd be there.

---

[1] Here's a bit of social history. For those who weren't around then, Keynsham occupied a special place in the hearts of British teenagers in the 1960s. This nondescript town on the edge of Bristol gained a mythical status thanks to a Radio Luxembourg advert. Unbelievably – and this was the era of the early Beatles and Rolling Stones – Luxembourg 208 was the only radio station to play non-stop pop music.

Luxembourg was a commercial station, and the most frequently broadcast advert was for Horace Batchelor's Infra-Draw Method. The Infra-Draw Method had nothing to do, as was popularly inferred by young boys, with a method of birth control, but was a supposedly foolproof scheme for winning the football pools. The advert culminated in Horace Batchelor, spelling out his address letter by letter

K–E–Y–N–S–H–A–M. The advert was so unbelievably naff that it became a cause celebre. Viv Stanshall and the Bonzo Dog Band even named an album after it. Such was the impact of Horace Batchelor's slow West Country drawl that even ten years later the mere mention of Keynsham would be greeted with howls of laughter, and elicit the response 'How do you spell that.' Try mentioning Keynsham to anyone born before 1955 and see how they react.

For a big man Mr Blunt was surprisingly light on his feet; he moved in his enormous suit like a ship under sail. Once, in the further reaches of the building, I had come across an empty corridor that had been newly covered in green carpet. Unexpectedly, and before I could stop myself, a primeval urge, hidden for generations, welled up from some deeply recessed gene and took control of my body. I ran and rolled over and over on the freshly laid greensward. For a minute I was a child in an ecstasy of dizziness rolling down a grassy bank. I lay on my back on the floor and savoured the woozy feeling in my head. I breathed deeply, dreaming I was in a field with the summer sun warming my face. I could smell the sweet grass; I could hear the bees fly by. But then a cloud obscured the light. I opened my eyes to find Mr Blunt peering down at me with a quizzical look on his face. His fat face was so close that I could smell coffee on his breath. It was one of those moments when a logical explanation doesn't help.

'I was just testing the carpet,' I said.

Mr Blunt said nothing and, with his suit flapping, carried on his way.

Mr Blunt gave a little grunt as he turned a page of my file. There was a brass bell, the type favoured by hotel receptionists, on his desk. I looked around the room. It was furnished with regulation civil service chairs and filing cabinets – all grey, all soulless. On the floor was a square of swirly carpet – the sort of carpet that a cat could throw up on and you wouldn't notice. But there was something different about the room – the ceiling seemed higher. Indeed, Mr Blunt seemed higher! I looked at the floor, and then I saw it. The legs of my chair had been cut to make them shorter. They had been hand-sawn; there were jaggedy splinters round the edge. Mr Blunt must have done this himself. What was this man's game? It was so ridiculous that I almost laughed aloud. I was beginning to wonder which was worse – being drunk or being hysterical.

I tried to think of something else... I imagined Mr Blunt on a Friday afternoon enjoying a moment of calm satisfaction as he allowed himself the luxury of reflection. He is doing well; he can clearly see his future. He imagines a golden staircase leading ever onwards and upwards. His plan is working, all he needs to do is to hit his targets and a place is assured – yes, assured – in Regional Office. Regional Office! He savours this thought, visualising the Regional Director's room. It is decorated like a palace – he'd never want to go home. And then from Regional Office – and here his golden staircase disappears into the clouds – to Head Office in Tothill Street, London.

Yet a tiny nagging doubt brings him back to the realities of this Friday afternoon. Targets. Targets – always increasing – always more difficult to achieve.

He always finishes his week with an empty in-tray. He scans a couple of circulars and moves them into the out-tray for his secretary to file. He picks up an application form. He is momentarily pleased; there is always something satisfyingly voyeuristic about an application form. Address, place of education, exams, interests, career details – a life summed up in four pages. It takes a glance at this particular form, however, for Mr Blunt to be disappointed.

Is he really the only person in the world who genuinely wants a career with the Ministry of Work? Nobody puts the Ministry of Work as first preference on their Civil Service application form. They all want the glamour jobs: Diplomatic Corps; Treasury; Customs. The real dreamers want to work for Meteorology in Bracknell. Not a chance. The Meteorology Office only recruits four people a year. So it is the no-hopers, the Met Office rejects, who end-up being offered jobs at the Ministry of Work. Mr Blunt is surrounded by wannabe TV weathermen.

I could imagine him looking at my application form. He stares at it; it is obvious from the scrawling handwriting, the spelling mistakes and the sheer paucity of thought that the application form he holds in his hand isn't from somebody who genuinely wants a career in the Civil Service. This is a freeloading student on the lookout for temporary work. Why do they waste his time? Why don't they stick to bar work? But he knows the answer to this. Because bar work is too much like hard work – that's why. Sybaritic students searching for the easy option. You have to watch these people; make sure you always have the upper hand. He has had enough of them. As soon as you've trained them, invested money in them, they've disappeared – probably to a beach on the other side of the world. Even worse, this particular applicant possesses the most spurious qualification in the whole academic pantheon. As far as Mr Blunt is concerned a degree in Sociology is a degree in trouble-making.

But targets, targets, targets. He has his targets to meet. Even long-haired, insolent, here-today gone-tomorrow students have their place on his golden stairway.

He writes in his rounded hand on the top of Max Redcliffe's application form. No interview required. Start ASAP.

At last Mr Blunt looked up from his studies and stared at me.

'Now where were we before we were interrupted ...'. Mr Blunt hesitated as if he was choosing his words carefully '...by your sudden illness? Ah yes.

How do you think you are doing, Mr Redcliffe?

'I think I'm settling in pretty well.'

'Do you?....' Silence.

'Yes, I'm getting the hang of the systems and enjoying working with the team.'

'Hmm...,' Silence.

'Yes I do, and I'm getting the hang of PI day.'

'So I hear,' said Mr Blunt with a mocking sneer.

Wait a moment, I thought, I seem to be doing all the work here. I was beginning to feel like a dog let loose by its owner – to see where it would run. And thus uncover a hidden stash of bones.

Rather than expose any secrets I now decided to say no more and sit it out. Silence. In the lull Mr Blunt looked down at my file. The file appeared to have expanded another inch since we last met. What was in that file? How could there be so many pages? For a moment I felt flattered that there could that much to write about me. Mr Blunt coughed and shifted his shoulders.

'So?' Mr Blunt intoned.

'So?' I repeated, 'what?'

'Is that all you've got to say?'

'What was the question?'

Pause. 'Miss Klebb tells me you have an attitude problem towards the claimants.'

The bitch! I was surprised. I'd done my best – though on PI day, when the heat was on, it was sometimes difficult to show claimants the empathy and support that they deserved.

'Well, maybe that is the case,' I had to concede, 'sometimes the stress on the counter can get a bit intense.'

'I think we're talking at cross-purposes here. What I'm saying is that you're too soft.'

I was astounded. 'Too soft? According to who?' Was I hearing right?

'Yes, you're seen as a soft touch. I've warned you about this'

'How can I be a soft touch? These people have fallen on hard times.'

'Hard times! They're having a laugh.'

'They're desperate. They need all the help we can give them.'

Mr Blunt interrupted. 'You need to understand that you have to make an example of these people. It's the principle of the matter; the foundations of our society would crumble to dust if we allowed these Giro-jockeys to freeload the system. And despite your fears,' Mr Blunt added sarcastically, 'I am sure the Inland Revenue have got things in hand.'

'Anyhow,' Mr Blunt continued 'we are getting away from the point. I haven't got time to indulge in namby-pamby intellectual theorising. We're here to discuss your personal development.'

Mr Blunt folded his arms and pushed out his rotund chin. I sensed that this topic was now closed.

'I want to talk to you about your appearance. I can remember you on your first day. I thought how smartly you were dressed. I thought, 'that man is setting a good example.' Unfortunately, I note that your state of attire seems to have deteriorated since then. I blame it on Ash Hill. I can't understand why Kastrina chose him as your mentor, he's so untidily dressed.' And then Mr Blunt said something I hadn't heard for many years. ' I want you to get your hair cut.'

Deja vu. I was being addressed by my father. I could hear the old man, sitting in his Parker Knoll Recliner, shouting at Donovan on Top of the Pops – 'get a bloody haircut!'

My father would recite, 'In my day, hair that went over the collar meant one of three things; you weren't fit to serve in the armed forces; you were a conscientious objector, or you were a nancy boy. The last person to have long hair was Oscar Wilde,' at this point he would turn and glare at me, 'and we all know what happened to him.'

Believe it or not, in the 1960s when I was a teenager, long hair was a political statement; it was a rejection of the establishment and a sign of revolutionary solidarity. When David Crosby sang 'I almost cut my hair,' I knew that he was going through a real bummer. And what was the first thing the police did when they arrested Nevil Sponge for conspiring to corrupt public morals? Booked him in for a mandatory visit to the prison barber.

As a kid I'd feared the barber even more than the dentist. I could remember the conversation from long ago. 'How would young sir like it?'

Sitting in the shiny black leather chair, with the aroma of exotic unguents heavy in the air, I would be lulled into a false sense of security.

'Just tidy up round the edges and leave the front.' A simple enough request. But I should have known. Unless it was a short, back and sides he was deaf to whatever style I requested.

'You kids think you can do what you like,' muttered Barber Brooks as he severed my Beatle fringe. I looked despairingly at myself in the mirror; the humiliation! Even my beautiful Chelsea boots couldn't disguise the fact that my hair made me look like an evacuee. And I still gave him a tip.

Why did I put up with it? He was my Dad's hairdresser; I'd always gone there. As soon as I was old enough to go down the High Street by myself I ditched the bastard. No more barbers – the Unisex salon was the future for me.

Over the years I closely studied Mick Jagger and John Lennon to see what they were doing with their hair. Collar length; shoulder length; with sideburns; without sideburns; covering the forehead; centre parted – I had observed and endeavoured to adopt, usually with disastrous results, all these styles. I remember the shudder of horror when John Lennon appeared to have temporarily lost his way and his Abbey Road shoulder length mane was brutally hacked for the Instant Karma period. While this new style looked dangerously as though it had been borrowed from the skinheads, in retrospect, Lennon had, of course, invented a new trend – Socialist-Worker radical chic.

There was one little problem with all this. My hair, while not being exactly curly, wasn't straight either. While girls could iron their hair for the Sandie Shaw/Cher look, boys were left facing a style crisis. So this is where Bob Dylan came in. Bob's curly hair achieved greatness in 1966 with the Blonde on Blonde album. As ever Bob broke all the conventions; his groundbreaking hair sent out a shiver of confusion that made the straight-hairs envious. 'Judas' cried a proto-mullet head in the audience at the Manchester Free Trade Hall. Even Eric Clapton in a crazed moment that he was later to bitterly regret, went for a disastrous perm. You could imagine Eric's horror when he came to, and looked in the mirror – granny takes a trip.

So I was surprised by Mr Blunt's demand – I thought the battle of the barnet had been fought and won ten years before. 'Are you a boy or a girl?' I was only asked that on a monthly basis now. But, well, this was the civil service – things moved at a slower place here; they were still using waxed Ibcol bog paper.

'A haircut. I'll see what I can do.' I said in a flat tone of voice that acknowledged Mr Blunt's request but didn't promise any action.

'Now, back to the matter in hand. I think it's time that we introduced you to the services of our training department. They run a three-day A.R.F. course that you will find highly beneficial.'

Mr Blunt pulled out a pad and wrote on it in his big round script.

'It certainly helped Lee Woods. It brought out a new confidence in him. He came back a changed man. It was as if Lee had grown-up over night.'

He folded the form and put it in an envelope which he sealed with a lick from his blancmange-coloured tongue. At which point I averted my eyes.

'Give this to Miss Shrimpton in Training.'

I almost expected Mr Blunt to say 'You'll be as right as rain in no time.'

'Mr Redcliffe, you need to realise that these people are sucking this country dry – they are chronic malingerers. Now, is there anything you want to ask me?'

'Yeah, I just want to check the status of my employment.'

'Status! You're here. What more do you want? Be grateful for that.'

'I thought I was covering for somebody else.'

'Remember, I rescued you from the dung heap – I'd hate to see you return there. Play the game and you can rest assured that your past is safe with me.'

Mr Blunt raised his large clenched hand and slammed it down on the brass bell.

'Thank you Mr Redcliffe, that will be all,' he said curtly, turning his attention back to my file.

## ~ NINETEEN ~

I was on a late tea break. My weeding in the Cabbage Patch had taken longer than expected. I'd made the mistake of asking Owen how long he'd been working at Union Street. I'd forgotten that this was the one question Ash had told me not to ask.

'Longer than I like to think.' he replied in his sing-song voice. 'Of course, I can remember the blitz. That must be about 35 years ago. The frightening thing is it seems like it was only yesterday. Good Friday 1941 was the night the bombers came over. We all thought we were going to die, we really did. I was in lodgings in Bedminster. I'd only recently come over from Wales. I met with a lot of prejudice in those days.'

'What do you mean?'

'Well, people in this city don't like the Welsh. They say we're taking their jobs, you see. Or worse. Anyhow it was better during the war – they were more worried about the black G.I.s than us. Our nearest shelter was in some caves – caves, can you believe it. There's a network of them just across the river. Of course, they're all closed up now.'

'So that's where we were, in the caves. There were waves of bombs throughout the night. From the thumps and shakes it felt like they were falling very close. By the end of the night I was covered in a fine grit that had fallen from the roof of the cavern. Well, next morning, I came out of the caves and looked down along Welsh Back to the city centre. It was a sight I will never forget. The beautiful city of Bristol was devastated. Some of the buildings were still on fire; but worst of all, it was the ancient churches – three of them, St Peters, St Nicholas and the other one – I think it's part of a bank now – I can't remember its name. They were absolutely gutted. It broke my heart.'

'Of course, I couldn't get into work until later on in the day. Well, I tell you, I walked over Bristol Bridge up the High Street and along to the Pithay. Everybody was giving a hand digging for missing people. It was like a human ant heap, people scurrying everywhere; I've never seen people working so hard. They wouldn't stop; they couldn't stop. It was life and death. I'll never forget that foul acrid stench. And the bodies of children – like little broken dolls. Max, I saw some dreadful sights.' Owen was silent for a moment.

'Anyhow, I'd got to the Pithay, I went round the corner by the chocolate factory and there was the Labour Exchange – that's what it was called in those days – standing absolutely unmarked amongst the devastation. It was a miracle. I have to tell you, for a moment I was a little disappointed. Really! I was! All those beautiful old buildings gone and the only thing left standing was this ugly monstrosity – along with the police station, of course.'

'And let me tell you the most amazing thing. The chocolate from Fry's factory next door had melted and run down the gutters and collected in an enormous pool right outside the main door of the office. By the time I'd got there it had set solid. It must have been ten foot long and about a foot deep. Well, with a couple of mates, we levered this great slab of chocolate out of the ground, put it on a stretcher, and took it down to the basement. It wasn't as if it was looting – we could have been shot for that – it was only going to go to waste. We cut the edges off where it was gritty and shared it out. There was nothing wrong with it – I was still eating it, when the war ended.'

I didn't know whether to believe Owen. As Ash had said, working in a twilight world does some funny things to your brain.

'Now, let me show you my Gloucestershire Cricketers....' I had to leave.

I scanned the chattering mass of faces in the canteen. As I knew nobody else in the room, I decided to risk sitting with the anarchists.

'Is this chair free?' I asked. The anarchists were in a huddle talking earnestly.

The three of them looked up simultaneously. They appeared surprised that I had asked to sit by them.

'Freedom, that's what we're fighting for, comrade,' said Che, gesturing with a wave of his hand for me to take a seat.

'Thanks.'

I drank my tea and tried to listen to their conversation. They were difficult to hear as the three of them leant across the table speaking in low tones, with their heads almost touching.

I could just about pick up phrases like 'street action', 'bourgeois bastards' and mention of somebody who appeared to be called 'Steve Ignorant.' I also heard dark mutterings about 'the milk snatcher' who had recently been chosen as leader of the Conservative Party. They were particularly angry about the back-to-front victory sign that Margaret Thatcher had given when she was elected. 'Did you see what she did? said Bolton Bob, 'Milk Snatcher was telling the country to fuck off. That cow needs sorting out before things get out of hand.' This showed surprising prescience for it would be another three years before Margaret Thatcher was to embark on her stone hearted sovereignty.

Apart from getting pissed and having a ruck I didn't quite know what anarchists were about. I don't think they did either. To my trained sociologist's mind they seemed a mite short on analysis. There had been a couple of Anarchists in my seminar group at University. They wore heavy black proletariat clothing. They were frighteningly earnest and would interrogate the lecturer with unnecessary aggression. I could never understand their questions – let alone the tutor's answers. Even in the seminar room they were prepared to back up their political thesis with not-so-muted threats of physical violence.

I once tried to discuss the Nevil Sponge dialectic with them. I thought they'd view him as a comrade in arms, but they were surprisingly dismissive, describing Sponge as a middle class, self-justifying hippie tosser.

At peace demonstrations, with their black flags, they would form a dark and menacing cohort, which seemed to be at odds with the aim of the protest. At one time I had lived round the corner from an anarchist bookshop. The Black Flag had unpredictable hours and was invariably closed. Perhaps that was the intention – an ironic statement about the exploitation of retail workers. Basically, anarchists were all a bit serious for me – when the revolution came it didn't sound as if it would be a bunch of fun.

But more shocking than all this revolutionary talk was the anarchists' attitude towards time-keeping. Bolton Bob looked at his watch and said: 'Hey, comrades our 15 minutes is up. We need to get back to work.' I couldn't believe what I'd heard. I didn't imagine Che Guevara filled out a time sheet.

'Max, I thought you might like to know about this,' said Astral as she passed me a memo from Regional Office.

My attempts to engage Astral in dialogue were at last making headway. Over the previous weeks, during snatched conversations, she had told me how she had come to be working at Union Street.

Astral had left school at 16. She had wanted to continue studying, but her parents were having none of it. There were plenty of jobs for girls like her at the nearby paper mill, or even better, at the tobacco factory. At Wills' you could smoke as many free ciggies as you wanted during your tea break. Packets were left on the table in the canteen alongside the salt and pepper and brown sauce. They had a weekly allowance of cigarettes to take home as well. It was supposed to stop people nicking them from the production line. It didn't though. If you went into any pub in Bristol there would always be some small time hustler in a backroom selling packets of Number 6 on the cheap.

Astral, however, aspired to more than the cough and smoker's face that went with the job of a leaf stripper in the new factory at Hartcliffe. But what could a girl from Brislington with two O Levels do? She'd fancied being a primary school teacher but with her qualifications teaching was out. So there was only one thing for it – nursing.

But it didn't turn out as she'd hoped. Although she'd been warned by Aunty Maureen, who had worked at the General, about nursing with its long hours and low pay what she hadn't been told about was the doctors. They liked the nurses, especially the pretty ones, to be at their beck and call and not to answer back. 'Nurse Weekes' they would say to her 'get this, fetch that, bend over here, stroke this.' They treated her, like their patients, with contempt. So after six weeks Astral packed her bag and left the nurses' hostel. It was only a short walk down the hill to the Ministry of Work.

I looked at the piece of paper Astral had handed me. It announced: Health and Safety Representatives Wanted. First Aid Training Offered. I read the details; eight half days training were offered plus a very generous, considering my current financial circumstances, £25 a year salary increment.

In theory, a first aid course is always a good idea – being handy with the Elastoplast is an undeniably useful skill. There was, however, one problem with this. I was so squeamish that I couldn't even look at a tomato juice without feeling dizzy. But it wasn't just the sight of blood that got me going – the mere thought of it sent my head spinning and my ears ringing. I'd fainted in doctors' surgeries, on dental couches, and most memorably – especially for the woman sitting next to me, and in whose lap I woke up – in a cinema. She was wearing a sable fur coat. It was rather nice.

So it was a measure of just how keen I was to impress Astral that I promised I would immediately request an application form for the First Aid training. 'Thanks, I'd be really interested in doing that,' I said enthusiastically.

One of my occasional tasks was to take forged Giros to be photocopied in the regional office across the road.

It was a good opportunity to nose about. Once I'd even sneaked a look into the Regional Director's room. I'd never seen an office like it. In the civil service there is a strict hierarchy of interior decoration. Ash had told me that there are sixteen grades of office defined by quality of carpet, chairs, desk, notice board and wastepaper bin. This one must surely have been right at the top. The office was furnished like the dining room of show-home in an up-market housing development. But bigger. The regional director had a carpet so thick that you needed a rake to brush it. There was an oval meeting table with six regency striped chairs, a leather Chesterfield sofa and a desk with nothing on it but three telephones – black, white and red – and pictures of what I assumed was the Regional Director's family. Except for the three telephones, there was no sign of papers, files or anything to do with work. The confidence of the man. It made Mr Blunt's office look like a garden shed.

The Giros, which had been dusted for fingerprints, were wrapped in clear forensic envelopes. Over time I'd begun to recognise a pattern. Certainly, there was nothing sophisticated about the techniques used to defraud. Invariably, the Giros would have been clumsily altered – the most common scam was to merely add an extra nought. The heavy-handed amendment – often in a different coloured ink! – could have been spotted by even the most myopic Post Office counter staff. The Giro would be confiscated and the culprit would be even further up merde creek without a paddle. With no means to pay the fine they'd end up doing three months in HMP Horfield. What was the point? This form of fraud was so pathetic and desperate that I could only feel sorry for anyone who resorted to it. And, of course, a criminal record meant even less of a chance of getting a job.

I collected the forged Giros from the fraud squad 'operations room.' Bart and Feltch bustled round the office like a pair of beagles. They were always in a hurry – busy, busy, busy, 'outta my way you, I've got an important job to do.' They were perversely fascinating; it was like watching the playground toughs to see who they would pick on next. While everyone was making finger-down-the throat gestures behind his back Bart would strut about like Freddie Mercury with a wedger. Kastrina didn't help, what with her fawning, and pressing her breasts against them. Of course, they both made out that they'd had her in the back of the Department of Work's Ford Escort (not at the same time – but then again there was a rumour, which Kastrina never denied). Even Ash doubted this. Doing it in the back of an Escort? You'd earn your Advanced Karma Sutra badge for that one.

When they weren't scrutinizing forged Giros, The Hounds of Hell were out on the prowl pursuing what they called their 'shit list'- claimants who combined working and signing. They didn't have to search far. Nearly every bar, restaurant, café and cleaning agency employs at least one dole cheque two-timer. Usually these demi-fraudsters are working in such dead-end, low paid, crap-jobs that they HAVE to sign-on to eke out even the most basic standard of living. So the Hounds of Hell were professionally employed – it was in their job description! – to frequent strip clubs, massage parlours, greasy spoons and drinking clubs; the sleaze joints that they'd be hanging around anyway.

'I don't mean to pry,' said Ash, 'Are you really going to do that First Aid training?'

'Yeah, worth £25 a year. Not bad, eh?'

'There's a number of things that you need to consider before you embark on a course like that. Its not just practising your osculation skills on blow up dolls, you know. The £25, you have to earn that.'

'What are you saying?'

'Sometimes you have to put your skills into practice.'

'No problem,' I lied.

'I don't think you've fully thought this one through.' Ash said this in an annoying school-teachery tone that indicated he was now in mentor mode.

I lied again. 'As it happens, I have.'

Ash continued:'You know that benchwarmer J. Kelly?'

'There's loads of J Kellys. Which one?'

'You know, not well known for his fastidious approach to personal hygiene. Stinks of cat food.'

I knew who he was talking about. 'The one with the big matted beard?' I asked.

'Big matted beard WITH STUFF IN IT. That's him, Well, not so long ago, he was found unconscious in the signing-on hall and Lee, who's also a First Aider, had to do a bit of mouth to mouth resuscitation. Personally, I don't think Kelly had collapsed at all; I reckon he just having a deep alcohol induced nap. Anyhow, Kelly came round quickly, and was so pleased with the attention he was getting that he reciprocated with tongues. I've never seen Lee move so quickly. Kelly claimed he was still dreaming.'

I could feel reverse peristalsis in my throat at the thought of this.

Ash continued. 'Unfortunately, it's a cruel fact that the people you are going to help are those that you least want to get close to. First Aid is not for a blennophobic like you. In my view it's best left to the Angels of Mercy like Astral.

'What's a blennophobic?'

'Look it up.' Sometimes Ash could be so annoying.

'Thanks for the advice. I'll bear in mind what you've said.'

## ~ TWENTY ~

I didn't, as had been predicted by Ash, make a complete prat of myself during the Christmas dinner. In fact, at the time, I reckoned my relationship with Astral was shaping up nicely.

Much to everybody's surprise, Kastrina didn't insist on going to Le Hotpot but booked the Christmas meal at an Italian bistro in Broad Street. The restaurant was in a cellar with a vaulted roof; there was a church-candle mustiness in the air which I quite liked. It was sort of romantic; well, it was better than I'd expected.

I positioned myself at the long table so that I was placed next to Astral. Unfortunately, Lee was sitting on Astral's other side. I was having trouble with my resolution to be nice to Lee. Like charming a snake it was proving to be a tricky act.

The meal didn't start well. It was a few seconds before the waiter recognised us – but when he did fear spread across his face. His eyes widened with recognition, and then glazed over with terror, as he realised that he was taking an order for Noel pizza – with extra cranberries – from the very person that handled his dole claim. Even in the candlelight I could see his complexion turn a waxy white. Instinct would tell most people to run, which was what he probably did, for the waiter wasn't seen for the remainder of the evening. Indeed, judging by the slow speed of the service, I guessed that the majority of the staff had left in a hurry by the back door.

Lee was regaling Astral with tales of his prowess on the football pitch. It reminded me of when Lee told me he was a 'gas head'. I'd mistaken this to be a refreshingly honest euphemism for stupidity, and thought that he was confessing to being an 'air head'.

Astral was turned away from me; she had her left elbow on the table and rested her jaw in her cupped hand as she listened. I had a good view of her back. It was a gorgeous silky back. She wore a backless dress that showed she wasn't wearing a bra.

It was just before the dessert when I felt the Niersteiner beginning to take hold. Astral was now looking particularly alluring. She was generating an aura of warmth and softness. I stretched out and casually put my arm across the back of her chair. Astral, who was still talking to Lee, pretended not to notice; at one stage she leant back on my extended arm but carried on listening to Lee. I could feel the gentle velvet undulations of her backbone against my forearm. I thought I felt a slight, ever so slight, shifting movement of Astral's shoulder as she acknowledged my proximity.

Lee asked Astral for a dance. As she got up to move to the dance floor Astral turned to me. 'See you in a while,' she said.

They looked so incongruous together; petite Astral and hulking Lee moving together on the dance floor like beauty and the beast. Astral had placed her handbag on the floor as a marker over which Lee was not to trespass. Occasionally she'd look over at me and smile. At one stage she waved and gestured for me to join them. If I was going to be dancing, it would be with Astral alone – a dance floor ménage a trois wasn't what I had in mind.

I watched the action closely. Elsewhere Kastrina was dancing provocatively with a heavily moustachioed man she had picked up from an adjacent table. He was open collared and had an enormous gold ingot round his neck engraved – I could make it out, even at this distance – with the letters G.I.B. The evening wore on. The manager went up to the DJ and pointed at his watch. The DJ held up two fingers. Time to move. I got up from my chair, and weaved my way across the floor to check that I'd read the situation correctly.

'No Woman, No Cry' I mouthed to the DJ.

The DJ shook his head and shouted – 'Sorry, mate, only a couple more tracks, then I've got to close.'

It was time to strike. Get in for the penultimate track and then move seamlessly onto the smooch. I stuck out my chest, wiggled my arse, flayed my arms in the air and pranced onto the dance floor.

*All right now, baby it's awwlriiight now....*

Yes! The timing was impeccable. Before Lee had realised it, I was in full Mick Jagger strut dancing with Astral. I'm not the best of dancers, but I knew this song well enough to sustain six minutes of hip wiggling and arse waving as I slowly circled round Astral – ready for the kill. Astral was enjoying herself. Bending forward towards each other we mouthed the words together:

*I took her home to my place*
*Watching every move on her face*

Our lips were almost touching; I could feel Astral's sweet breath.

And then the music was straight into Nights in White Satin. The DJ was a genius. The transition was so smooth that we were into each other's arms without any hesitation, without thinking about it. We were hanging onto each other as one. Her warm soft body fitted well; our hips moved together as we swayed to the Moody Blues' surging rhythms.

*Nights in white satin*
*Never reaching the end*

Well, the words weren't up to much – but it was the all enveloping mystical feel of the song; the swirling melatron, a sound that you could get lost in that made it so right for the moment.

*And I love her, I luuuuve herrrrr.*

And then it was over; the lights were up and the music had stopped. But we didn't want to stop; we continued shuffling round the dance floor clasped together, eyes closed, still moving to an imaginary beat.

I murmured into Astral's ear, 'Do you want to come home to my place?

'Yeah, that would be nice' she whispered. We felt so right. It was so easy; it was meant to be. But then I felt Astral's body tensing.

'Oh God, Lee promised me a lift home.'

'Come home with me?' I pleaded.

'I can't let Lee down.'

Through half-closed eyes I looked over Astral's shoulder. There was King Kong staring straight at us and looking none too pleased.

'Yeah, I suppose you'd better get a lift with Lee.' I looked into Astral's eyes and kissed her on the lips. 'Another time then.'

Astral held on to my hand and returned the gaze. 'See you tomorrow,' she said, as she fluttered her lips against mine.

While Astral was collecting her coat Lee sidled up and said, 'I saw that.'

'What?'

'You know what I'm talking about – I know what you're up to.'

'For God's sake Lee, what are you rambling on about?'

'She's too good for you – just keep away from her.'

Sensing that this conversation was going nowhere useful, without saying anything more, I turned and went to get my coat.

I ached with frustration as I walked home through the cold December night. Yet there was hope. I reckoned I was in there. A shag was just over the horizon.

## ~ TWENTY ONE ~

Lee had put an opaque plastic cask the size of a small barrel on his table. It was a cold, dull day. Despite attempts at conviviality, the Ministry of Work was a melancholy place to be on Christmas Eve.

For what must have been at least twenty minutes I had been staring at a blank M.O.W. 589. In addition to the usual morning-after-the-night-before feelings of nausea and vertigo I was also coming to terms with a new emotion in my life. I couldn't stop thinking about Astral. Her fragile beauty; our smooch the night before; the smell of camomile in her hair; the oneness that we'd shared during our dance. How can you love a woman you barely know? All too easily, it would seem.

I needed to plan my next move carefully. I'd been longing to carry on in the Cabbage Patch where we had left off last night but to my disappointment Astral had phoned in sick. I wasn't going to see her now until after the New Year.

I thought about our next date. Where should I take her? A restaurant? That might come over as too formal; like I'd expect us to do it afterwards as a matter of course. A pub? Maybe. But I didn't think Astral was much of a pub person. Cinema? Quite good. Lots of opportunity in the dark for exploration. And if the conversation drags we could always watch the film. Or how about something sophisticated, a bit unusual, certainly something Lee would never do. I'd got an idea.

'What's in there,' I asked pointing at the container on Lee's desk, 'cleaning fluid?'

'Don't be a div,' replied Lee, 'that's five gallons of top grade Kingston Black – the champagne of ciders, the best stuff money can buy. It's not for amateurs.'

I unscrewed the cap of Lee's container, bent over and sniffed. The pungent reek of ammonia made my eyes water. This was the sort of stuff that made your teeth fall out.

'If it's all the same to you I'll stick with the Newcy Brown,' I said.

'Fine by me, I wasn't offering it to you anyway. I haven't got enough to go round.'

'You tight bastard.'

My resolution to be nice to Lee was doomed from the start. He was such an arsehole. I'd been so near to making it with Astral last night. And then Lee comes along and sticks his fucking great flat face in the way.

Nobody was sure where Kastrina was. 'She's probably with the Hounds of Hell in the Cabbage Patch helping them with their enquiries,' Lee suggested with a smirk on his face.

'I don't think that's a very nice thing to say about our supervisor,' Cynthia protested.

Without shifting his stare from his hand of cards, Ash added 'Piss off Lee.'

We weren't expecting to do much work.

'Nobody in their right mind is going to register on Christmas Eve,' said Ash.

'Except for Jehovah's Witnesses,' I added.

'What?'

'They don't recognise Christmas.'

'Really?'

'Yeah, my parent's have a window cleaner who is a Jehovah's Witness – last year he cleaned our windows while we were having Christmas dinner. We were all wearing party hats and he was out in the cold staring at us through the window.'

'He was probably expecting a massive tip.'

'No, he wouldn't even come in and join us for a mince pie'

'What he'd already seen through the window must have put him off'.

The team had devised a rota to answer the phones, while Ash organised a game of cards. To add to the party mood Cynthia had supplied a range of crisps, Twiglets and Cheesy Footballs.

I was opening my fifth can of beer when I was called to the counter.

It was unusual to see the Fresh Claims room empty. Normally, at this time of day, it was buzzing with a fug of the usual sad and desperate people. Today, on Christmas Eve, apart from one man huddled at the end of a bench, the room was empty. The dirty cream gloss paint on the walls accentuated the cold. Two ridiculous drooping streamers, made of pink and blue paper chains, criss-crossed the ceiling. I noticed the man was wearing dark blue work overalls and guessed he must have come straight from work.

I greeted the man cheerfully: 'Hi. How can I help you?'

The man spoke even before he'd sat down 'What am I going to tell her?'

'Tell who?' I asked.

'My wife. What am I going to tell her when I get home this evening? When I walk through the front door, what am I going to say?'

The man handed me a folded piece of paper. 'Read this.' I opened the letter. Three short typed paragraphs announced that due to a headcount reduction his employer would be releasing him to seek employment elsewhere. I had seen those duplicitous words so many times before; the double standard of releasing... to seek employment. It was as is they were doing you a favour. Releasing! Releasing what exactly? A slave? A prisoner? Those words were so clever – and so demeaning.

'That's my career, ended,' said the man. 'Thirty-one years and all I get is this. A letter. A bloody letter. A bloody letter on Christmas Eve. This was the last thing I was expecting. Do you know when the foreman gave me this I thought it was my Christmas bonus.' He gave a broken laugh and continued. 'The manager didn't even give it to me himself. The coward.'

The man went on, 'I've got to go home and tell my wife. We were going to be wrapping presents this evening. How do I tell her on Christmas Eve that I'm out of a job? I don't know what I'm going to do. I really don't know what to do.'

I wanted a clear mind for this. This man deserved more than being signed-on by a half-cut civil servant. The man's world was crumbling. He was in shock; his face looked pale and waxy. I reached over and touched his arm. I thought the man was going to cry.

In the background, a door opened and I could hear laughter and shouting as C Section continued with their revels.

'You'll get redundancy pay – that'll keep you going for while.' I said, trying to think of something to say that was reassuring. The man didn't seem to hear.

'Thirty-one years I gave that company. I've been with Prentegs Engineering all my working life, I started with them as an apprentice.'

'You could retrain at the Skill Centre.' I had to stop myself from calling it the Gulag. 'The Job Centre can tell you about schemes.' I hated myself for reciting this crap. The man wanted his job back. Not the dole. On Christmas Eve.

'Headcount reduction! What sort of language is that? I did a skilled job – precision engineering. Now it's been automated. You press a couple of buttons and it's all done for you. I'm too old to retrain now. I'll never get another job.'

I didn't know how to respond. I took the man's details and explained what would happen next. The man got up from his seat. I knew it was a stupid thing to say, but I said it nevertheless. 'Anyway, have a happy Christmas.'

'Yeah,' the man replied flatly – 'and you.'

The man turned and walked slowly – as if he had no particular place to go – out of the room. It was getting dark outside now. This hunched man looked like the loneliest person in the world.

I walked back to C Section. I now felt too sober. I picked up a paper cup, and without asking Lee, filled it with his cider. I downed the contents in one.

'Hey, who said you could do that,' shouted Lee.

I refilled my cup and drank again.

'Fucking hell, that really does taste like piss.'


On my first day back after the Christmas break Kastrina asked: 'Did I see you holding hands with a claimant? A male claimant.'

I was surprised she'd seen me.

'I was trying to comfort the man; he was distressed,' I explained. 'And anyway I wasn't holding his hand, I was touching his arm.'

'I suggest that you keep your pillow-biting inclinations for outside of work.'

'For Christ-sake Kastrina – it was Christmas.'

'I don't care if it was pancake day. You're not paid to touch people. If you want to do that sort of thing join the Samaritans,' sneered Kastrina unhelpfully.

I wanted to reply that the Samaritans didn't touch people either – but that wasn't the point.

'You're so naive Max,' continued Kastrina 'He was like all the rest of them – a professional Giro jockey.'

'Kastrina, he'd been working with the same company for thirty-one years. Thirty-one years and made redundant on Christmas Eve. That doesn't make him a professional Giro jockey. He'd got to go home and tell his wife that he no longer had a job. Some Christmas present.'

'Didn't take him long to get down here though. Signing-on on Christmas Eve! Now that's what I call dedication – dedication to scrounging.'

# TWENTY TWO

'Who the fuck's he?' said the woman standing in the doorway. I was concentrating on double-checking my files. At the previous week's team meeting Kastrina had warned there had been unacceptable mistakes on PI day. 'There have been too many people waiting round the counter – you need to get 'em in and get 'em out.' Even Kastrina didn't mess about on Thursday afternoons.

Somehow I knew that the voice at the doorway belonged to Justine. I also knew she was asking about me. I continued with my work. I didn't look up, I'm not sure why, but I pretended to ignore her. Maybe I wanted to hide the fact that her reputation had preceded her, and that I was curious to meet her. Maybe I already felt intimidated.

I could sense that Justine was moving towards me. As she stood by my table. I could smell a rich perfume that had the scent of dark red roses.

'Hello,' she said in a tone that indicated she expected me to know who she was.

I raised my head. Justine wasn't what I had been expecting. I should have known not to trust Lee. She certainly wasn't a typical cider head. Even a cursory look revealed that she was far from durty. She had long dark hair and an olive complexion that radiated a Mediterranean sensuousness. Indeed just one look was enough to show she possessed something that nobody else in Union Street had – she had style. With her well-cut clothes she wouldn't have looked out of place in somewhere like Sneyd Park, Bristol's most exclusive suburb.

I got up from my chair.

'Hi, I'm Max – I've been covering for you while you've been away.' For a reason that I couldn't understand, I found myself speaking in my best middle class West London accent. 'Are you better? Sounds like you've had a rough time, glad to see you're back.' Why was I talking like this? My clipped English made me sound like character from a 1950s Ealing Comedy.

'You don't speak like you're from round these 'ere parts. Where do you live then?'

She had style – until she opened her mouth.

'Redfield.'

'Oh my gawd!' she laughed derisively.

'What's wrong with Redfield?'

In truth, I knew exactly what was wrong with Redfield. Even the most glittering city has its arse-end. And that was where I lived – Redfield; a dull Victorian grid of streets where the air reeked of dry roasted bones from the fertilizer factory.

'I ain't got nothing against Redfield as such. It's not so much a place, it's more somewhere you go through to get to somewhere else.'

'Well, I live there and it suits me fine.' I was struggling to think of something good to say about the area. 'It's got some good pie shops,' was the best I could come up with.

Justine slowly nodded her head in a manner that implied what a wanker. 'Maybe it has. But you can't exactly get the full taste on Church Road, can you now?

'Taste?'

'Cider.'

'Ah.'

'How long you been there then?'

'A few months.'

'Got a lady friend?'

'What's it to you?'

'I'll take that as a no then.'

'Take it how you want.'

'Now what was your name again?'

'Max.'

'Max, that's a funny name. What's that short for? Maxwell?'

'Something like that.' I didn't feel that this was a good moment to reveal that in a fit of suburban pretentiousness my parents had named me Maximillian Octavius Redcliffe.

'Got your silver hammer then?' I'd heard this comment, a reference to a lame Beatle's song, too many times to even smile.

'Very humorous,' I said with a straight face.

'Well, excuse I for not laughing. Especially as you're the little git who's taken my job.'

I could hear my voice sounding posh again. 'I think you'll find that you've got that wrong. I'm only here on a temporary basis.'

'That's not what Mr Blunt told me.'

'What did Mr Blunt tell you?'

'He said that you are now on a permanent contract. And I've been given another job to do.'

Permanent contract. I didn't like the sound of that. The permanent bit was especially alarming.

'Well that's the first I've heard of it.'

'I can't help that. Ask Kastrina.' She turned to Kastrina and said. 'Hey Kas; Maxwell's got a permanent contract, hasn't 'ee?'

'Oh, I've been meaning to tell you Max. It quite slipped my mind. You are now on a permanent contract. Well, there's just a couple of formalities to go through and then you will have passed your probationary period. Congratulations.'

'Oh great! Anybody else want to tell me something of earth shattering importance that I ought to know about?'

'Yer, your flies are undone.'

'Oh piss off Lee.'

' So before Redfield, where did you come from?'

'London.'

'Oh, London is it?' Justine said sarcastically.

'Ruislip actually. Have you got a problem with that?'

'No, I'm just asking myself what the likes of a college boy from London is doing in Union Street.'

'I'll tell you. I'm trying to get some money to go travelling.'

'We're all doing that.' She turned to Lee and shouted 'aren't we Lee?'

Lee looked up. 'Err ... yes,' he said unconvincingly.

'And who said I've been to college?'

'You've got college boy written all over you – you look like a wet fish straight out of the sea.'

I'd been beseeching cosmic forces that Kastrina was a one-off. Having met Justine, I was beginning to realise that the power of prayer sometimes just isn't strong enough. First Kastrina, now Justine. Stone hearted bitches the both of them.

## ~ TWENTY THREE ~

'Well this is different,' said Astral as she looked round the room.

'Is it?'

'I've never been to a tea shop before.'

'You're having me on.'

'No. Have you been to a tea shop before?'

'Yeah. Loads of times.'

Astral started laughing.

'What's so funny,' I asked.

'This.You!'

I was beginning to feel that I'd made a big mistake. I'd thought a cup of tea and a buttered toasted teacake would be just the thing. We could then see how things develop. No hassle.

'Max, you've misunderstood me. It's nice. I'm just not used to this sort of thing. My aunt sometimes comes here though.'

I'd spent most of my youth in tea shops. Maybe not teashops. More expresso coffee shops. After school I'd meet my mates at a little Austrian styled place, the Blue Danube, before I caught the bus home. In the Midlands I'd sober up in Brucianni's – an Italian coffee bar that also sold Amaretto biscuits. But Broadmead didn't have a coffee shop. It was either the Concorde Café or Cardrews. Neither had the romantic Dr Zhivago ambience that I was looking for.

'I thought we could go out sometime.' I laughed nervously.

She was surprised. 'What? You and me?'

'We had a good time at the Christmas party. Just see how it goes. No big deal.'

'I enjoyed the party.' We were both silent for a moment. Astral took a sip of tea. I was getting nervous. This wasn't going as I had hoped. I could feel pinpricks of sweat on my back. I could hear Ash lecturing me on his Darwinian view of relationships. Eventually I said, 'Stupid, isn't it.'

'No. It's not stupid....' she said emphatically. I was pleased to hear this. '... No, it's only that...' she paused and looked at me... 'You don't know then.'

'What don't I know?'

'Who I'm going out with.'

'I though you said that you weren't going out with Lee.'

'Of course I'm not going out with Lee. Lee's like a brother.'

'Who then?'

'I'm going out with Kayne.'

I wasn't sure I'd heard her right. 'Kayne?'

'Yes, Kayne. Kayne Bender from the finance section.' For a moment I had to hang onto the table as I felt myself falling into a dark void.

'Kayne Bender?' I repeated.

'What's wrong?'

I hated Kayne Bender. He's a streak of shit I thought. 'Nothing. He's a nice guy.'

'You said that as if you didn't mean it.'

I'd heard all about Kayne Bender with his smarmy good looks. Twice a week, in the evening, he worked for Parker and Barker in their warehouse. Rumour had it, he was popular with the managers.

'I do mean it. He's okay.' How come I didn't know this?

'Do you really think he's okay?'

'Sure, he's all right.' I hated Mr Back-Door man. I'd always hated him. Now I hated him some more. 'How long have you been going out with him?'

'Since the New Year. We bumped into each other on College Green. You know how it is on New Year's Eve.'

I knew exactly how it is on New Year's Eve. Where was I? Why wasn't I bumping into the most gorgeous girl in the world on College Green? I was in Ruislip. That's why. Ruislip. The one night I should be in Bristol and I'd gone to stay with my parents. Watching Andy – fucking – Stewart and his ridiculous bagpipe infested Hogmanay Hootenanny on the TV.

On the pavement outside the teashop Astral said, 'Can I ask you something?'

'Sure.'

'Don't tell Lee about Kane. He doesn't know.'

'He's bound to find out.' I would wait for the right moment to tell him.

'See you tomorrow,' she said. It was dark and I was shivering. I watched her as she walked away. She got me into this situation. She owed me more than this. Didn't I get a consolation prize or something?

She must have sensed my look, because she turned and smiled. I gave a weak smile in return. I felt sick.

## ~ TWENTY FOUR ~

It was only when Joy's screaming reached an annoying pitch that I began to pay attention. Charles, one of the trainers, calmly pronounced 'Time out.' But to no effect.

'You pompous ignorant little shit,' Joy shouted.

'I'm sorry but I don't have to take this behaviour from you anymore,' said the man from Yeovil. He then looked over to Charles for support.

'Yes, time out, Joy,' said Charles.

'You think you can treat me like dirt, don't you? But you can't.' Joy was acting as if she was possessed; she was shouting and swearing and shaking.

In the firm but caring tone used by nurses to patients as they come round from anaesthesia Charles said: 'Joy. Time out.'

But Joy was sailing now. She was right into the role, there was no pulling back.

I was on the third day of the ARF1 course, and this was the first time anything interesting had happened. The morning's session included role-play, a technique that had been introduced to the group as 'a powerful new psycho-drama training tool recently developed by a North American university.' The idea was to act out difficult situations we might have to deal with. If we encountered problems we could call 'time out' and suspend the action. Course members were then asked to make suggestions about what to do next.

Before we started Charles had warned that role-play could be dangerous; sometimes participants over-identified with the character they were acting. At the end of the session we would be given downtime when we would have the opportunity to de-identify with the role.

This particular role-play was about handling pressure on the counter. The counter clerk – played by the man from Yeovil – didn't have the right

110

paperwork at hand and was incessantly interrupted by phone calls and colleagues asking trivial questions. Nobody, however, considered how this was affecting Joy, who was playing the claimant. After her conversation had been interrupted for the fifth time, she had snapped.

I watched with fascination as Joy slammed her fist on the counter: 'I want my money,' she hissed through clenched teeth.

Here we go I thought. She's really getting into it now. I recognised the cry of 'I want my money,' like a dog baring its teeth, as the danger signal. It was the howl that comes from the tangled frustration of being refused what you know you are due, when you need it most. Get to this stage and there's no going back. The cry of 'I want my money' invariably means that something is about to blow.

The man from Yeovil was uncertain what to do. Should he take time out? Or should he carry on with the exercise? He shifted back in his chair and folded his arms. He looked sideways over to the trainer and then back at Joy.

'Time out,' he said.

'You smug bastard,' Joy replied. And then she sat back. For two seconds there was silence as she appeared to re-enter the real world. But then, suddenly, she lurched forward and with one last jolt, grabbed a heavy grey stapler, and lobbed it into the man's face.

'TIME OUT,' shouted Charles.

'Jesus Christ,' said the man from Yeovil, holding his jaw. His mouth was smeared with blood. He seemed unaware that a front tooth was flapping loose.

'Somebody stop the woman,' he shouted, holding his forearm in front of his face as he stood up and backed away from the desk. 'She's gone mad.'

But it was all over. 'Sorry about that' said Joy, 'I got carried away.' For a moment she was calm, and then her face creased up and she started sobbing.

I'd started the course feeling optimistic. I was glad to get away from the office. It gave me a break from C Section, which was becoming, in Ash's words: 'a sexual hothouse.' Where he'd got that thought from, I'd no idea. For me it felt more like a deep freeze.

A week's training would be a change. I was keen to discuss ways of working with the Claimants' Union and consider the Wages for Housework debate. I also needed time to come to terms with the news that I was now on a permanent contract.

Though I'd learnt to be wary of his recommendations, Lee had said innumerable times how much he'd enjoyed the ARF1. In fact, Lee used any mention of the course as an opportunity to boast that he'd pulled. I was sick of hearing how Lee had ingratiated his way back to the hotel where the out-of-towners were staying and had pressed his attentions on an innocent clerical assistant from Newton Abbott. I even knew the poor girl's name, Rachel Thompson. Ash reckoned this was the first time Lee had got his end away. No wonder Lee had returned to Union Street ponging of Denim, 'for the man who doesn't have to try.'

This was the first time I'd been on the fourth floor in the upper-sanctum of the education training room. The stairs to it were blocked by a chain from which hung a sign that enigmatically stated: Do not ascend unless authorised. The training room was better furnished than anywhere else in the building. There were soft chairs, and for once the walls were not covered in institutional gloss paint. At the far end of the room was a mock-up of an old-style signing-on counter, which apart from the lack of a screen and the absence of the reek of piss was authentic enough for the purposes of role-play.

The Civil Service Trainers were a different breed. They were very, very shiny and clean. They wore brilliant, biologically cleaned, white shirts and were immaculately dressed with perfect ties and uncreased jackets. I'd seen them at Union Street as they leapt Bambi-like up the stairs, two at time. You could be sure that their breath smelt of peppermint. They were at ease with flip charts, multi coloured marker pens and all the other accoutrements of the training room. With their ample personal skills I had to admire their confidence and enthusiasm. Not only were they good at talking, but they also appeared to listen. 'Thank you for that,' Charles would coo as he wrote on a flip chart in a rounded school ma'am hand. For all their easy familiarity I felt that I couldn't trust them as far as I could chuck a dog. I hated them immediately.

On the first day I had scanned the room for talent. The course members were an unappealing mix of older male civil servants and young girls who appeared to be missing the compassion gene. I was surprised at how annoyed I was by this. How come an arsehole like Lee got to pull? I could imagine Lee's first question when I returned on Monday. 'Did you score then?' I'd have to lie. 'Lee, I'm exhausted, I had to fight them off'.

But then again, I reassured myself, Lee's threshold of taste was rock bottom. Rachel Thompson was probably the local bike. The story was changing in my mind as I thought about it. Yes, office slag, definitely. Not – as I had first surmised – some sweet sixteen year old west country virgin.

About the only person I thought I would like to get to know was a henna-haired woman named Joy Squirrel. She introduced herself to the group as being interested in massage and a type of exotic dancing that I had never heard of, but apparently involved a pole. As for the rest of them – I was shocked. They were all so hard-nosed. Like Mr Blunt and Kastrina they hadn't got the imagination to empathise with the claimants. When I tried to put forward a moderate view about trying to get a work-life balance I was shouted down as if I was a member of the Baader-Meinhof terror group. The Ku Klux Klan would have a field day recruiting from the Ministry of Work in the South West. I was beginning to realise Kastrina was not a one off – if you know where to look there's a whole army of them out there.

Things got off to a bad start when Charles, the chief trainer, introduced the programme on the first day by saying that some people thought that ARF stood for Attitude Re-Focusing. Although this was a joke, I felt that the jest had an uneasy ring of truth in it. The themes covered were not as I had hoped. Topics that were run up the flagpole focused more on taking away benefits from the economically inactive than giving. The course was a mixture of presentation and discussion groups with guest speakers to liven it up. I was not surprised therefore when, on the second day, Bart and Feltch were unleashed to talk about their work as Shadow Economy Investigators.

After all Charles's wishy-washy talk the Hounds of Hell were at least startlingly honest. In their dangerously distorted view of the world all claimants were scroungers – and should be treated like scum. Everybody who walked through the door of Union Street was under suspicion. They regaled their audience with tales of the desperate, the sad and the unexpected and revelled in their victimisation of the unfortunate. 'I'm proud of what I do,' smarmed Feltch, 'I enjoy it, I think it makes a difference.' Exactly what the difference was, I was unsure.

Feltch spoke about the two-way mirror in the 'goldfish bowl', the room next to Baxter's desk. 'It's amazing what people get up to in the interview room when they're alone,' he said without specifying exactly what. The horrible leer on Bart's face gave an indication of what he was implying.

I remembered the muffled snigger I had heard when I was completing my application form. I wondered if I had been watched.

Bart explained some of the tricks of the trade. 'Look at the claimant's hands when they sign-on. Watch out for splatters of paint, or scabs from boiling chip fat.'

'If they're in a rush make them sweat it out,' said Feltch. 'Summon them to the interview room on the pretence of checking their details. People on the dole have plenty of time. If they're in hurry, it's a sure sign that they're up to something. If they say they've got something urgent to do – like go for an interview – call them in, make them wait.'

'The interview excuse – oldest trick in the book that. We see it all the time,' echoed Bart.

A man with thin whiskery hair, fawn slacks, grey socks and sandals asked how they tracked down the cheats.

'Easy, most of the time we rely on tip-offs from the public. There's a lot of settling of scores out there. More likely than not it's people who are narked with their neighbours. They see the guy next door scuttle off to work, and ten minutes later the postman delivers a Giro. Why should they get away with it? They don't reckon it's fair. I'll tell you what, it's amazing who writes to us. You won't believe this, but I was extracting a confession a couple of weeks ago and showed the accused a copy of the anonymous letter that had been sent to us. He recognised the handwriting straight away. He should have done,' Bart was laughing now, 'it was his mother's.'

'It's true, I swear,' added Feltch, who was shaking his head in mock disbelief, 'His mother had grassed on him!'

I wondered if the Giros I'd photocopied, the ones that were so clumsily altered, were typical forgeries – or whether they were the worst of the bunch.

'What about forging a Giro. How easy is it to do that?' I asked.

'Give us a break,' said Feltch, theatrically raising his eyes to the ceiling, 'a four year old child with a box of crayons could do better than most of the fakes we handle. Ninety percent of the forgeries are the work of incompetent amateurs. If they're very clever they'll skim the Giro with a razor and rub on a bit of Letraset. But they're the exception. Most cheats aren't that smart. Normally they use a rubber, write over the original, screw the whole thing up so it looks like the dog's chewed it, and then take it to the little old lady at the sub-post office hoping that her eyesight isn't up to the mark. Well, those little old ladies can be pretty sharp. They're on the phone to us before you can say Old King Cole.

I tell you, for the majority of people we deal with there's only one way to go and that's down – down among the low-life.'

I couldn't help feeling that there was something intrinsically wrong with this approach. Wasn't the point to get people back into work?

'But what if they've got children to look after?' asked Joy Squirrel.

'Well they shouldn't be signing on, should they? They're not available for work.'

'What if they have to go to the dentist?' I asked, half expecting the reply that they shouldn't have any teeth. But they didn't even bother to respond.

'People are too lenient. Benefit fraud is not a victimless crime,' said Bart. 'Put it another way – you wouldn't stand by and watch an old lady being mugged. In my view not enough convicted fraudsters are put in prison.'

'How much would that cost the tax payer?' I asked. 'I thought the idea was to save money.'

'Stop winding us up, Max,' sneered Feltch. While Bart added in a tone that was both humorous and threatening, 'Yeah, Redcliffe, we're watching you.'

On Friday afternoon, as I ticked the boxes on my evaluation form, I thought about what I'd learnt. At least I'd survived with my personality intact, and as far as I could tell I hadn't turned into Lee Woods's doppelgänger. Admittedly I hadn't pulled, but then again I had higher standards than Lee; I wasn't remotely interested in a one-night stand with the office nympho. More interestingly, thanks to Bart and Feltch's talk, the course had sparked a most unexpected line of thought. I now had an idea to cling onto in those dull empty moments; I had the seed of a plan that could well be my salvation. Maybe Attitude Re-Focusing wasn't such a bad title after all.

## ~ TWENTY FIVE ~

I stood under the enormous and forbidding entrance arch and scanned the dark street. By now it was second nature. It was no big deal. Just as others clock off, I check the road to see if anybody is waiting to kick the crap out of me.

Justine was also leaving the building. 'Where you off to?' she asked, as she tied a patterned silk scarf round her neck.

'Home,' I replied.

She gave a short sarcastic laugh. I wasn't sure why. 'Yeah, me too,' she said.

'See you then.' I said as I started to walk away.

'Wait a moment. Fancy a drink?' she asked.

'They're not open yet.'

'They are if you know where.'

'Where then?'

'My little secret.'

'Oh come on.'

'Are you interested or not?'

I was surprised and flattered by this. Thankfully, my initial impression of Justine had proved wrong. At work I'd observed her with some of the more unpredictable claimants and was impressed how she handled them. She had an innate wisdom that comes from the sort of experiences you don't get when you are brought up in Cherry Tree Avenue. A drink with Justine sounded like an excellent idea.

'Not tonight thanks,' I replied.

Was I stupid? I'd recently been ditched by my fantasy girlfriend. The last thing I wanted to do was to go back to an empty flat in Redfield with only a transistor radio for company.

'Who says there's going to be another night,' said Justine.

The way I was feeling, to go for a drink with Justine would be the best

116

thing in the world. I wanted to be in the company of somebody fun, somebody sensuous, somebody who would return my gaze with a smile. Somebody I could reach over to and touch.

'Fair enough.' I said as I began to walk away. 'I've got to be going. See you tomorrow.' I was being such a wanker. It wasn't as if I was in any position to play hard to get. Why was I doing this? Was it because I was scared that she was too savvy for me? I was shouting at myself: 'Wake up Max. This is an opportunity you need to grasp. Chances like this don't come along often.'

'Max.'

I turned. 'What?'

She gave me a wide disarming smile that revealed her perfect white teeth.

'Look, I'm just trying to be friendly. I know you're going home to an empty house.' She was right. I was so unsettled in my gloomy room above Denise's Hairdressing Salon that I'd never even unpacked the cardboard boxes that contained my few possessions. The place stank: a horrible cloying odour seeped through the floorboards from downstairs and hung in the air. I wondered if my clothes smelt of hair lacquer. I couldn't tell.

But at least it covered up the smell from the bone factory a couple of streets away. In the summer – and there was going to be plenty of summer this year – the air was thick with the gut wrenching stench of carcases being roasted to dust.

While I loved Bristol, Redfield, with its mix of pie shops, bingo halls and betting parlours, depressed me. I needed to live somewhere else, somewhere that lifted the soul, that made me feel good to be alive when I stepped out of my front door in the morning. Given the choice I would have lived in one of Clifton's elegant terraces. But my paycheck wouldn't stretch to that.

'Well thanks for your concern,' I said.

'Tell me. How long ago was it that you left London?'

'I left Ruislip five years ago. But if you're asking when I left university, that was a couple of years ago.'

'You are so up yourself. You had to get that in, didn't you?'

'What!!?'

'You know what, you arsehole.'

'What???'

'University.'

'Oh, for Christ sake!'

'Okay, forget that. Let me put it another way. Am I right in thinking you don't know our fair city too well?'

'Maybe.' I wasn't sure where this conversation was heading.

'Well, I'm going to make you an offer. I'm going to take you on a little tour. Not tonight, seeing you're otherwise engaged. But some other time – I'm going to show you the world according to Justine.'

'Sounds intriguing. The world according to Justine. Do I need my passport?'

'Just your wits and your wallet. You won't be asked for any ID where we're going. Now, I like cider and jazz.

'Jazz?'

'Jazz, it's the Bristol sound...'.

I thought it was best if I saved my views on Jazz for another time.

'...But don't go getting any other ideas, mind – pie-eating college boys aren't my cup of meat.'

'I didn't say I ate the pies.'

'Well you know what I'm saying.'

'You've got no worries on that count.'

'Good, I don't want you getting the wrong idea. So here's what I'm suggesting. We'll do the Clifton Iron. Its like the Aintree Iron but bigger – and harder. And of course they don't have real cider up in Liverpool.'

'Sorry, I'm not following you.'

'Don't you worry, you will. So we'll start off at the Corry Tap, move on to the Oak, then over to the Albion, down the hill to the Eldon, along to the Prince of Wales, maybe drop into the Mardyke – and finish up at the Sundown Club. On the way I'll tell you about my plans to go travelling, my quest you could call it – and you can tell me about yours. You up for it? Or are you scared of having a good time?'

'I'm always ready for a good time.'

Justine moved nearer and touched my arm and said 'Let me know when you've got a space in your busy diary, and then we'll sort something out. See ya.'

For a moment I wasn't too sure if I should have kissed her.

Justine walked round the corner and headed off to Clifton; I strode with renewed vigour in the opposite direction.

I was looking forward to my evening with Justine. By then I'd have time to get my shit together – like have a bath and think of some things to talk about. I thought about Astral for a moment. Astral and Kayne Bender – I hated that. It was time to move on.

I looked left and right, checking if there was anyone hiding behind a bin, waiting to drag me down an unlit alleyway. I felt good. Justine had put another idea into my mind. Maybe a pie for supper wasn't such a bad idea after all.

## ~ TWENTY SIX ~

Kastrina watched me with a cold predatory stare as I walked across the room to my seat. There was a note on the table written in her hand. It read 'Report to Mr Blunt at 8.30 am.' It was already 9.00 o'clock. 'Is it?'

'What's this?' I felt uneasy about an unexpected summons to the 2nd floor.

'You are in BIG trouble,' Kastrina replied.

'Big trouble? What do you mean?'

'Don't come the innocent with me, Max. You know exactly what it's about.'

'I don't.' And I didn't.

'Well, there are two policemen waiting for you.' She was enjoying this.

'Two policemen?' I hoped that Kastrina hadn't noticed the tremor in my voice. 'What do you mean, two policemen?'

'Well not policemen – detectives. Plain-clothes anyway.'

'What!'

'Its been nice knowing you Max,' she said holding out her hand mockingly.

I wasn't feeling up to this. The previous night I'd spent a long and grimy session at the Olde E', a dodgy boozer in Montpelier, and was now suffering from severe dehydration.

My route to Mr Blunt's office took me past Baxter's reception desk. Baxter looked up from his work. He'd been deep in thought, fantasising, I guessed, about his latest project. The day before he had told me about his idea involving slightly sticky notes that could be attached to documents without causing surface scuffing when removed. As if.

'They've got the riot squad waiting for you upstairs, Max.'

I didn't feel like Baxter's little quips at this particular moment.

'They'll need more than that to keep me under control.'

I rolled my shoulders in an attempt to loosen them and walked as casually as possible. I knocked on Mr Blunt's door and without waiting for an answer, entered. Mr Blunt was talking to two men. Both were well built and dressed in trainers, jeans and thick-ribbed cardigans.

'Redcliffe, I want to introduce you to these gentlemen.'

Lounging back in their chairs, neither of them got up to shake hands. They were not, judging by their relaxed manner, employees of the Ministry of Work. I nodded a hello. I recognised the type – Starsky and Hutch.

'This is Detective Inspector Fogerty and Detective Inspector Rogers. I think you may be able to help them with their enquiries.'

'Hi.' I could feel the blood draining from my face like the colour being sucked from an ice-lolly. Was this, at last, the nemesis that Mr Blunt had been threatening? There was nowhere to sit. I put my hands in my pockets and looked at the two Detectives, waiting for what was to come next. The Detectives seemed to be in no hurry.

It wasn't that I didn't like the police. Sure, they had a job to do. It was just that they spent too much time concentrating on the wrong things. Like hassling ME.

Just the other week the Bill had turned a good evening into a downer. It was about 3 am and the streets were empty. I was returning home after a session at the Dugout, a pleasingly seedy subterranean dive in Park Row, feeling relaxed and at one with the world. I had been walking along, running my hand against the vertical bars of some railings, slap, slap, slap – it was the sort of thing that a child would do with a stick, only I hadn't got one, so I was just using my hand – flap, flap, flap. A prowler car drew up and a cop got out.

'What are you doing?' He wasn't rude; I just didn't want this attention. It had been a good night. I didn't want it spoilt.

'I'm going home.'

'It's a bit late to be going home.'

'It's never too late to be going home.'

'Don't get funny with me.'

'I'm not. What's up?'

'I'm asking the questions – you just concentrate on giving me some answers. What's your name?'

'Max Redcliffe.'

'Date of birth?'

6 March 1952.

The policeman spoke into his radio – '5692 to base. Run a check on a Mr Redcliffe, first name Max, date of birth six of the third '52. Over.'

'So, Max – where have we been tonight?'

I didn't like the way the policeman called me by my first name. It was too familiar; I felt I was being patronised, treated like a kid. Also, what's with the 'we'?

'Seeing we're on first name terms, what's yours?' I asked.

'Police Constable 5692.'

'Is that really what you like to be called?'

'By people like you, yes.'

I could see that I wasn't going to get far with this approach.

'I'll call you 5692 for short,' I said. I knew I was pushing it; I was watching for the signs to pull back. The policeman didn't seem phased.

'If you must. Now, let me repeat my question. Where have you been tonight, Max?...'

'If you really want to know, I've been to the Dug Out.'

The policeman looked straight at me and in a caring way asked, 'Is there something you want to tell me? You can make it easy for yourself, if you want.'

I could hardly believe this; this was unexpected heavy stuff. One minute I was as happy as a freak in shit, the next I was being invited to confess all sorts of unimaginable crimes. I didn't like these situations.

'What's this about?'

And so it went on. Even to the police it was obvious that I wasn't the Clifton Rapist. In the grand scale of things, being stopped by the police was only a little thing, but I went home feeling pissed off, nevertheless.

They eyed me up. The big one, Rogers, was chewing gum; the other was so slumped in his chair that he was almost lying flat on his back.

'Mr Blunt has been telling us all about you.' said Fogerty. He knows, I thought. Of course he doesn't know. How could he?

'Not all bad, I hope,' I tried to joke.

Fogerty laughed, turned, and smiled at Mr Blunt. Mr Blunt, who seemed uneasy with this bonhomie, gave a strained smile in return.

The big one leant towards me and said, 'We need to speak to Philip Tone. Mr Blunt tells us he's one of yours.'

I felt the muscles in my shoulders drop with relief. It was as if a giant elastic band that had been tightening round my chest was released. How paranoid can you get? But then again, I wondered if Mr Blunt had been checking me out for his own agenda.

'Oh, that's all right then,' I said, 'I thought you were after me.' As soon as I said this, I regretted it.

The detectives laughed. 'Don't worry, we leave parking tickets to the

Traffic Department.' Mr Blunt stared at me and nodded his head.

Ha, bloody ha, I thought – not so much Starsky and Hutch, more Laurel and Hardy.

'What did Philip Tone do to demand this special attention?' I asked, changing the subject.

'At this stage I'm afraid we're not at liberty to reveal the nature of his misdemeanour. Let's just say that it involved a bicycle and leave it at that.'

Pathetic.


A stooge for the police; Ash didn't say anything about this being in the job specification. But what was I to do? I was still feeling shit-arsed from the night before. I couldn't think straight.

While the detectives sat hidden behind the shoulder high screens I ran through a last minute check to see that my files were in order. I couldn't believe that they were going through all this hassle for such a stupid offence. Fortunately Tone wasn't due to hand over his UB40 card for another hour. I would be able to come up with a plan by then.

I'm always surprised that fugitives from the law continue to sign-on when they know they are wanted by the police. Judging by some people's behaviour you'd think it was written in the Geneva Convention that you can't be arrested when in possession of a UB40. I'm going to break the Official Secrets Act here. It's so obvious, I'm not particularly worried about legal repercussions. Here it is: there's a well-worn path between Union Street and Bridewell. When the police are hunting somebody on the run, the very first thing they do is to check with the dole office. Now there's a surprise!

One of my claimants, Harry Scoot, even featured on Police 5. Shaw Taylor had done the full bit including an identikit picture that made Scoot look like an unshaven maniac out of the Texas Chain Saw Massacre. You'd think anybody in that situation would go to ground. But not Scoot. There he was, standing patiently in the queue. It seemed as if he'd come in to show off. 'Look at me; I've been on Police 5. I'm a TV star.' I noticed he signed his papers with an unusual flourish – as if he was giving an autograph. Of course, he was pulled immediately. Well, he certainly got the attention he was craving. Two months later his photograph was on the front page of the Post along with half a column about his recent activities. He got five years.

Hopefully Tone wasn't going to be so stupid. But then again did he have any inkling that Starsky and Hutch were on his case?


Shitting hell! He's early! 10.45 and I could see Tone at the back of the queue. And I still hadn't come up with a plan. Tone was looking relaxed. He showed no sign of being aware that he was being hunted down for his cycling misdemeanours.

I looked over my shoulder. Starsky and Hutch were hidden behind the screens. Tone was getting nearer with each claim I handled. I had to warn him. Perhaps I could slip him a note as he handed over his UB40 card – Get out of here, the Fuzz are after you. But Tone was normally so spaced by this time of day that he would probably misinterpret what was going on and attract attention to himself. And then we'd both be screwed.

Tone was now third in line. I tried to make eye contact. Look at me. Look at me you bastard. And then Tone noticed; he glanced at me and gave a nervous nod. He was probably wondering why this guy was staring at him in such a peculiar way. I held the stare, and made a slight flapping hand gesture that I hoped would be interpreted as 'go away'. Tone looked puzzled and slightly uneasy. It was clear that my hand gesture had been misinterpreted. I looked behind me. Laurel and Hardy were still out of sight round the corner waiting for my tip-off.

Lee was walking past.

'Lee, mate, do me a favour. I'm desperate for the loo, can you take over for a moment?'

'Make it quick, I've got some important filing to get on with.'

'Back in a couple of secs.'

I hurried past the detectives.

'No sign of him so far; back in a moment.'

I was away from the counter for about five minutes. By the time I returned to my seat, Tone had been signed on and was nowhere to be seen.

Ninety minutes later the doors were closed and the signing-on hall was empty. I was tidying-up my papers when the detectives ambled over.

'Didn't show up then?'

'Nope.'

'Let's have a look at his file.'

I ran my fingers across the files and pulled out Tone's. This was going to be the difficult bit.

'Here we are. Oh my God, what's happened? Jesus! How the hell? He's been in! And he's been signed on. I don't understand it.'

I pointed to the initials against the signature. LW. Lee Woods.

'It must have been when I went out to the loo. I handed over to Lee. Perhaps he didn't know. I thought everybody had been told.'

'Let's have a look,' demanded Rogers, grabbing the file from my hand. He flicked through the papers. He didn't seem pleased.

'You've wasted my bloody morning.'

'I don't understand how it happened.'

I could feel Roger's anger. I could sense his fists tightening. Any moment I expected to be thumped.

'Is he some sort of friend of yours?' asked Rogers.

'What?'

'Is this Tone some sort of friend of yours?'

'What do you mean?'

'I reckon you set this up; I reckon there's something funny going on here.'

'Look, it was mistake; you need to speak to Lee. He was the person who signed-on Tone.' I felt a tinge of guilt about this; I didn't want to get Lee into trouble, but then again Lee knew nothing. He'd be okay. In fact, for a moment, I allowed myself a little chuckle. I liked the idea of Lee being interrogated for information that he didn't have.

'You're the mistake, pal.'

'I'm sorry, it wasn't my fault.'

'Fucking civil servants! I tell you one thing, the next time there's a bundle over here and you need help, don't expect us to drop everything and come running to save your scrawny little arse.'

Rogers and Fogarty started to walk away.

'We need to check some files when we get back to the station,' said Rogers in a voice loud enough for me to hear. 'What do you reckon, start with the Perverts?'

'Drug users first, I reckon' replied Fogarty.

## ~ TWENTY SEVEN ~

'So what are you doing here in this shit-hole?' asked Bolton Bob.

Although I was largely ignored by the anarchists, as the months dragged by, they did at least begin to acknowledge my existence. Today was a milestone; this was the first time one of them had initiated a conversation.

'Trying to get some bread together for travelling.'

Bolton Bob didn't seem impressed. I wasn't surprised. I didn't think of anarchists as being great travellers. All that black clothing – they'd really feel the heat. Besides, travelling, with its potential to exploit the locals and impose an alien western culture, was probably denounced as a degrading bourgeois activity.

'If you're going through Afghanistan,' said Bolton Bob, who appeared to assume that all travel meant the hippie route to India, 'my mate Chad knows a nice little caravanserai in Mashad. It's in the Bit Guide. I'll get the details for you.'

'Well, thanks anyway but I'm not going to India, I'm heading for South America.'

Bob stroked his straggly beard. He seemed interested in this. 'Oh I get your drift, man,' he said drawing air through his nose in an exaggerated manner. 'You've got to be careful though, it can be a heavy scene in Columbia. You can get banged-up for bloody-ever if they catch you with a bit of splutter.'

'What?'

'Splutter?'

'Splutter what?'

'Splutter and choke. Coke.'

'Ah, coke. Yeah. Well, I think I'll stick to the leaves rather than the powder,' I said, wondering about the politically correct slant on coke sniffing. 'Good for altitude sickness.'

'Che Guevara used old charlie to alleviate his asthma when he was in Bolivia,' added The Other One.

'That was the only good thing that came out of Bolivia for Guevara,' said Bob.

I felt I needed to set the record straight before, in the eyes of the anarchists, I metamorphosed into a drug mule straight out of the pages of Snowblind.

'This will probably come as a surprise to you guys, but cocaine isn't exactly my main reason for going to South America. There's something that I've been wanting to do since I was a kid. I dream about it all the time. I've always wanted to check out the rainforest. Not just visit the rainforest, but live in it, really experience it.'

'Experience the rainforest!' repeated Bob, mimicking my southern accent. 'You bloody ponce.'

Uh oh. I knew I'd made a mistake here. I doubted whether experiencing the rain forest was a concept that featured in the Anarchist Cookbook. It was a bit too touchy-feely for them. I looked at Che for support. Surely somebody from Cheltenham called Jeremy would understand what I was talking about. Che failed to respond.

'Well did you hear about what happened to that entomologist guy?' added The Other One. 'He certainly EXPERIENCED the rainforest. You'd think butterfly collecting was the most harmless pastime known to man...'

Bolton Bob interrupted, 'Excuse me, but can we try to avoid the gender stereotyping?'

'Apologies comrade.' The Other One started again: 'Butterfly... collecting...' he looked at Bolton Bob and Che to check that he was using the correct terminology.

Bolton Bob swore under his breath. 'Bourgeois Bastards.'

The Other One stopped. 'Let me start again.' I could see that he was getting flustered.

'You would think that the ...bourgeois activity of butterfly collecting is the most harmless thing known to ...to man AND woman.'

It was Che's turn to interrupt. 'I don't want to sound pedantic but shouldn't that be 'women and men?'

'Oh for fuck's sake, you tell the story.'

'Hey cool it. It's your story.'

'Can I continue then?'

'Sure, tell it exactly as you want to.'

'Thank you. So there was this person, who happened to be a guy, in the jungle, collecting enormous fluorescent turquoise butterflies.' The Other One emphasised each word as if he were addressing an audience of four year olds. 'The butterflies were the size of your fist, they were. When he'd caught them he would pin them out on a board to dry. Not a good idea actually; the Indians didn't like it...'

Che coughed. The Other One corrected himself.

'...You see, the Native Americans thought these butterflies were the spirits of their ancestors. So one night, to appease the gods, they crept into his tent, threw a big fishing net over him, dragged him outside, and pinned him to a board with spears. No more collecting butterflies for him. Bad scene.'

'Wow,' exclaimed Che. I couldn't decide whether he said this in approbation or horror.

'You're kidding,' I said.

' No, it's true – it was in the News of the World last week.'

'But that's horrible.'

'And of course,' added Che, 'the great man himself, didn't get to use his return ticket from Bolivia, did he?'

'I didn't know Larry Wallis had been to Bolivia,' said Bob.

'I'm not talking about Lazza, you asshole. Forget the Pink Fairies I'm talking about Guevara.'

'Oh, yeah, right. Bummer. South America is a real dodgy place.'

I was starting to view the anarchists in a new light. 'Well thanks for the advice, guys. So that's three things I need to cross off my South America 'to do' list: cocaine smuggling; butterfly collecting and revolutionary activities.' I counted these out on my fingers. 'Anything else I should avoid while I'm there?'

'Look, Man,' said Bob, 'I don't want to put you off these things – it's just best to be aware of the consequences.' This was a surprising response from an anarchist – a group of people not particularly well known for their cautious approach to life.

'Very considerate of you, thanks.' I replied.

'So what's the score? When are you going?' asked Che.

'Dunno. Soon. I've got it all planned. I'm going to give myself time to get acclimatised. I've heard about a little community from San Francisco that's set up in the rainforest where I can ease myself in, get used to the heat and the culture. Maybe learn a little of the native Amerindian lingo. It's called Jonestown.'

'Jonestown? That doesn't sound like the ultimate, full-on jungle experience.' said Che.

'Maybe, but that's where I'm heading. It'll be a good start.'

'Just one thing,' added Che, 'Steer away from the llamas. The cocaine and altitude can combine to create a heady cocktail that makes a llama seem very attractive to a lonesome traveller on a cold night.'

'Thanks, I'll bear that in mind.'

Che looked at his watch. 'Time to get back to work, comrades.'

Cynthia, who had been sitting quietly at the same table, said 'I've read about Jonestown. It's a Californian cult. I wouldn't go if I was you.'

Cynthia had just given me what would turn out to be the most important piece of advice I would ever receive in my life. But I wasn't listening.

As Justine was leaving the canteen, she stopped, leant down and whispered conspiratorially into my ear. A deep fragrance hung in the air.

'Change of plan, we're going to start with jazz. See you at the Duke on Saturday – 9.30 – Bog End.'

'Okay' I replied. I wasn't sure whether to feel delighted or nervous.

## ~ TWENTY EIGHT ~

The big heat had started with a few freakishly warm days after Easter. For over a month now there hadn't been a cloud in the sky, and every day was a little bit hotter. This weather was different. It wasn't the hazy warmth of an English summer – this was a full, open-the-oven-door scorcher.

As I traipsed to work in the short-lived cool of the early morning I noticed the pavements had become greasy without their frequent scouring by rain. By 11 a.m. the city air was thick and oily. Yet even this brilliant heat never permeated the gaol-thick walls of Union Street where, like an underground cavern, the temperature remained at a constant 68 degrees.

I hated being incarcerated inside. The smell of sun lotion and the tanned limbs of the claimants made me dream of Greek Islands, blissful golden beaches and aquamarine seas.

I shouldn't be working in weather like this, I thought.

Ash and I were running a last minute check on our claims in a dim room next to the signing-on hall. To ease the boredom I mentioned my surprise that so many people were desperate to get a job. I thought that would get him going.

'Yeah, despite what Blunt says, and all that crap you read in the newspapers, very few claimants are in it for the long-term. Mostly it's through no fault of their own that they've lost their job. With luck the majority have the skills and initiative to quickly pick up something else.'

Ash was right. I'd noticed that most people came and went in the space of three or four weeks. I was beginning to realize that slackers and lie-in-bed activists were in a very tiny minority.

Ash continued, 'Most people can't cope WITHOUT work. What was it Freud said? Family and work are the bedrock of humanity.'

'Freud got a lot of stuff wrong.'

'But not in this case. You know what he meant, Max. Time, like nature, abhors a vacuum. Work gives people a structure to their lives. There's something about idleness that drains the human soul. I've seen many people who in the absence of work become confused and flounder. It's a frighteningly easy descent down the slope to a state of suspended limbo. Off the slab and into the slop bucket. It's single men who are the most vulnerable.'

'Not this single man. When I was unemployed I could get on with a bit of real living.'

I remembered an earlier, more gentle life, when I would enter a transcendental state where chores that should take minutes stretched out for hours and tasks that should take hours would drag on for days. A visit to the launderette, rather than being a domestic duty that is slipped in between other activities, could be strung out to fill a whole day. And a pretty satisfying day at that.

'You're the exception, Max. Besides I think you're using the term living in the loosest sense. Most people would call it asleep-at-the-wheel time wasting. While most people subscribe to the work ethic, you're more into the shirk ethic,' Ash laughed.

I feigned a hurt voice. 'Hey, I thought you said we were in this together.'

'You're the sociologist, you know all this. Not only does work supply money; just as important, it gives a routine and a social life.'

'But not for everybody. I'm not the only one who's happy watching the river flow. You ought to read what Nevil Sponge has to say.'

Ash made a snorting noise that signalled his disapproval. 'Nevil Sponge wrote all that nonsense way back in the 60s. He was pandering to an audience of lazy gits, telling them what they wanted to hear. These days he's back in Australia running a publishing empire selling porn magazines. He's the biggest capitalist bastard of the lot now.' Ash was right about the porn empire – though I wasn't pleased to be reminded of the fact.

I could hear distant shouting in the street; some psychobillie probably heading our way.

'Well what about the PIs? Most of those benign lunatics can't cope with everyday living, let alone the harrowing world of work.'

I'd seen so many people try to navigate their way through the benefit system and go under. Only yesterday I'd watched Blow-Job Lil, stick thin and bruised, in Fresh Claims. There was shouting, abuse and tears as she failed to understand the formalities of being given a number, waiting in a queue for a couple of hours and then going through the form-filling process. Invariably, at the vital moment when her number was announced, she had briefly left the room for a 'bit of business'. She returned, unaware that her moment had gone, and spent the rest of the day waiting, only to be told at the close of play that her number had been called hours ago. She left dazed and frustrated, swearing never again to waste her precious time on you fucking ejits.

'This place doesn't exactly help. The trouble with this organization is that we can't just leave them alone. We're the Ministry of Fear, state funded bullies. We kick the vulnerable when they're down. Why don't we just let these people get on with their idiosyncratic lives? What's wrong with that? Just leave them alone. Surely it's cheaper to give them a weekly Giro than bang them up in gaol?'

'Or,' added Ash, 'we send them to do forced labour at the Gulag.'

Ah, the Gulag. Anybody who had been unemployed for over six months could be summoned to undertake forced labour – a Government Sponsored Training Scheme – at the Skill Centre, AKA the Gulag. The Skill Centre (the eastern front) was in a dour suburb called Fishponds. Not as bucolic as it sounds, Fishponds was endowed with a chilling mythology. I'd heard tales of specialist doctors who administered electrodes to help overcome ergophobia related illnesses. A terrified man had told me about his visit. He was a carpet fitter who was suffering from crippling spasms in his legs. The doctor had recommended the removal of his kneecaps. 'But won't that be dangerous?' the carpet fitter had asked. 'No problem. It just means your legs will bend both ways. It could be useful.' 'But I wasn't planning a career in the circus.' I felt slightly uneasy to notice that nobody ever returned to the dole queue from Fishponds.

'Yeah,' I continued 'or set the Hounds of Hell on them.'

'Which is invariably Kastrina's approach,' Ash concurred.

We lapsed into silence. I think we were both surprised that we'd agreed on something.

Suddenly, without warning, a frosted pane of glass in the window near my table shattered. The street shouter! Another pane splintered, and then another. Bang! Bang! Bang! It happened quickly – but became deeply embedded in my mind ready for repeated replay. A mystery assailant was walking along the street, systematically breaking the window panes. Not with a brick, however. I looked on with fascination as an increasingly damp scarlet hand punched out one pane of glass after another.

'What's going on?' I said, feeling slightly faint.

Ash leant back in his chair. He seemed remarkably unconcerned.

'What are you complaining about? We need some fresh air in here.'

At that moment Mr Blunt burst through the door. He must have heard the sound of breaking glass. He walked across the room and stared at a box of claims that had been left directly under the now broken windows. 'There's blood all over the files,' he exclaimed. He turned to us angrily. 'What the hell have you been doing?' he demanded, looking directly at me.

'Grolier hasn't taken his pills today,' Ash calmly explained.

'Well don't do it again,' said Mr Blunt, still staring at me. Sometimes I felt so helpless.

## ~ TWENTY NINE ~

I weaved my way through the crowd. This was the bit I hated; waiting in a pub, alone. I tried not to look like some loser stood up on his first date. The Bog End was the side of the bar by the doors leading to the gents' loos. According to Justine, it's where you get the best sound. I recognised some of the faces around me, but not enough to say hello. I pressed up against the bar, in no hurry to be served.

I wasn't so sure about the world according to Justine. The band were hammering out an awful, chunka, chunka, chunka, New Orleans number. I had never quite got round to confessing to her that I hated trad jazz. A man with a goatee beard and a nicotine stained face was imploring Rosie Lee come back... to meeeeee. The trombonist was so fat his stomach wobbled in time to the music. If this was the Bristol sound somebody ought to turn it down – or, even better, off. I would have paid good money to be across the road in the Granary with the air-guitar-playing heavy metal head-bangers shaking their long greasy hair to Uriah Heap.

I'd never known anybody like Justine. Nearly all my friends in Ruislip had been to Grammar School and then to University. Ruislip was that sort of place; knee-deep in wankers. Even podgy little Reg Dwight had been to the school just down the road in Pinner. Justine had an edgy energy which I enjoyed. She was fun to be with and also a little crazy. I thought we could have some interesting times together.

Justine had been brought up on the toughest estate in Bristol. She didn't know where her Dad lived, and she had an idea, though she couldn't be sure, mind, that her Ma was on the game. She certainly had a lot more 'uncles' than her friends. As for her brothers, they were a couple of wasters. As soon as they were old enough, they were both banged up in Horfield, the local nick. The height of their ambition was to share a cell together.

Justine had learnt from an early age that there was nobody around to look after her. If things were going to happen in her life, it was up to her. She'd left school – which had taught her nothing except how to fight and lie – at 15. A year later she did what most girls on the estate did; she got married. 'I married Wayne Skuse. Nobody could believe it as our families had been fighting for generations. Don't ask me why, we just did. You should have seen the wedding; it was like the Jets and the Sharks. You could have cut the atmosphere with a Stanley Knife. To be fair, out of respect for the occasion, everybody behaved themselves. Well, Jayce had his car torched, but nobody gave a tinkers-toss about that, we all knew he had it coming.'

What she didn't do though, was have a baby. She was far too smart for that. She'd left the escape hatch open, unlike her friends who had their babbys, got their flat from 'the housing' down the road from their Ma, and were never going to leave the estate.

Where was she? Perhaps she had chickened out. The noise was becoming unbearable. People were shouting to be heard above the music. Chunka, chunka, chunka, oh Rosie Lee ...won't you come back to me. There was a whoop from the front and a surge towards the podium as a small guy in a bowler hat – a bowler hat! – was dragged on stage. 'Ladies and Gentlemen, all the way from Pensford...' The rest of the introduction was lost in a cheer from the crowd at the Bog End. Then there was a reverential hush as the man put his clarinet to his lips and blew a tune that I faintly remembered from my childhood. A black and white picture of a lonely girl on a cold pebble beach came to mind.

The leader of the band signalled for a change of pace. A blonde middle-aged women with thick orange make-up started to sing. 'Pardon me boys, is this the Chatanooga Choo Choo'. Oh really...

Justine lurched towards me, staring into my eyes but saying nothing.

'Where the hell have you been?' I shouted.

There was an unusual look about her face, a pinched look that I had never noticed before. She reached up and put her arms round my neck, and with her hands behind my head pulled me down to kiss her. She pressed her lips to my mouth and gently pushed her tongue forward. And then, to my surprise, she blew a swig of warm brandy from her mouth into mine. Momentarily shocked, I tried to jerk my head back, but Justine had anticipated this reaction and held my head firmly to hers until we had both enjoyed the heat of the alcohol and the soft pressure of tongues.

I was reeling. 'That was a nice surprise,' I said. Thankfully it wasn't cider.

'See you later,' said Justine turning away and disappearing back into the crowd.

That was the last I saw of her for the rest of the evening.

## ~ THIRTY ~

The crowd slowly unpicks itself. As the months went by I began to recognise my more distinctive long-term claimants. The Union Street veterans included Ras Nacho who despite being registered as a playwright could only sign his name with a cross; the beautiful Saphran, a devout Catholic cross-dresser; the Polish bag-babbler Mrs Golunski; little-miss-posh-girl Arabella Smythe, always late for her 9.30am signing – we all knew about her bar job at the Dug Out but didn't have the heart to formally introduce her to the Hounds from Hell; and the Kinsale twins – identical names and identical signatures – pulling some sort of scam, but I couldn't figure out what. One thing was for sure, I never saw them together[2]. And Otto Grolier. Otto Grolier! Otto Grolier was the most unpredictable of the lot – a crazy messed-in-the-head benchwarmer whose behaviour depended on whether he was taking his medication. I rarely got any real hassle from him, however. 'I think you should have this,' he said as he pushed a dead

---

[2] One evening I was jerked out of my torpor by a most unexpected sight on Top of the Pops. The Fighting Ghandis, a West Country punk band, known more for their brooding machismo than musical abilities, were grinding out their latest anthem. As the camera focused on the lead singer, there, on the neck of his guitar, as bold as the neon lights of Weston-super-Mare, was the lettering Kinsale Brothers.

So that's what the twins had been up to – guitar making. I was perversely pleased, telling myself that I had played a significant role in the success of the Kinsale brothers' mystery enterprise.

In Ash's view, it was thanks to the dole that there were so many creative types around in this country. Despite all its faults, where would all the artists, actors, musicians and writers be without the state sponsorship offered by their weekly Giro? Indeed, a band from Birmingham was so grateful for this support that they named themselves UB40. Sure, there were numerous dreamers who still couldn't hum a tune or paint their nails, but where would creative geniuses like George Orwell, Francis Bacon and Eric Clapton be if at some time in their life they hadn't been able to make that weekly journey to the labour exchange. If you were to stop these handouts the creative juices of the country would evaporate.

Years later I would boast, 'Ah, the Kinsale brothers, guitar makers to the famous. Yes, if it wasn't for me, they wouldn't be where they are today.'

pigeon over the counter. He seemed to like me.

Did I say that most of my claimants wanted to work? Well let me amend that. Some of my claimants were total bastards. And dangerous with it. The pimps and dealers were far too smart or busy to be bothering with the mundanities of regular employment. They'd got their work well sewn up – it was just that the Inland Revenue didn't know about it. They were the ones who would arrive by taxi and stride to the front of the queue, and with unquestionable authority – or menace – demand to be signed on immediately. They'd got stuff to get on with, and unless you were Kastrina, you knew for your own safety at the end of the day, it would not be a wise thing to refuse.

It was the NFAs that I got to know well. The NFAs – No Fixed Abode – or as Ash said, No Fucking Allowance – were daily signers. Why, when they had lost their home, they were made daily signers, I wasn't so sure. It seemed typical Ministry of Work thinking – like I said, when somebody's down, you might as well stomp on them.

Anyhow, their brutal lives on the mean streets were a not so merry-go-round that centred entirely on drink, drugs and the dole office. Sometimes the NFAs moved in packs, with a more experienced hand helping fill out the forms. But mostly they were solitary figures, illiterate and damaged – teetering on the brink of becoming non-people. I often wondered at what point they had fallen from grace. My own empirical research indicated that there was no pattern. Given the wrong circumstances it could happen to anybody. Nobody is exempt. That poor bastard could be me, I sometimes shuddered.

Of course, for those who have the inclination, the opportunity to get out of your head is always lurking. Even in the 1970s, an innocent age before crack cocaine, there was a small clan of lank, pasty-faced needle freaks, who paced the streets. For some the siren song of powerfully alluring pleasures called, as did the opportunity to slide into the abyss.

Dr Glazier was a victim of the wrong circumstances. The Doctor liked the taste of his own medicine too much for his own good and had been dismissed from his post in the hospital. For the first couple of months his habit seemed to be under control; he was charming, if a little distracted, and well groomed. He was the ideal claimant.

But then, one day, he queued at Enquiries and asked to be registered as a PI. He had no money for his rent and had been thrown out of his exclusive flat in Victoria Square. The monkey was on his back. As I amended the Doctor's Clifton address to No Fixed Abode, I felt I was signing his death warrant.

Each night on a park bench or under the Arches is a step further away from normality. His life moved down a gear. And as if the disturbed sleep wasn't bad enough, nightly harassment from the police, from skinheads and fellow PIs quickly took its toll.

I remember one summer evening, several years before, I missed the last train – the 11.50 pm from Marylebone – back home to Ruislip. I wandered round central London for an hour wondering what to do. I had a return train ticket but no money. Eventually I found a stray deck chair in Green Park and curled up as best as I could to keep warm. Within half an hour I was disturbed by a big flashlight being shone in my face.

'You can't sleep here,' the policeman said.

'I've got nowhere to go.'

'You've got to move.'

'Where can I go?' I said, wondering if there was a nice warm police cell waiting for me.

The policeman was unexpectedly helpful. 'Head up to the statue of Achilles, the big bloke with the sword and shield, just opposite the Hilton on Park Lane. We don't get up there until 4 o clock. You might grab a couple of hours' sleep.'

To my surprise there were hundreds of people clustered round the base of the statue; it was like a refugee camp. Anybody who sleeps rough in London, and doesn't know the ropes, is sent there. It makes the work of the police easier to corral the amateur vagrants all in one place. And keep the cells clear for the hardcore trouble-makers.

At four o' clock a squad of police arrived. This time they used what looked like a second world war spotlight mounted on the back of a truck to wake us up and move us on. The sleepy crowd dispersed as first light was breaking. I only had an hour to kill before the milk train left for the suburbs.

After just one night of homelessness I had felt sick and dizzy from lack of sleep. Imagine this happening night after night. You enter a never-never land of constant tiredness, an impossible world that is so fuzzy round the edges that you can't think straight. For some it can be a release. You don't have to think ahead – you can't think ahead, you survive for the minute. There is now no chance of getting a job; the preoccupation is the search for safety and a little something to sustain you through the long cold days and the even colder nights. At this stage it is tempting to think you've reached rock bottom – the land of the living dead. But it is possible to sink even further. Ah, but what did I know?

One day Doctor Glazier hobbled into Union Street without any shoes. He told me the previous night someone had stolen them. He was out cold and didn't notice they were missing until he woke to the grey dawn. Somebody's idea of a joke. You don't think about the importance of shoes until you're without them. The hassle, the humiliation of finding another pair, a pair that fitted, was not particularly funny. It took him several desperate days to find a replacement.

The decline of the Doctor was rapid. He had hollow glazed eyes, his hair grew long and within three months had gone grey. He then suffered what I thought was the ultimate humiliation – it was the defining point that indicated that he wasn't just an outsider, he had left the human race. He was no longer one of us – he was an animal. But not even animals do that. One evening, round Christmas time, he never quite made it to the public convenience. He shat himself.

I saw him in a doorway on Park Street. He was hunched up and crying, his trousers were thick with shit. People crossed the road to avoid the stink. Nobody gave him money, they didn't want to get that close. That was the end of his life.

During that Christmas the thought of Dr Glazier haunted me. I was ashamed that I too had passed him by. I wondered whether this was the end of the line for him.

But, in the New Year, something amazing happened. I was astounded to see, in my queue, a resurrected Dr Glazier. I was later told that he'd been rescued by a kiss-of-life angel who had taken him to the temporary homelessness accommodation and given him the full Christmas check-up and make-over. His old clothes had been cut off, he'd then been bathed, fed, re-clothed and even given a haircut. I realised that while shitting yourself might be social excommunication, it doesn't kill you.

It could have been worse, at least Dr Glazier didn't have Kastrina after him.

'If anybody sees a man with a bandaged fist let me know, I want to speak to him.'

'You're kidding.'

'I'm not,' she said angrily.

'What are you going to do, deduct money from his benefit?'

'I just want to have a little word with him. Make him realise how much he's inconvenienced us. In fact, I might just inconvenience him – by making him a daily signer. I've also notified the police – they owe me a favour.'

'You couldn't be so mean.'

'Just watch me. I don't think he'll be signing-on again in this town in a hurry.'

I didn't tell Kastrina that it was Grolier she was after.

It wasn't always bad news. Over the months I watched the slow climb back to a state of self-esteem of one, damaged, lonely man. A daily signer, I'd noticed him at Union Street with bundles of bags, bottles and newspapers. He spent his day collecting this stuff. He was a busy man. As the summer drew on he seemed to grow in confidence. From being mute, he'd mutter a few words about the weather, 'ot, in' 'it an' 'at' being his stock phrase. And then one memorable day he wheeled into the signing hall – he didn't dare leave it outside for fear of it being nicked – a sparkling new trailer the size of a large wheelbarrow. It had four inflatable tyres, varnished wooden bodywork, and red wheels – it was the business.

How he'd got his truck nobody knew, but the man now had a purpose in life. From then on, I would see him all over town, hurrying along with his little red wagon collecting his stuff. He had created his own job, he was in control; he appeared to be a contented man.

## ~ THIRTY ONE ~

The city streets were sizzling. I had never experienced anything like it in this country. It hadn't rained for three months. By midday the temperature was in the mid 30s. 'Far out – the thermometer's sweating,' Ash noted on a particularly sticky day.

The heat even permeated the signing-on hall which had acquired a rancid locker room stench.

There was talk about the water running out. The rivers were low, and the Chew Valley reservoir that served Bristol was virtually a dustbowl. A village that had been submerged for twenty-three years was revealed. Previous inhabitants returned to collect souvenirs; one man brought back a chimney pot from his home, another rescued his old garden gate. The Water Board had drawn up a contingency plan that involved sending a boat to the Arctic, harpooning an iceberg and towing it back to the Albert Dock at Avonmouth. In some parts of the country the water supply had already been cut off, and people had to trudge through the heat with buckets to collect their rations from a communal tap.

I was so concerned about this decline to third world standards that I'd even put a brick in my loo cistern to save water. I was also particularly keen to support the 'Save water, bath with a friend' campaign. I briefly wondered if Astral shared my passion for water conservation. Probably not. But Justine might.

The heat was certainly getting to Baxter.
'Did you see them?' asked Baxter in an agitated voice.
'Who?'
'The men.'
'The men?'
'Yes, two of them. In protective clothing.'
'Baxter, what are you talking about?'

'You know, protective suits, white baggy plastic suits, and a helmet. Protects you from germ warfare. Though they weren't wearing the helmets.'

'And they were here?'

'Yes, only a few moments ago. It's something to do with the top floor, I reckon.'

'Did they go up to the top floor?'

'No, they asked for Mr Blunt.'

'And did Mr Blunt deal with them?'

'He did, and he was very secretive. I didn't hear it all but I heard him say something like 'Come in quickly, I want as few people to see this as possible.'

'I'm not surprised,' I said, laughing, 'they were probably here to perform his lobotomy.'

'No, Max, this isn't funny, I think there's been a nuclear spill on the fifth floor.'

'Baxter, I think we'd know about something like that.'

'There's no reason why we should. There was no particular rush to warn the public when there was that radioactive leak from Windscale. In fact I seem to remember it was exactly the opposite. There was a cover up. The public wasn't warned at all.'

'But Baxter, that was a nuclear power station, this is a dole office. There's a difference.'

'Well, I've always wondered what happens at the top of the building. What about the sign saying Do not ascend unless authorised. You can't tell me that's not sinister.'

'Baxter, that's the training department. You've been up there yourself.'

'I feel most uneasy about what's going on here. There's more to this than meets the eye. I don't like it. I must have a word with Mr Blunt'.

'Yeah, you do that.'

In the out-weirding-the-claimant stakes, Baxter was now right out in the lead.

# THIRTY TWO

I spotted the buff coloured sheet of paper on my table as soon as I walked into the room. Report to Dr Hammer in the medical room at 2.30 pm, today. The note was signed E Blunt.

'Hey, Astral, who's Dr Hammer?'

Ash interrupted before Astral had a chance to reply, 'Dr Hammerstein? He's the department quack. Comes over from the Gulag now and again.'

'I've got to see him this afternoon,' I said.

'What for?' Prickly heat getting to you?'

'Very funny, Ash... I don't know.'

'It's probably a routine medical,' said Astral. 'I'm sure it's nothing to worry about. They sometimes do a random sample to make sure that you haven't picked up anything since you started working here. It's the pens. Never suck your pen.'

'Ash has told me all about the pens...and the sweets ... and Ed Chicken and tepees.'

'Poor Ed Chicken! He's a lesson for us all.' Astral obviously didn't know the truth about Ed.

I turned and faced Astral, 'Tell me,' I asked, 'What's the Doctor like?'

Ash butted in again. 'You hear tales. But don't you always. It's like school doctors – you know, broken needles, cold hands, and unnecessary requests to go through the coughing routine. You ought to take a urine sample with you. Anyhow, all I know is that when I saw him I thought he was the biggest charlatan that ever walked the earth. Don't be deceived by his bedside manner, he appears charming and talks posh. Don't tell him anything confidential. He's in cahoots with Blunt. Oh, and watch your kneecaps.'

Lee chipped in 'He talks posh to cover up his Swiss accent; rumour has it that he's in the employ of one of them large pharmaceutical companies. He tries out the latest drugs on people. Uses us like guinea pigs. Don't let him shove anything up your arse.'

'It could be to do with your application to become a first-aider,' said Astral.

I smiled at Astral. 'You're right, I expect that's why he wants to see me.'

I was reluctant to tell her that my application form was still sitting unsigned in my drawer. And that's were it would remain.

The medical room was in one of the further reaches of the building. It smelt of bandages and antiseptic and was sparsely furnished with a desk, a couch and a screen on wheels.

'Ah, Mr Redcliffe do come in and take a seat.' Dr Hammer looked me up and down in a professional manner.

I pulled a warm plastic bottle out of my pocket and put it on the desk.

'What's this?'

'I've brought you a drink,' I heard myself saying.

Dr Hammer reached forward to take the bottle.

'Don't. I was joking. It's my urine sample.'

'Ah, I see,' said Dr Hammer giving a strained smile. 'How are you feeling, Mr Redcliffe?'

'I'm feeling fine.'

'Mr Blunt has asked me to examine you. He is concerned about your health.' Dr Hammer spoke with the flawless middle England accent that is frequently adopted by immigrants on the make.

'What do you mean?' I was beginning to feel uneasy. Mr Blunt taking an interest in my health? Perhaps I was too healthy.

'He fears that you're not well. You are fortunate to have such a caring and considerate manager.'

'I'm sure I am.'

'Good. I want to ask you a few questions. Have you had any headaches, or sudden flashing lights in front of your eyes, recently?'

'No more than normal,' I said with a hint of sarcasm that seemed to be lost on the doctor.

'No more than normal,' Dr Hammer repeated. 'I see.'

I thought I'd better explain. 'It's from the light shows at concerts. I sometimes get flashbacks. Also hissing ears. Everybody gets that, don't they?'

'That could be significant. What about tastes? Do you ever get strange tastes in your mouth?'

'It depends on what I've been eating. The other day I had a pie that wasn't too good.'

'Mr Redcliffe, I'm not a man to beat about the bush, so I'll come straight to the point. Mr Blunt said that you nearly fainted in his office and then, later on, he found you thrashing about on the floor. He said that it was lucky that you hadn't harmed yourself. By the way he described it, it seems that you were experiencing what we call a grand mal.'

'What?' I said, alarmed.

'There is nothing in your notes about a propensity for fits. Have you had these fits before? How are your temporal lobes?'

For a moment I had no idea what the Doctor was talking about; and then I remembered my mad lapse on the carpet.

'Oh, I know what he's on about. It was when I was rolling on the carpet.'

'Yes?' Dr Hammer was looking at me with interest. 'Tell me more.'

'It was just one of those things – one of those things you do on impulse.'

'Yes?' It was obvious that rolling on newly laid carpets was not the sort of thing that Dr Hammer did on impulse.

'I just saw this carpet and rolled on it.'

'I see. Mr Blunt said that you were writhing in an alarming and uncontrolled manner. He said that when he spoke to you, your eyes were glazed and you were babbling incoherently. Mr Blunt is worried.'

I was becoming worried myself. 'It wasn't a fit; it was just something that I did. I don't know why, I just did it. Haven't you ever had an impulse to roll on a lawn, or down a grassy slope?'

'No. Never. I leave that for my dog to do.'

I wanted to suggest to Dr Hammer that he ought to, that it might loosen him up.

'Mr Redcliffe, I think we need to take this seriously. You may have I.C.D.' The Doctor's tone of voice had lowered.

'What?'

'Impulse Control Disorder.'

'Impulse Control Disorder – this is ridiculous.'

'Not at all. Denial of the problem is one of the symptoms. What happens if you have one of these episodes near some machinery, near the photocopier for instance. You could do yourself some serious harm. You could damage expensive machinery.'

'But I wouldn't roll about near a photocopier. I'd only do it on a large expanse of carpet.'

'But how can you tell? These sorts of attacks are unpredictable. What would have happened if you were driving a car?'

'You don't understand, I knew exactly what I was doing.'

'Well, what about the broken windows then?'

'The broken windows! They weren't anything to do with me! Mr Blunt knows that.'

Dr Hammer sat back. He was no longer listening.

'Mr Redcliffe, I think it is you who do not understand. Fits like these can be dangerous. You probably don't even know when you've had them. Luckily for you, you work for a sympathetic employer. I am here to help. Now, I can understand why you haven't mentioned this before. Some employers are wary of taking on staff with a condition such as yours. But I can help – Mr Blunt specifically said that I must do all that I can to make sure you stay in the Department. Eric, Mr Blunt, is a good man; he has your best interests at heart. Of course, once this goes on your personal file employment elsewhere will be difficult, if not impossible. But the Department will look after you.

For a moment a mist of despair descended. I felt powerless; this turn of events was so unexpected. I stared helplessly at the Doctor. I felt as if I was in a dream; I wanted to shout but no sound was coming out of my mouth.

Dr Hammer stood up and with a sweep of his hand indicated that I was to leave.

'I can see that you are shocked by this – but it is best to get your problems out in the open. We can then face them together. I will see you again soon when we can talk about medication. Don't worry, this won't affect your probationary period. I can assure you, Mr Redcliffe, that your position with the Ministry of Work is not under-threat.'

That was the last thing I wanted to hear.

## ~ THIRTY THREE ~

'So Ash, what's the plan?'

'...Sixty-nine, seventy, seventy one – hang on a moment – seventy two, seventy three, seventy four, seventy five. Done.' Ash was checking to see that all the claims were in his box. 'What?'

'You said you had a plan.'

'Uh?'

'To get out of here. Your plan to get out of here.' After my appointment with Dr Hammer I felt I needed to do something. Formulate a strategy. Urgently.

'I told you on your first day – don't even start working here. That's the best plan.'

'Yeah, well, I didn't quite understand what I was getting myself into.'

Ash shook his head and said laconically. 'You should have listened, man.'

'Okay I should have listened. I'm listening now, though.'

'Hmm.' Ash thought for a moment. 'Have you seen those adverts on the London Underground?

*If u cn rd ts ctct us abt trg fr a jb in Computers.*

I could read that, straightaway, no problem.' Ash said this in a manner that indicated he was rather pleased with himself.

'Com'on Ash, everybody can read those adverts.'

'Maybe. But you know what I'm saying.'

'No, I don't.'

'Training.'

'Training! That's a crock of shit,' I retorted. 'You and I spent three years at University and we're both stuck in this cess-pit. If that's your route to salvation, I'm not impressed. I've been on that trip.'

'Listen. I've thought about this a lot. I'm going to summarise many years of thought here. Are you ready for this?'

'Ash, I'm giving you my full attention. But keep it short.'

'Okay, well as I see it there are four ways to get on in life. Well, five if you include theft and violence, but being a man of peace I'm not into those – well, not yet, anyway.

'Think about the people who are successful in this world. Really successful – top of their league. What do they have in common?'

'They're all capitalist bastards?'

'You are so predictable. Apart from that?'

'Greed?'

'Maybe. But I'm thinking of something else. I'll tell you. What they have in common is sleep – or lack of it. Not only do they work hard, they also work long, long hours. They can do this because they don't need sleep. That hippie guy who owns Virgin Records, contrary to popular belief, doesn't spend all his day spaced out on a water-bed. He gets up at the crack of dawn and gets on with the job. All the great world leaders – Churchill, Kennedy, Napoleon – were high energy people... they never slept.'

'Never?'

'They'd catnap for short periods. Einstein slept 15 minutes every four hours. That was it.'

'What about Bob Dylan?'

'He's the exception. Bob needs more sleep than most. He needs to dream a lot. But he's not exactly a world leader, is he?'

'He is in my eyes.'

'Look, are you sure you want to hear this?'

'Yeah, sorry, carry on.'

'Of course the sleep deprivation drives them crazy in the end. But that's beside the point. What I'm saying is that to really succeed in this life you need a specific type of high energy. Which I haven't got. Neither, going by your narcoleptic behaviour, have you.'

'Ash, when you dish out the insults, they're of the highest quality. First, what was it, blennophobic? Now narcoleptic.'

'Blennophobic. Do you know what it means, yet?'

'Something about fear of slime – doesn't everybody have that?'

He gave a sinister laugh. 'Not everybody, my friend.'

'Anyway, what do you mean, my narcoleptic behaviour?'

'I mean your habit of sneaking down to the Cabbage Patch.'

'That isn't necessarily sleep.'

Ash ignored my innuendo and continued. 'Basically, anything that involves employment after five o'clock is not my scene. Nor yours. The night shift, that's for Dracula.

'So, onto the second route to success.' Thankfully Ash, true to his promise, was going through this at quite a pace. 'The second route to success is to use your social contacts. That's why the middle and upper classes have it so cushy. With their old school ties and their Masonic weirdness they're way ahead before the likes of you and I have even got out of bed. Unless, Max you are hiding some aristocratic connections, which, judging by your low bred behaviour, I doubt, you can also forget nepotism.'

'Very perceptive Ash. But also unnecessarily rude.'

'The third is down to good luck. I bought five Premium Bonds in 1967, or it could have been '68. Not a whisper. I could be waiting forever for my lucky break. So, what I need to do is take my destiny into my own hands. In short, create my own luck.'

So far, so obvious.

'And how are you going to do that?' I asked, leaning forward with anticipation. This was going to be Ash's star turn. For the last six months he'd been straining to share his philosophy about the world of work. It was a perspective, I guessed, that had been formulated after many years of inhaling jazzers.

'Okay, prepare to have your mind well and truly blown. You are going to have to re-think everything about your life after this...'

Just at this moment, however, Astral walked into the room.

'Anybody got a pen I can borrow?' Astral asked cheerily. Ash's lifestyle master-class was temporarily put on hold.

'Here have one of mine,' I said as I reached over the table and grabbed a biro Lee had left beside his filing box.

'Thanks Max. Oh, and how was your appointment with Dr Hammer? Have you got the First Aid Training booked?' She was standing with her back to the window.

'Nearly. There's a few formalities that need to be sorted.'

'What sort of formalities are we talking about?' Ash asked sarcastically. I could sense his frustration at being interrupted. I bet Karl and Fredrick never had this problem when they sat down over a pint of vodka to discuss the Communist Manifesto.

'Bad news, I'm afraid. There's a bit of waiting list.'

'Bit of a waiting list! First Aid has never been that popular before.' I knew Ash was trying to stir it.

'Yeah, I was disappointed. If I wait too long I'm afraid my enthusiasm might just go off the boil.'

'Maybe I could give you some preliminary instruction,' Astral volunteered. I noticed that the light shining through her blonde hair had created a halo round her head.

'Yeah, that would be good.' I was trying think of something that we could do together, something hands on. 'Some bandaging practice might be helpful.' I suggested. Ash was looking at me. He was trying not to laugh. Astral was at the door. She turned. 'Max, we'll talk about this later. Bye.'

'You dirty bastard,' howled Ash. 'Bandaging practice – what the hell is that?'

'No idea!' We both laughed. But only briefly. Ash was keen to continue the conversation.

'So where was I before we were interrupted?' asked Ash. I reckoned he knew exactly where we were, but I didn't want to appear too keen.

'You were talking about taking destiny into your own grubby little hands.'

'Ah yes. The fourth route to success. This is the one I'm banking on. And it's open to everyone. Even you, Max. So here it is; many years of thought and experience condensed into one short phrase.' The pitch of his voice had lowered and he was speaking slowly. 'And the short phrase is: Getting the knowledge. That's what it's all about. Getting the knowledge. And before you make some facile comment, I don't mean becoming a taxi driver. I'm thinking of getting quality training, real skills, the things that are in demand. The sort of expertise employers are gagging for.'

I shook my head. I was disappointed; for a lifetime of thinking this seemed to be lacking in substance.

'Been there, done that.'

'But what I'm coming to, is getting the right sort of education. Tell me, Max what did you think you were going to do with your Micky Mouse sociology degree? Make a career out of studying football hooligans? Fat chance! No, you've got to acquire the skills that are in demand. You only have to look at your claimants. Excluding the dossers and tossers, the ones who want to work and can't are those with no skills – or the wrong skills.'

'Yeah, but I've had enough of education – it was good at the time, but I can't face all that again.'

'It's up to you. I reckon a college course is a lot easier than working your nuts off twenty-six hours of the day.'

I still didn't get it. If Ash had all the answers, why was he working here, with these evolutionary failures?

'And when, exactly, are YOU going to do this life-enhancing course?'

'When I'm ready Max – and I think I'm going to be ready soon. I just have one little obstacle in my way at the moment that I need to sort out.' Ash reached over the table and pulled a grey filing box in front of himself.

'Do you know what the future's going to be about?'

'Instant mashed potato?' I said thinking about a TV advert I'd recently seen.

'Interesting, but I was hoping for something a bit more profound than the root vegetable dialectic.'

I thought hard for a moment and dragged up some half-understood sociology. 'Well Marx predicted the workers taking control of the means of production. Unfortunately the rise of the middle classes has put an end to that.'

'No, I'm thinking about something totally different. A positive symbiotic relationship between man and machine, that's what the future's going to be about.'

'What's that mean?'

'I'm talking about computers, you retard. Every other item on Tomorrow's World is about computers. You don't need to be Nostradamus to see the way things are heading.'

'Working with the N.E.R.Ds. I couldn't handle that. Those computer guys give me the creeps.'

'One day you'll remember this conversation and realise how right I am.'

Ash started counting the contents of his next box. 'One, two, three... And I tell you one thing, I won't be doing this any more.'

'Yeah, and I won't be peeling potatoes.'

## ~ THIRTY FOUR ~

Shit! Another letter on my table. I was learning to dread these notes. But on further scrutiny this seemed different. On the envelope, Maxwell Redcliffe, was written in a flamboyant – female, I guessed – hand. I opened it with trepidation.

*Max*
*Make it a shower!!!*
*Justine*

I could feel myself smiling. Yes, a shower was a much better idea.

## ~ THIRTY FIVE ~

'What we need, Maxy Boy' announced Ash as we walked through a desolate inner city area of Bristol, 'is more excitement in our lives.' Ash, in the way that he knew best, was trying to cheer me up.

We had spent a gloomy evening in an empty pub grandly named the Montpelier Hotel. The run-down ambience of the Montpelier Hotel was not uplifting. I felt the title 'hotel' was an overstatement for an establishment that offered 'dormitory accommodation for the working man'. The seating in the bar was un-upholstered, and a gallon jar of pickled eggs stood sweating on the counter. The clientèle was mostly corked-up Irish; republicans, judging by the rebel songs on the jukebox. Although we were obvious outsiders, we didn't get any hassle. The real attraction of the Mont' was that it hosted frequent late night lock-ins. But not tonight, everybody had collapsed in the heat.

'I don't know why we bother with that place,' I said, 'it's a dive...'

'Forget it, it's time for me to introduce you to one of the city's more exotic locations. I'm now going to show you to the most far-out club in Bristol. Good dope, bad girls.' Knowing Ash's taste in these matters I wasn't about to get too excited.

It was a sultry night. As we walked through an empty Portland Square, I could feel the bass through my feet even before I could hear it. Ash was taking me to the Sundown.

'Here's what you've got to do. Hang about, act cool, and let me handle the guy on the door.'

We joined a dozen people queuing in a dimly lit nicotine stained corridor.

'Max, relax – try not to look like you're casing the joint for a bust,' Ash whispered.

Ash pushed his way to the front and began talking to an enormous West Indian guy who I assumed was the doorman. A variety of handshakes were exchanged and then Ash beckoned to me to come forward.

'Ashton, I want you to meet my mate Max. Max this is Ashton. Ashton's THE man round here.'

The noticeable thing about Ashton, who I'd seen many times in the queue at Union Street, was his hat. It was a hat with attitude. I had never seen a hat like it. It was like a flat cap, but instead of being made with tweed or some material like that, it was silver patent leather. It was a hat that was so ridiculous, so uncool, that it challenged you to make a comment. It said: 'Mess with my hat and you mess with me.'

I wasn't sure how to do the fancy give-me-five stuff so I stuck out my hand and gave Ashton a traditional firm handshake.

'Pleased to meet you,' I said, feeling as straight as a line of squaddies. Ashton smiled, crushing my hand in his massive fist. No doubt about it, you wanted Ashton as an ally, not an enemy.

'Hey Max, you my friend,' Ashton drawled. I wondered whether Ashton was taking the piss. 'You get down de bar, you're holding t'ings up, man.' And with that we were in.

At the end of the corridor there were steps that led down into the darkness. The basement of a semi-derelict building on the edge of St Pauls wasn't quite what I had expected of the most far-out club in the Bristol.

It took a while for my eyes to adjust. I peered through the gloom; the room was small, sticky and dark. There appeared to be a warren of rooms leading off into the unknown. Although I couldn't see much, I liked what I could smell. The music was so loud I could feel the air vibrate; it seemed to be doing something to my stomach – vital internal organs felt as if they were being shifted around. It was clear that this was not the kind of place you came to talk – communication at the Sundown was limited to a more basic, physical level.

A corner of the room lit up from the flare of what must have been at least a twelve skin spliff.

'He's lighting a bloody bonfire.'

'Just take in the ambience,' said Ash. 'It's the vibe that's special. Okay, at the moment it doesn't look much, it's early though, things don't hot up 'till much later. Stuff just gets passed around. There's plenty for everyone.'

There were a number of things that you had to learn quickly about the Sundown. There were rooms at the back that you didn't go into. They were reserved for the regulars. At first sight it looked all very innocent; a murky room, lit by pools of intense light, was set aside for elderly West Indians to play dominoes. There was high-pitched raucous laughter and the rattle, click and bang of the pieces as they were slammed onto the table.

Was this for real? Or was it a front for something else? Perhaps there were things going on in the darker corners that you didn't want to know about. These were rooms that a white boy working in the dole office would be well advised to steer clear of.

At one stage the DJ grabbed a microphone and in a thick patois sang over a beat that was so heavy on the bass that I could see my drink ripple.

The procedure for buying a drink was curious. There was a hefty wooden barrier the size of a railway sleeper placed about a metre away from the bar. One of two girls, who were standing in the intervening space, passed you your drink once you had shouted your order to the barman.

'Licensing laws', Ash explained, 'they can serve drinks all night so long as they provide a waitress service. Technically the two girls are waitresses.'

I have to confess that I was still feeling on edge; I imagined suspicious eyes looking at me, working out where they'd seen me before. A Huggy-Bear type, wearing – even in this heat – a long patchwork leather coat, brushed past. Ash must have sensed my unease. 'Don't worry, you'll get into it. It takes a few visits to get to know the people, but once you're accepted, you'll dig it so much that you'll want to be here every night.'

What happened next didn't help. As I was waiting to be served, somebody standing behind me put their hands over my eyes. For a very brief moment I was totally freaked.

'What the fuck?' I shouted, struggling to free myself. I then realised the hands were small, and soft, and the person pressing into my back was female.

'Guess who?' whispered a vaguely familiar voice.

'Justine!?'

This was good. Perhaps Justine was by herself. I'd seen a couple on the dance floor – they were virtually doing-it with their clothes on. 'It's called whining' Ash had explained. It looked fun. Justine would probably be up for that...

The hands were lifted and I turned round. Not Justine. What was SHE doing here?

## ~ THIRTY SIX ~

'Where are we going?'

'You'll see.'

We had spent the remainder of the evening at the club smoking and drinking and I was now too out of it to know what was happening – or to care. Even after the swelter of the Sundown the air outside was warm. It was just right. It was one of those delicious nights when you feel that you could walk and talk forever. Once, on such a night, I had tried to walk to the horizon – to see what the view looked like from there. It had seemed logical at the time.

To avoid the concrete-heat of the shopping centre we strolled through Castle Park, with its bomb-gutted church and its mess of car parks. As we wandered by the riverside she put her arm through mine. Was this a sign of affection? Or was I being led somewhere? But she seemed different tonight; she talked about her horse.

'Bareback riding is absolutely the best,' she sighed.

We leant over a wall and stared into the blackness of the docks. At least being near water gave the illusion of coolness. I heard a plunk as a rat slid into the oily river. I could smell the comforting aroma of yeast from the brewery on the opposite bank. To our right a fig tree incongruously clung to the river wall. Owen had told me about this tree; another of his dubious tales. Three hundred years before, St Peter's Workhouse had been famous for the fig tree in its courtyard. Although the workhouse which had stood near this site was bombed in the blitz, this self-seeded plant remained. Because of the hot summer this was the first time in many years that the tree had borne fruit. I picked a fig and carefully folded it open. I took a bite, but spat it out – it wasn't ready yet.

'Where are we going?' I repeated.

'We're just walking.'

She guided me along King Street; the cobblestones shone in the yellow streetlight. I had never before seen the street empty. Even at this time of night- it must have been 3 am now – soft music drifted from an upstairs open window above the Duke. Somebody was having trouble sleeping in the heat.

There was something I had to ask: 'Err, what about your bloke?'

She didn't flinch. 'He's away all week. On the road, you know. Sales.' She was silent for a moment and then added, 'We have an open relationship.'

At the end of King Street she pulled me across the road to a roundabout that was covered in low spreading bushes. 'Right, here we are,' she announced.

## ~ THIRTY SEVEN ~

I woke up feeling like shit. Merely turning my head to look at the alarm clock sent the room spinning. I was on the edge of a whirlpool – one move and I'd go down. Lying on my back I manoeuvred myself to the side of the bed and carefully shifted my legs from under the sheet to the floor. With the help of my right hand I gently pushed my body to an upright position. But the effort of sitting was too much. I slumped forward and held my face in my hands. From this position, through my fingers, I could see my knees. They were dirty and grazed. For a few seconds I pondered the significance of this – and then the events of the night before hit me like a cyclone.

A frightening vision haunted me. I remembered car lights sweeping across the canopy of vegetation. I was looking down at a face. For a brief second, I saw, as if caught in a strobe light, eyes shut tight and a mouth orgasmically contorted.

'Oh fuck!' I howled as I fell backwards onto the bed. A new nausea swept through me.

How could I have done it? How could I have done it on a traffic island? It was so horrible, so sordid. What had I been thinking? Why hadn't I said 'no'? Why had I said 'yes'? Did I say 'yes'? Did it matter? Of course it fucking mattered! I felt sick. And most of all I felt ashamed. A one night stand with the office nympho. Any self-respect I had just ran screaming out the door. How could I have done it with Kastrina?

The events of the night before came slowly into focus. I remembered the traffic island opposite the Green Rooms, off Queen Square, that is covered, not with the usual ranks of municipal planting, but with shrubs. I didn't know what the plants were, but they were big enough to provide a dry and secluded space underneath. She led me to a shallow hollow in the ground – the sort of indentation that sheep make under thorny moorland hedgerows. Yet, with an absence of sheep in the city centre, I wondered how this indentation had been created. And more to the point, I wondered how

Kastrina knew of the existence of this hidden den? How often, I asked myself with increasing alarm, had she prowled the clubs, pounced, and dragged her innocent victims back to this squalid lair?

What a hypocrite I was. With Kastrina! Yet last night she had seemed different. She was softer and kinder. But was that because I had been so far-gone? In truth, I'd been gagging for it. I'd used her; she'd used me – it was as simple as that. So what? And, I reasoned, why should anybody know? Ash had been the only person to see us leave together. I knew I could rely on Ash's discretion.

As I slipped back into a fitful sleep I had one thought in my head that, mantra-like, I muttered over and over again. Nobody must know – this must be an absolute secret. NOBODY MUST KNOW.

## ~ THIRTY EIGHT ~

'**S**o did you do it?' asked Lee, who was sitting next to me at the counter.

There was a lull in the queue. Although signing–on officially stopped at 11.30, we usually stayed at our boxes to catch up with the late signers until the doors were bolted at noon.

'Do what?'

'You know.' Lee replied with a sickening smirk on his face.

'Lee, what are you talking about?'

'Do IT?'

'It?'

'Yeah, IT?'

'What?'

'Hump. Did you hump her?'

'Lee, I find your take on life obtuse at the best of times – at this particular moment you have totally lost me.'

As Lee spoke the next word, his grin got even bigger – his mustard coloured teeth were exposed to the back of his mouth. They were glistening – he seemed to be blowing bubbles.

'Kastrina,' he drooled.

Ah. Despite pleas to some greater unknown force, deep down inside I knew that this beastly act would come back to haunt me. In truth I had been waiting for this moment. Had some passer-by seen us shagging? Even in a small city the size of Bristol anonymity is never assured. Everybody moves in tight little circles and news travels quickly. Your indiscretions soon catch up with you. Despite all that I had hoped, I knew somehow Lee would find out. And I knew Lee would make a bloody great banquet of it.

I wanted to say Kastrina had been different that night, that there had been a temporary truce in her revenge-driven vendetta against the rest of the world, but I knew Lee would neither listen, nor understand.

'Well, what about Rachel Thompson?' As soon as I said this, I knew I'd made a mistake.

'What about Rachel Thompson? Well, I'll tell you about Rachel Thompson. First she was a bit of class. Second she wasn't my supervisor. And third, I didn't shag her brains out on a roundabout in full view of everybody. I don't think there's any comparison between my rather special moment with Rachel Thompson and what you did with...' and here hesitated for effect, 'Kastrina.'

'It wasn't a roundabout, it was a traffic island. And, if you must know, we were very discreet.'

'Oh yeah!' Lee sneered. 'If that's discretion I'd really hate to think what you get up to when you're acting a little bit reckless.'

I knew I'd lost this one. Retreat is sometimes the best policy. I casually gathered together my pens, stamp and box of claims and, even though it wasn't yet twelve o'clock, I walked away from the counter with as much nonchalance as I could summon.

'Piss off Lee,' I said as I walked past him.

I could hear him laughing as I walked out of the door.

## ~ THIRTY NINE ~

Although Ash's warning on my first day of threats and violence from claimants appeared to be exaggerated, I did find that I was increasingly greeted – more likely shouted at – in the street by complete strangers. Groups of street drinkers would shake their bottles at me in a friendly enough way in what I liked to interpret as a toast. One morning, as I walked to work, an enormous roar erupted from a man across the street:

'Hey Dole Man, are you goin' ta work?'

I did my best to ignore the drunken Scotsman and carried on walking.

'Well I'm not. I'm gonna get drunk. I bet that pisses you off.'

I had to grin. 'It does,' I said to myself keeping my gaze locked firmly forward.

'How the hell did he know?' I asked Ash.

'Come on, there are no secrets in this world. You might think there are. But there aren't. Take my word for it.'

'Did you tell him?'

'Give me some credit, man. For a start how am I supposed to know that you shagged Kastrina's brains out on a traffic island?'

'There, you said it as well.'

'What?'

'Shagged her brains out.'

'Oh, that was Lee's expression. And on a traffic island. I know it's built into the human psyche to do it in as many different places as possible – but a traffic island! There are limits you know!'

'It was very secluded traffic island.'

'Max, by the very nature of what it is, no traffic island is secluded. Anyhow, I have to say that if I hadn't heard it from you I wouldn't have believed it.'

'Nor would I. And I was there.'

'Doing it.'

'Yeah, All right – doing it.'

'With Kastrina.'

'Oh, for Christ's sake Ash, just shut up.'

'Don't worry, we've all been there.' Ash had dropped the mocking tone in his voice.

'What do you mean?'

'You haven't joined a particularly exclusive club, that's all I'm saying.' I could see that Ash, in fact, was saying a lot more.

'You too?' I understood. 'Christmas, huh?'

Ash gave me a sideways glance and shrugged. 'Just leave it.'


I wasn't looking forward to meeting Kastrina. So, as I returned from the canteen with Ash, it was with a mixture of fear and relief that I saw her in the distance, strutting along the corridor, deep in conversation with Mr Blunt. I wanted to get this over and done with.

'Here come the pyscho twins,' muttered Ash, apparently oblivious to my trauma.

As Kastrina and Mr Blunt drew near I managed to give a thin nervous smile. There was no reaction from Kastrina – not a flicker, not a glimmer; her face was set as hard as rock. She walked past with no acknowledgement of my existence. How does she do that? I asked myself. After such an intimate encounter, how can you not show any sign of emotion?

'Are you all right?' asked Ash. 'You look a bit peaky.'

'I'm not feeling too good. I think it's Doris's rolls; they've been sitting around in the heat for too long.'

At least, I thought, it could only get better. But then I hadn't yet spoken to Astral.

## ~ FORTY ~

I'd been pissed off with Justine for leaving me in the lurch at the Duke. Later, she'd apologised in what I felt was a half-hearted sort of way. She'd met an old friend, and when she saw me at the bar she thought I seemed to be enjoying myself. I don't know how she got that idea. Anyhow, I calmed down. You can't be angry with Justine for long. And tonight I was grateful for Justine's company. I needed somebody who could help me take my mind off the mishap on the roundabout and the ensuing humiliation.

As we walked into the Orchard's public bar we were hit by a crescendo of shouting. It was Wednesday night. Justine and I had already had a few bevvies at the Ostrich, a dockers' hangout that was thriftily furnished with a job lot of old Bristol bus seats. The Orchard, which was on Spike Island, a slither of land between the harbour and the River Avon, was a loud pub. The room went quiet for a moment as the dole-scamming clientele recognised us, but their attention quickly wandered back to the matter in hand.

'So where are you thinking of travelling?' I asked.

'You know how some people want to swim in the seven oceans,' Justine replied.

'Yeah, that's a cool idea,' I could imagine Justine emerging from a tropical sea.

'Well, I've got an idea like that. I want to travel to the five continents and drink cider.'

'Oh great!' I laughed.

Justine grinned. 'This is a serious pursuit,' she said.

'I don't doubt it is. But are you sure cider's available across the globe? Isn't it just a European thing?'

'Look, wherever you have apples you have cider.'

'I suppose so.'

'I've already done some research.'

'I bet you have.'

'Normandy cider, easy. South America – I've read about the West Country community in Patagonia, they must make the stuff. South Africa, no problem.

'Cape Apples' I shuddered. 'You can't eat them. Totally verboten.'

Justine looked at me quizzically and carried on. 'Australia – I bet it's a staple drink, like Fosters. That just leaves Asia – and here I'm not too sure.

Justine had got me thinking. Apples…Orchards…

'Garden of Eden!' I shouted. 'Although I don't remember the Bible specifically saying that Adam and Eve were cider heads, I bet you they weren't averse to a drop or two of fermented apple juice. And they were somewhere in Asia.'

'Well, there you go then, that's my trip sorted,' said Justine rubbing her hands together.

'Er, I don't want to be a downer Justine, but you've missed the Antarctic.'

'Shit! The Antarctic, I'd forgotten all about that. Nothing grows there, does it?'

'Certainly not apples.'

'I'll just have to take a flagon of Scratch with me. I'm not having my trip ruined by a poxy continent like the Antarctic.' I liked her pragmatism.

Justine got up. 'Back in a mo,' she said, 'I need to speak to somebody.' She walked to the back of the room. I could see her talking earnestly to a wiry man with sun bleached hair and eyebrows. The next time I looked she'd gone.

In the short time I had spent in Justine's company, I had come to realise that Cider houses are in a league of their own. The décor is stripped down to the minimum – bare flagstone floors, wooden seats, brown and cream walls, splots of nicotine stain on the ceiling, and, of course, a jar of pickled eggs, like biological specimens, on the counter.

According to Justine, after you've had a few pints there's nothing more satisfying than the bouquet and consistency of a pickled egg. First there's the tang of vinegar. This acts as a wake-up call to the taste buds telling them something special is about to happen. Then there's the firm rubbery bite of white followed by the cloying texture of the yoke. All this in one mouthful. No wonder the pickled egg is the preferred late night snack of the cider drinker.

I studied my pint with a dash. Although I liked the thought of rough cider- it was a natural product that epitomised the West Country – when it came to drinking it, I wasn't so sure. Justine would eulogise over the delights of a taste or two of Kingston Black. 'Look, it has the pale colour of an autumn morning in it,' she would say, holding it up to the light. She'd then take a swig, roll the liquor round her mouth and swallow. 'Arr, that be good. Liquid dew drops – with a long lingering finish. My, you can taste that fruit.' I saw things differently. However much I tried, I could never pick up the tastes that Justine so graphically described. I didn't like the diaphanous bits floating in it, and not only did it look like piss, to me it tasted like piss. The dash of lemonade helped though. 'The more you drink the better it gets,' Justine assured me. I wasn't sure that I wanted to get to that stage.

A couple of years before, Somerset Cider had planned to discontinue the production of Scratch and focus on a more commercially viable apple-based product. There was an outcry. They didn't realise the scale of the monster that they had created. It was only after a crazed mob of cider drinkers descended on the Weston Zoyland Cider Works and strung the chief blender upside down over a 10,000-gallon vat that the company relented. (In retrospect harming the very man responsible for blending the precious brew was not a good idea – but cider does that to you.)

I looked around; across the room two guys and their girlfriends were talking and laughing. I thought I recognised them from somewhere, probably Union Street. One of the guys, an enormous man whose head appeared to grow directly out of his shoulders, glanced over, nudged his pal, and shouted something. His mate, whose massive riveter's arms were so densely tattooed that they appeared blue, bellowed a reply. Although I couldn't make out the detail of what was being said, I somehow felt it was about me. I nodded in acknowledgement.

There's also something about cider drinkers – and it's not just their lack of teeth. Statistics, if you are to believe them, show that there are more gutter-huggers in cider pubs than any other drinking establishments – gin palaces included. When I first came to Bristol I was struck by the round and florid West Country faces. The complexion was not due, as I first naively thought, to honest toil in the fields but to an excessive consumption of 'rough cider.' Rough cider can be a devilishly strong, face twisting drink; a cruel master that flays the complexion, churns the guts and even worse, scrambles the brain. I had seen the ambition of many a poor boy at Union Street cruelly terminated by his craving for a 'taste'. Even more frightening were the female cider heads. Blowjob Lucy, who hung round the laundrette offering 50p tricks, was legendary.

I didn't have to look far for the evidence of cider's health threatening characteristics. Slumped nearby was an enormous man of indeterminate age with a red beard that went right up to his eyelids. He was as near orang-utan as a human can get without stepping outside the Homo Sapiens gene pool. His trousers were ripped, and to my displeasure, it appeared that he wasn't wearing any underpants.

In an attempt to avert my gaze I contemplated a collection of local pictures that must have spanned many years. Hanging on the wall was a gallery of black and white and sepia tinted photographs of ships sliding gracefully down a slipway into Bristol's harbour. While the majority of photographs were old and fading, there were several of more recent events.

You see, the Apple Tree quenched the thirst of the labourers from the port's only remaining shipbuilding yard. Most of the clientèle were deaf from the constant hammering of their trade.

Justine had told me that when they launch a ship the pub stays open all day. The last boat to go down the slipway was a tanker for transporting Guinness from Dublin. 'Now that was an opportunity not to be missed. Cider and Guinness, Poor Man's Black Velvet, the black and the golden, what a drink! A twelve hour sesh! Man, we really launched that ship!'

That was a year ago. The order book was now empty and the yard was in limbo, struggling by on the occasional re-fit. There had been a knock-on effect on the neighbourhood. Spike Island was now in terminal decline. With its soured earth and landscape of empty factory sheds it felt like a relic from another time. Not so long ago the life-blood of the city pumped through here; twenty years earlier the air would have been heavy with the sweet smell of tobacco from the bonded warehouses, or scented by the leaves from Brooke Bond's tea packing factory. Now the tattoo parlours, the knocking shops, the glimpse of cranes over the rooftops, had all gone. Only the bitter dust from the coal-yard floated in the breeze.

I was feeling good; the evening was going well. At least Justine had turned up at the Ostrich. On time. And seemingly sober. And if she knew about my encounter with Kastrina she wasn't saying anything about it.

But where was she now?

Five minutes later Justine reappeared and sat down opposite me with her back to the rest of room.

'Where the hell have you been?' I asked. 'I was beginning to think you'd done a runner. Again.'

I wasn't prepared for what was to come next.

'Max, don't say anything – just listen.' Justine's demeanour had changed. She was leaning forward towards me – so that nobody else could hear. 'And don't look at the men in the corner. I said DON'T look at them, you prat. In the toilet a girl warned me my boyfriend was going to get a right belting.'

'I didn't know you had a boyfriend.'

'Don't be a div, Max, they're talking about you.'

'Me!'

'The girl asked me why you'd been staring at them. She wanted to know what our fucking game was? No, Max, for God's sake DON'T look at them. They've recognised you from Union Street. She said as soon as you step outside the blokes are going to give you a hiding.'

I should have known; things were never straightforward when you were out with Justine.

'It's not my bloody fault,' Justine said, as if she was reading my mind. 'This is what you do. Go to the toilet out the back, there's a side door on your right that leads into the yard. Just leg it. I'll see you in the Nova in 15 minutes.'

I felt uneasy about this. 'What about you?' I wasn't being particularly chivalrous. Surely she was used to going out with guys who enjoyed a bit of a bundle. What would Justine think of me if I ran away? 'I can't just leave you here.'

'I can handle those guys –my brother shared a cell with one of them. It's you who's in trouble. Just get up and go. Do it now.'

What happened I wondered, as I ran for my life along an alarmingly deserted Cumberland Road, to that romantic evening I'd been planning? It was only when I was within a hundred yards of the Nova that I dared look over my shoulder to see whether a man with no neck was thundering after me. My heart was pounding and I was dripping with sweat. It appeared that nobody was following.

Justine's flat was on the top floor of an elegant, but decaying, house in Royal York Crescent. It was a world away from my own empty room with its thinning lino and Baby Belling in the corner. But as we climbed the stairs each floor became less palatial – smells alternated between student cooking and old lady's 4711 cologne. By the fifth floor – in a previous age this would have been the servants' bedrooms – the surroundings were far from salubrious. The shower and loo were in an enclosed wooden cubicle on the landing. That'd be interesting. Justine's room was small, neat and cosy, with a low roof that sloped towards a dormer window. The walls were decorated with framed impressionist prints. From the window you could see across the docks and the Cumberland Basin to a distant church tower on a hill across the valley. I caught a glimpse of the lights reflecting from the water of the harbour far below. I could even pick out the route along which I'd just run for my life.

Justine had a single bed, which surprised me.

'Who needs a double? I used to live in a caravan – this bed's enormous compared with that. If I'm going to sleep with somebody I want to know where they are.'

Justine poured out some Scratch for herself while I opened a bottle of Hirondelle.

'Careful not to mix it, mind,' warned Justine.

I rolled a J and we lay back on her bed. Through the warm night air I could hear the faint rumble of traffic from the Cumberland Basin.

'I've got something important to tell you.' Justine said seriously. But then she sniffed the air. 'What's that smell?' she asked.

'Fear probably.' I laughed.

'No, it's something else.'

'Com'on, it's been a hot day,' I said defensively.

'No, it's not sweat.' Justine sniffed my shirt.

'Oh God! It's that disgusting bone factory,' I said, horrified.

'No, it's like...' she sniffed my shirt again, 'it's like pear drops. No. It's hair spray... It's cheap hair lacquer.'

'You're probably right. My flat reeks of the stuff. I suppose its better than smelling like a crematorium.'

She shook her head. 'You're funny.'

I sometimes wondered why Justine bothered with me. Once she said. 'I've watched you with the claimants. You do your best, your heart's in the right place. You may not know your head from your arse, but one day you'll sort yourself out. You'll do all right, Max.' There were times when I had to hang onto those words.

I kissed her.

'Don't forget there's a drought on,' she whispered.

'I think it's about time we started conserving some water,' I replied.

She never did get to tell me what was so important.


The whirr and rattle of a milk float woke me. For a while I lay listening to the dawn chorus. While in theory I liked Justine's expectation of closeness, I was a light sleeper, and frequently woke as she shifted in her dreams.

At 6.30 I dressed silently. I looked at Justine – with her face relaxed in deep sleep she looked like another person. She was more peaceful, more beautiful, than I'd ever seen her. I pondered whether to wake her, but kissed her gently on the forehead, and left without disturbing her.

I stepped out of the house onto the wide regency promenade. The city was still. I walked through the empty tree-lined streets past italianate villas to Park Street and the University Tower, past George's Bookshop, and then down the hill to the Centre and the docks. I'd learnt to love this city. It had such a deep history. As I moved through the landscape past graceful churches funded by god-fearing medieval merchants and elegant Georgian terraces, so at odds with the squalid slave trade that funded them, my mind was transported back to past times. I stood for a moment by Neptune's statue and stared across a grey sheet of water towards acres of abandoned sheds, rusting cranes and rail tracks leading nowhere. I wondered how this landscape looked in its heyday. There wasn't the slightest gasp of a breeze. The early morning sky was deep blue. I could tell, even at this hour, it was going to be another stifling day.

It was only 7.15am and I had an hour and a bit to spare before I was due to be in work. I wanted to wash away the smoke, sweat and passion of the previous night. As I boarded an empty bus and headed out of town to Redfield to shower and shave and change my jeans and shirt I noticed some small muscle twisting my stomach. It was Thursday, PI day, and I needed to be feeling my best.

## ~ FORTY ONE ~

I saw Astral walking ahead of me. I was keeping in the shadow of the buildings. Even at this time of day the direct sunlight brought me out in a sweat. I walked faster and caught up with her. I thought we could discuss the arrangements for our bandaging practice.

'Going to be another hot one.' I said. I didn't want to seem over-keen.

'Go away.' said Astral. She was staring straight ahead.

'What?'

'Just go away.'

'What's up?'

'I think you're horrible.'

'Astral, what are you talking about?'

'You know exactly what I'm talking about. Go away Max.' She broke into a half run. I increased my stride to catch up with her. We were jogging side by side.

This was ridiculous. The last time we'd spoken she'd been positively coquettish. She turned and glared at me. 'It makes me sick to think about it. How could you? Is that what you do? Go to the Sundown and pick up any old tart that takes your fancy?'

How had Astral found out? Through Lee probably. He'd be sure to exaggerate and embellish the details.

But at least she wasn't talking about the previous night with Justine. I was relieved about that. Even so, not in my wildest nightmares had I expected the news of my encounter with Kastrina to be so much in the public domain. The bush telegraph in this city is like a loud hailer. And fast. The way things were going I was expecting to open the Evening Post and see my indiscretions listed under Births, Deaths, Marriages and BONKINGS.

Jogging in this heat was stopping me from thinking straight. The sweat was now running down my back.

'What you've heard, is not true. It's Lee's fantasy, not mine.'

170

'You keep Lee out of it. He's a friend. Not like you.'

'Its not like Lee made it out to be,' I pleaded. Thanks to Lee, in Astral's eyes I was now, I guessed, an alfresco-obsessed sex-crazed pervert. 'Sure we met at the Sundown. But what happened wasn't important.'

'Wasn't important! You...you shagged Kastrina's brains out on a traffic island and you tell me that it's not important.' I was surprised at Astral's language; this wasn't her usual turn of phrase.

'Astral, it meant nothing. I promise.'

'You always slagged her off, and took the piss out of her. You're a two-faced hypocrite.' Tiny beads of moisture had appeared on her upper lip.

We turned the corner by the police station. We were in the full hammering sunlight now. The big arch of the dole office entrance was in sight just 100 metres away.

'But what about the bandaging practice?' I asked.

'You disgust me.'

Astral broke into a run. I stopped. My private lapse was such common knowledge that I felt ashamed of my weakness, of my superficiality. And if I was honest with myself, I also felt a tiny bit smug.

As I watched her running in her platform shoes I asked myself why she was behaving like this. While I'd been expecting a hard time from Kastrina, I hadn't anticipated heavy shit from Astral. What's it to her? I turned to cross the road to get my early morning cup of tea from the Concorde Café and looked back at Astral's tottering figure in the full sunlight. Perhaps she cared after all?

## ~ FORTY TWO ~

The doors for the P.I. session were opened on time at 2.00pm. There was the usual rush to get a place in the queue.

The previous week I'd asked Kastrina about the tune she hummed.
'Why do you always sing 'Here Comes the Sun' on PI day?'
'I've changed the words'. 'Here comes the SCUM dee da de de...,' she sang:
'That's crass.' But I had to laugh.

To my left I could hear Kastrina demonstrating her hurt to help philosophy. Today she was coming on really strong. Which was unusual for a PI day.
'No, you can't sign-on early.... I don't care if you've got a job interview... phone the employer and tell him you are going to be late... the nearest phone box is across the road... it's not my problem if you haven't got any change.'
Another voice. 'I want my money.'
'I'm sorry but you didn't sign-on last week and now you'll have to make a fresh claim.' I could hear Kastrina explain.
'I forgot.'
'Your claim has now lapsed – go round to Door 3 and make a fresh claim.'
'But that's not fair.'
'It's the rules.' I couldn't understand why Kastrina was doing this. What had happened to her 'get'em in get'em out' directive?
'Where's my money?'
'If you make a fresh claim you can get a form to take to the DHSS for an emergency payment.'
'I want my money NOW.'
'Please, you're holding everybody up.'

'Where's my fucking money?'

'I've told you, your claim has lapsed.'

'You BASTARD!'

And with that he was on the counter, and reaching over the screen.

'You bastard, I want my fucking money.'

Ash and Lee were already in place, armed with the cleaner's brooms, ready to brush him back as he tried to grab onto the side of the screen and propel himself over. The screens were well designed – there was nothing to hold onto. Yet, somehow, with enough anger inside them, claimants had been known to cross the counter. The man was hanging on precariously to the top of the screen. Ash and Lee now had the advantage. Together they pushed; the man had nothing to hold onto and fell head first, nine feet down onto the hard floor. BUMKKK.

I heard that BUMKKK. It didn't sound good. I could remember that feeling from when I was a kid and had cracked my head on the pavement. That horrible, dull sensation when your head feels like it has the consistency of a watermelon – and the sudden realisation that your head is really rather precious, and that you need to look after it, and that it's hurting and throbbing, and woolly and you're worried that you might, this time, have actually hurt yourself, and this mussiness is not going to go away, and you just want to lie down, curl up in your mother's arms and go to sleep.

I had to draw my thoughts back to what I was doing. Keep the queue moving. There's only a flimsy plate of perspex between you and this mad mob. Just keep them coming. All the claims are in my box. I've got nothing to worry about. But, ever so slightly, my hand started shaking. My handwriting was going to pieces. It was the nerves.

'You bastards have hurt my mate. He's out cold.'

Although the colour had drained from her face, Astral, who was sitting to my left, was keeping it together. Just. She looked at me for a moment, as if she was expecting me to do something, but then called over her shoulder. 'We need first aid here. Quick.'

'We need a bloody ambulance.'

The hall had gone quiet. This was a bad sign. When PI day was going well it was a market place, a hubbub of friends greeting each other, discreet dealing in the corners and banter between the city tribes. This hush meant something was up; you could sense a natural order establishing itself. Them and us. People were checking to see that they weren't standing in the wrong place. There was a motion in the crowd like a wave sucking back before it breaks. Those ready for revenge, those ready for trouble and those beyond caring were assembling within striking distance of the screen. Others were shuffling towards the back of the hall, out of the way. I noticed one of the

Kinsale twins edge out of the door.

Mr Blunt had appeared behind the counter and was talking to Kastrina, offering her words of encouragement. 'We've got people at hand to offer extra support,' he was saying. Mr Blunt walked past me and quietly said, 'Reinforcements are ready out the back if things get out of hand. Stay at your post, Max.' And he gave me a smile, a real smile. In this moment of stress we all needed to believe in him. For the first time ever, I warmed to Mr Blunt. I didn't have time, however, to stop and think what form these reinforcements took. Owen? Baxter? Who was he kidding?

For a moment I thought everything was going to be okay. But then I heard the cry that I'd dreaded.

'Get the fucking bastards!' somebody whooped. And then came the surge as the first round of assailants stormed the screen.

Mr Blunt bellowed his order across the room. 'Stay at your posts.'

I tried to concentrate on my work. I'd got a job to do; I just wanted the bloody idiots to go away. They weren't helping anybody; in fact they were screwing up everybody's chance of getting a Giro. A boot swung past my face. Shit, somebody's over the top, I thought. Before Ash and Lee could restrain the assailant, the youth had kicked one of my filing trays into the air and onto the floor. Still standing on the counter, he lashed out with a foot, which Ash caught and with surprising speed, yanked. Lee had the lad by the leg and was endeavouring to pull him off balance. The assailant's legs were pulled from under him and he fell arse first onto the counter and then rolled onto the floor. Ouch! I could feel that injury as well. In an involuntary act of mutual sympathy I felt my hand moving towards my own coccyx. There were now scuffles all along the line of the counter; at least six people were over the screen.

I looked on in despair as my files were ground into the floor.

I turned to my right and saw Otto Grolier.

'Grolier?'

There was a glow of recognition in Grolier's eyes.

'Hi Man!' he said cheerfully.

This brief moment of recall dulled as Grolier's' eyes glazed over and he aimed a punch at my head. This was the first time that I'd ever been hit in anger by an adult. I was on the gritty lino floor. From where I lay I could see a corner of sky through the window – I noticed it was washed-out blue with the heat.

Where were Starsky and Hutch? Taking their time no doubt. Why wasn't Kastrina doing anything? And most important of all, where was Tina Turner and her limo when I needed her most?

And then a Doc Marten swung into my stomach.

## ~ FORTY THREE ~

Even though Ash had warned me that intimidation and violence was part of the job description, I had never believed it would happen to me. First the threat at the Apple Tree and now this. I was sure about one thing. I wasn't doing a job where I got beaten up on a regular basis.

As I lay on the floor waiting for Astral to perform her Angel of Mercy act, I wondered if I should hold my breath and pretend to stop breathing.

But Astral never came to my aid. Eventually it was Lee and Ash who dragged me to my feet and shouldered me round the corner to an interview room. To my annoyance Lee was laughing. They discussed whether they should put me on the floor or whether I should be propped in a chair with my head slumped forward on the table.

'Dr Hammer will be with you in a moment.' I heard Ash say cheerily. They left me on the floor.

Dr Hammer, who arrived five minutes later, felt my ribs, shone a light into my eyes and tut-tutted. 'That's your driving licence withdrawn, I'm afraid.'

'I haven't had a fit. I was beaten up. There's been a riot.'

'See if you can get up,' he suggested, ignoring what I'd said.

I stood up slowly and held onto the table. I could sense him looking with a professional interest at my legs. I thought about the doctors at the Gulag. What do they do with the kneecaps? Sell them for transplants?'

'Mr Redcliffe, the time has come for you to face up to the reality of your situation.'

I didn't have the strength to argue.

Ash told me how the scuffle ended. 'It kind of whimpered to a halt. Once they were over the screen the rioters seemed uncertain what to do. And of course they weren't ready for our secret weapon.' I could guess what was coming next.

'For a few moments Kastrina was uncharacteristically restrained. She sat like a wily old cat and observed the fight. But then she launched into action.

'RIGHT YOU BASTARDS! I'VE HAD ENOUGH OF THIS,' she shouted as she jumped off her stool.

She picked up an empty claim box and smashed it over the head of the nearest insurgent. Man, you should have seen the look of surprise on his face. The poor guy wasn't expecting that! He just crumpled. But that wasn't all. With all the concentration of a rugby player converting a try, Kastrina kicked the man in the groin. On hearing the crushed-gonad-induced-howl the assailants NOW knew exactly what to do. And quickly. Grolier and his scum chums scuttled back over the counter like a swarm of rats on a hot tin roof. But get this. What really blew my mind was they got back into line again as if nothing had happened. The brazen fucking cheek.'

'Dedication to scrounging,' I was alarmed to hear myself say. 'They must have realised they were messing up their chance of getting their money.'

'You're right. Not a good idea to stamp on the hand that writes the Giro. We picked up the claims from the floor and by the time the pigs arrived it was situation normal.'

'Apart from my broken ribs.'

'Broken ribs! Com'on, you've had a few days off. What are you complaining about?'

I wasn't badly hurt; Grolier's punch, which must have been with his damaged hand, merely knocked me off balance. Even the kick was half hearted. It was my confidence that took a knock, though. I took a week off work – not so much to heal my wounds, more as a point of principle – and to my surprise returned to a hero's welcome. Mr Blunt muttered some appreciative words regarding moral fibre and a mention in dispatches to Regional Office while Kastrina felt a bicep and said something unnecessary about not realising how hard I was.

Of course violence always leaves a mental scar. You never forget the face of the person who has thumped you – it's freeze-framed and stamped on your brain forever. The strange thing is that no such branding seemed to have taken place in Grolier's mind. The next time Grolier signed-on there was no acknowledgement of anything untoward having taken place. No knowing I-sure-kicked-your-butt look. No apology even. Absolutely nothing. It was as if the scuffle had never happened. 'He was probably so out of his head, he doesn't realise that he beat the shit out of you,' said Ash.

## ~ FORTY FOUR ~

I wrote the date on a UB40 and swore. 'Oh shit!' While the riot might have been a mental turning point it was Mid-summer's day that was to push me into formulating an escape strategy.

'What's up, man?' asked Ash.

'21st June. The twenty-bloody-first-of-fucking-June. Jeeesus. I just don't believe it.' I put my head in my hands and stared down at the table. To sum up my life: I'd got a shitty job; I lived in a foul flat; I hadn't got a car; I hadn't got a family – let alone a girlfriend. The future looked bleak. It wasn't as if I was spending my money on the things that most people take for granted – I didn't even smoke straights. Life's pleasures were few and far between. Though the night with Justine had cheered me up.

'What's so special about the 21st June?'

'June 21st. The Summer Solstice. Midsummer's day. I started working here to save money for the summer – it's Midsummer's day already. I've been here for nine months. And I'm still here. Shit!'

'Amazing that a shirker like you has stuck it this long, more like,' said Lee.

'Piss off, Lee.'

The reality was making me feel dizzy. Tick-fucking-tock. Every second of every day was hammered into my brain. How does time go by so quickly? The days and the weeks float by: mashed-out Monday; nothing Tuesday; anxious Wednesday; PI Thursday -the terrifying day around which everything else revolves, and then Praise-be-to-Mr Natural it's Friday. And onto the weekend. The wonderful, joyous, spirit-affirming weekend that is finished before you've even started. Surely this isn't all there is to life. Spending your whole time at work and looking forward to what? Old age, illness and premature death? There must be more to our time on the planet than this?

I couldn't believe I'd been at Union Street for nine months. Nine months of my life. And what had I got to show for it? Cracked ribs and a nasty yellowing bruise. Along with the capacity to shrug off abuse.

Ash pronounced his familiar mantra.

'Max, take it one day at a time'

'I think I've been taking too many days at a time. I need to get off this bloody roundabout.'

I looked down at the table and muttered to myself 'My life is now, I can't fritter it away like this any longer.'

'What's that you said?' asked Lee, who appeared to be enjoying my crisis.

Still holding my head in my hands, I raised my eyes and looked at Lee. Perhaps other people don't feel like this, perhaps they really are happy. Was Lee's only concern in life how to get into Astral's knickers? (Though I had to concede that such a thought was not without its merits.) Was that all Lee thought about – apart, of course, from being a Gas Head?

I could see that Lee was beginning to feel uneasy with my stare on him. 'What did you say?' he repeated.

I stared at Lee. I stared at Lee's ugly, cheddar cheese teeth and emollient hair, and concluded that, yes, thoughts about Astral's underwear were probably the limit of Lee's intellectual curiosity. I got up from the table.

'I said I'm outta here.'


Thanks to Otto Grolier and his nifty footwork, getting out of Union Street was now my top priority. When I needed thinking space I sought solace in the loos in the basement. They were so cold and malodorous that few people used them. I sat on the wooden seat. I'd often stared at the Civil Service regulation loo-roll holder monogrammed with a royal crest and debated whether to unscrew it and sell it. What would it be worth? I reckoned I could get at least 50p from Pauline & Doreen's junk shop on Stokes Croft. Today, however, I was oblivious to my surroundings.

Where had it all gone wrong? I wanted to be sitting at the kitchen table reading The Guardian; I wanted to be eating toast; I wanted to be skinning up; I wanted to be in a pub laughing with Justine – no, any half-reasonable girl would do; I wanted to be lolling on the grass in the park; I wanted to be reading J.P. Donleavy; I wanted an afternoon where I did absolutely sweet FA. In fact, I didn't care where I was. I just knew that I didn't want to be here.

How do other people at Union Street survive? Is this how old gits like Owen, shifting stacks of paper down in the cellar, felt? Did they start work thinking the whole thing was a joke, and then wake up one day and realise, oh shit I've just spent 30 years of my life stuck in a job that I hate?

Of course there was Astral's little friend, the unspeakable Kayne Bender who supplemented his day job with an evening shift of shelf stacking at Parker and Barker's. But Kayne did this, I found out, not so much for money and environment but for perks of a sexual nature. 'You see,' Kayne would say with a smirk, 'those prim female managers with their immaculate hair and their grey fitted suits like a bit of rough.' What all these women saw in this oily lothario was beyond me.

But I didn't fancy working the twilight shift, whatever the rewards. I thought about Ash's four steps to career progression. Well, five if you include theft and violence. And then I remembered the ARF course and what the Hounds of Hell had said, and my thoughts on the last day when I filled out my evaluation form.

In retrospect Grolier had done me a big favour. How's the saying go? 'If you want to rob a bank, work for a bank.'

I had always considered myself to be honest.

That's not to say that I hadn't been tempted once in a while. I remember years before when I'd been seduced by an easy opportunity. For months, I'd cased the joint. I'd observed the shop assistant's movements; I'd weighed up the angles, and checked out the blind spots. Then, in one moment of pure adrenalin, as quick as a cobra, I stretched over the glass counter and grabbed a mini chocolate bar. I must have been nine years old.

Ten years later, I'd nicked an LP from HMV in Oxford Street. The record was too big to hide under my coat; I just walked out of the store with it under my arm. And then I ran. Not straightaway. I allowed a few discreet yards before I really hoofed it. I ran and I ran. Down North Audley Street, back up another street, weaving through the traffic at Marble Arch, I didn't stop to admire my haul until I'd reached the safety of Hyde Park. It was only then, on a bench overlooking the Serpentine, that I allowed myself the pleasure of opening the gatefold cover to study the monochrome pictures of five hirsute men wearing prairie hats.

But something wasn't right. I put my fingers into the record sleeve. To my dismay there was no shiny black vinyl disc. Apart from a square of cardboard the sleeve was empty. I'd gone through that emotional roller-coaster to steal an empty record cover.

Later that afternoon I went back to HMV and bought the LP. And yet I was never able to listen to The Band without re-living those moments. It wasn't so much the guilt; I just didn't feel good. Maybe that was guilt. That wonderful feeling when you carefully lower the stylus onto your favourite track – and the brilliant thing about this album was that it was the first track, Across the Great Divide – was somehow spoilt. Ever so slightly, but spoilt it was. Every time I played it I felt a faint jolt. I'd got a guilty conscience and

I hadn't even nicked anything – apart from a cover. How stupid was that?

So that was my career as a thief; one Cadbury's Roses mini chocolate bar from Woollies and an LP cover from HMV. And I'd regretted them both. Those crimes were imprinted on my mind as examples of how you can feel when you commit a dishonest act. In the end, without even considering the moral arguments, I had decided that honesty was the best policy.

I was surprised, therefore, when, this sweltering summer morning, I seriously began to consider an idea that had been planted by the Hounds of Hell months before. Bart and Feltch had not only unwittingly sparked the beginning of a plan; they'd also provided me with a few helpful insights. I remembered one of them saying, 'Its like they do it for us.' In other words, Bart and Feltch were such comatose scumbags that if I wasn't grassed up, and if I kept my mouth shut, the chances of me getting caught were pretty slim.

I inspected the contents of the toilet bowl and pulled the flush. The time had come. Now what was it Ash had said about hot-wiring a dead claim...?

## ~ FORTY FIVE ~

The day after our night together Justine didn't come into work. She was away for a week, and then another. I remembered Ash saying something like 'she comes and goes.' Even so I had a bad feeling that her absence was because of me.

Two weeks later, Lee handed me a letter – it had Confidential written on the top left hand corner.

'You're not allowed to get personal letters at work,' said Lee.

I recognised the handwriting.

'What's it to you, Lee?' I asked.

'I could have opened it.'

'Go ahead,' I said handing the letter back to him. I couldn't be bothered with Lee's petty-mindedness. As I expected, Lee made no attempt to take it from me.

'Look Lee, what is it you're trying to say?'

'Just watch it,' he said. 'You're breaking the rules.' He could be such an annoying bastard.

I didn't feel good about this letter. I wanted to read it privately.

'Where you going?' Lee asked.

'None of your business.'

'What if somebody needs you?'

'Oh for fuck's sake, just say I'm weeding. Okay?'

I went down to the Cabbage Patch and sat on the sacks.

The letter was written on lined paper that looked as if it had been torn out of a notebook. It read:

*Dear Maximillian*

*Why didn't you wake me to say goodbye!*

*I'm writing this before I set off round the world. I have met a man to sail the seven seas with.*

*First stop St Malo tomorrow – for Normandy Cider. You take care*

*J.*

*PS I've brought a flagon of Scratch with me – for Antarctica, just in case!!*

So that was it. I felt sick. Was that what she was going to tell me? Why didn't I wake her? I'd never expected a long-term relationship with Justine. But one night. That was a bit swift.

It sounded as if I'd driven her to this. And who was this guy she'd gone off with? I could imagine him; some self-fondling chinless trickster in a blazer, white creased trousers and deck shoes. He probably wore a nautical cap with an embroidered anchor. Anchor! Wanker!

I lay on the rough sacks and reflected that we'd had a short but interesting relationship. Justine was frequently brutally honest. The week before she'd disappeared she'd given me her particular take on life: 'Max you are such an innocent,' she'd said while we were in the canteen. 'With your middle class background, your grammar school education and your nice manners, you have it so easy. Not everybody gets a chance to do A levels after their CSEs you know. Your life is a bloody doddle. Look at the other side of the counter. That's where life is hard. Most of them haven't stood a chance since the day they was born. Their parents – if they know them – have fucked 'em up, school has fucked 'em up, and now they're only able to do the lousiest, shittiest jobs. When you're like that there's only two ways to go – seek revenge or get out of your skull. Or perhaps both.' 'What about you, then?' I replied. 'Max, you know nothing about the real world.' Well, maybe. Though I wished she'd lay off me.

I suppose I wasn't surprised. I should have known when I saw the single bed. While a single bed requires physical closeness it shows little desire for long-term commitment. After all, you're not going to be shacking up with somebody who has a single bed, are you?

Over the following weeks I would take out Justine's note and study it. I'd miss her and wished her well. And at least she'd escaped the fate of Blow-Job Lucy and the other cider-heads. I felt sorry for myself. But in my heart I knew that it wasn't meant to be. Even so, I was now sorry we'd never said goodbye.

Okay. So what now? I wondered if Astral was still pissed off with me.

Maybe it was time for me to make amends with the fantasy girlfriend. Surely she had seen through that matron-pleasing Kayne Bender by now.

## ~ FORTY SIX ~

Ash spent the morning quietly muttering to himself, shaking his head and cursing. He'd had his JAR and looked agitated. He was chain smoking and every ten minutes he got up and walked round the table.

'What's up, Ash?' I asked.

'That fucking man. That fucking, fucking man.'

I didn't have to guess who he was talking about. 'Bad JAR, eh?'

'God! I dunno.' He sounded exasperated.

'Seems like you and me need to go for a drink.' I said. 'Give you a chance to unload.'

'I'd appreciate that.'

An hour later, over a pint at the Bay Horse, Ash told me about what he called the 'railway fiasco'.

'I'm not sure whether I'm reading the situation right. I'd be interested in your perspective. It's a bit personal, so you've got to promise to keep it to yourself.' I felt honoured. I'd never heard Ash seek advice from anybody.

'Get another round in and then I'll be able to give you my full attention.' I said.

Ash brought two pints back from the bar. We were sitting in a corner of the room; the high back of the settle meant that we were hidden from public view.

'So what's the story?'

'It's a weird scene,' said Ash as he opened his tobacco tin. 'I don't know what to make of it. It's all to do with something that happened a couple of years ago when I was living near Aberystwyth. Some mates and I used to live in this enormous gaff in the countryside called Ty Mawr. We're talking Dracula's Castle here; man, it was a groove. A ramshackle Gothic house; dark, shabby and spooky. The air was heavy with malice. Roger Corman couldn't have made it up.

'And you lived there?'

'The locals thought it was a hippie commune. Orgies, free love and all that
shit. Fat chance! Well, it was cheap. It had an entrance hall the size of a barn,
with a massive curving staircase, a billiard room, kitchens and larders and all
sorts of outhouses. There was even an old horse drawn hearse with plate glass
sides in one of the stables. We used to sleep in it for bets. The house was
cheap because it was in the sticks. And the place was falling apart – there were
some rooms you didn't dare go into for fear of crashing through the floor. It
was almost empty; it had little furniture or anything like that, no beds, no
carpets. I was lucky; at least I had a mattress, some of the other guys just
crashed in their sleeping bags. Living in a place like that is an experience. It
was great for getting out of your head, wandering around and getting lost.
And that was just in the house. The grounds, with acres of overgrown
rhododendrons, were even more extreme.'

Ash discreetly opened a film canister and crumbled some shit into his
rollie.

'I don't know how you can do that at this time of day,' I said.

'Lebanese. It's light stuff. It softens the edges of the afternoon. As I was
saying, I didn't have a car or anything so when I needed to go to University,
which wasn't that often, I'd hitch. We were so in the middle of nowhere that
getting to a road with some passing traffic on it was half the problem. The
nearest main road was a half hour trek over the fields and then we had to
cross a little railway line.'

Ash put his roll-up to his lips, spat out a few loose strands and lit up; stray
bits of tobacco flared, and then against all odds, the stick began to burn.

'Crossing the tracks was no big deal. Occasionally the train driver would
wave wildly at us, and we'd wave back. It was cool; people always wave at
trains. It was one of those little ones, just two carriages. Well, one Autumn
day, as Dan and I were climbing through the wire, this guy jumped out from
behind a bush. He was so agitated – he was shouting and swearing – that for
a moment we thought he needed help. Do you know who he was? He was
the railway police. The Fat Controller himself. He'd been waiting for us. We
pissed ourselves with laughter. 'Haven't you got anything better to do with
your time?' He must have been hiding behind that bush for days. But he was
serious. So serious that he bust us for trespass on railway property. We
couldn't believe it – it was so petty. It cracked us up even more.'

'We were fined twenty quid each. Now, that did piss me off. For that sort
of money I could live for a month.'

Well, at first, I thought I would go to the bank and draw out the dosh in
1p coins. I was going to stand in the courthouse and watch the bastards
count it all out. But then I thought this is stupid. I'm not giving my hard-

earned money to the Railway Police. That was my student grant. Who did they think they were? If they want my bread they can come and get it. So to cut a long story short I quit Wales and bought my bag of pennies to Bristol. It was no big deal; I'd finished my course at University and I'd been thinking of leaving for a while. The country life's fine in the summer, but winter in Mid Wales can be harsh. I knew that just keeping warm in that big house was going to involve a lot of woodchopping.'

Ash was silent for a moment and then, in a brighter voice, said 'Hey, did you know that the Welsh have no word for orgasm?'

The Lebanese must have been stronger than Ash thought.

'Is that your personal experience or is that a fact?' I asked.

Ash laughed. 'Sorry, that was just a thought that surged into my head. I've spent more time with the Welsh than I like to think about. I know their ways. '

'It's an interesting observation, nevertheless. Do you want to tell me about that as well?'

'No, I'll stick to the railway fiasco.' Ash offered me his tiny spliff. 'Are you sure you don't want any of this?'

I thought about what I'd got to go back to. Trays of files to be sifted through. An afternoon that was going to be fuzzy round the edges suddenly became rather attractive.

'Go on then.' I took a couple of drags and passed it back.

Ash scanned the room as if he was checking for something.

'What I'm saying is that I never did pay that fine and I've been wanted by the police ever since. I'm a fugitive. Max I'm a wanted man.'

Ash paused for the drama to sink in. The way he had said this, I half expected a sheriff's posse to burst through the door. 'To tell you the truth, I wasn't sure whether the Railway Police were the real McCoy, but it seems that their jurisdiction extends even beyond the Welsh borders. The really weird thing is that I get the feeling that that fat bloater Blunt knows all this. He makes mysterious references to my past, nothing specific, but he hints that he's aware of a secret that I wouldn't want people to know about. Although he doesn't come out and say it, it feels to me as if he's using his knowledge as some sort of veiled threat. In my J.A.R. this morning he asked me how I saw the future, and when I said I wanted to do something with computers, he said for somebody with a past like mine that would be a problem. And then there's my enormous file, what the hell is in that?'

During the telling of this tale I could feel myself become increasingly self absorbed. It was as if Ash had explained some universal truth. I scrunched up my empty cheese and onion crisp packet and put it in the ashtray alongside Ash's roach.

'I'm glad you've brought this up, mate,' I said, 'Because exactly the same thing is happening to me.'

As I walked back to the office the pavement felt nicely soft beneath my feet.

I sat down at the table, pulled a rack of files towards me and started checking the details. I couldn't concentrate. It was 2.30 pm and I felt sleepy. The sacks in the Cabbage Patch were becoming increasingly attractive. I couldn't hold out 'till tea break at 3.00. I needed to get up and do something before I fell asleep.

'Well, that's that sorted,' I said, to no one in particular.

'No need to shout,' said Lee.

I looked around. Kastrina was nowhere to be seen. Ash, meanwhile, was doing Enquiry Duty on the counter. Good luck to anybody who needed a sensible answer from him this afternoon. So it was just Lee and me. Lee was doodling on a pad of paper, deep in thought and oblivious to his surroundings. I didn't reckon I'd be missed.

I turned back to Lee. 'I can feel the call of the Cabbage Patch. '

'Wanker.' Lee replied.

'Sod it,' I said to myself.

I lay back on the sacks and gazed at a yellowing light bulb. I was feeling drowsy. It was quiet except for the far-off hum of some electrical equipment. I imagined I could see contorted faces in the outlines of the cracked paint on the ceiling. I drifted in and out of sleep. Was I really such a turn off? Astral had been a non-starter and now Justine had done a runner. A night with me and she disappears to the other side of the world. A guy could get a complex about this sort of thing. Chocolate! I needed chocolate. I wondered if Owen... I put that thought right out of my mind. I checked my watch – it was 3.30 already! I'd been lying here for an hour; I'd missed my tea break. I didn't feel like moving now – I'd stay here till it was time to go home.

I thought about my current situation. It all seemed so black and white. I had a simple choice; carry on forever at the Ministry at Work or get out. A plan began to slowly take shape in my thoughts.

So this was what I was going to do. First...

**Author's Note: The Ministry of Work have demanded – EVEN THOUGH THIS IS A WORK OF FICTION – under The Contravention of Fraud Guidelines (ref; 1966/507 paras 8-13) that the following twenty-six lines containing details about setting up a fraudulent claim be deleted from this book.\***

I also concocted – my mind was racing now – a shatter-proof alibi should the claim be discovered. I'd write a message on a MoW 459 and slip it in the back pocket of the claim. The note would say Congratulations – you've uncovered a bogus claim! If I were caught I would explain that I had trained as a sociologist and I was keeping my hand in with a piece of action research. I was evaluating how far I could go without being spotted. It would surely be of interest to the Hounds of Hell if I identified any weaknesses in the system. At the very least, I expected to get an incentive award for showing initiative and saving the Department billions of pounds.

I sat up. My mouth was dry. Could it really be that easy?

---

*Despite my unwavering assertion that this is a work of fiction my legal adviser nevertheless insisted that I submit my manuscript for scrutiny by the Ministry of Work lawyers. The Ministry of Work legal vultures probably felt obliged to demand that something was cut – so this is it.

## ~ FORTY SEVEN ~

It must have been a couple of weeks before I realised that Baxter was missing. At first I had assumed he was on holiday, and that the man sitting at the bottom of the stairs was on temporary duty. The temp seemed pleasant enough, but after a while I began to miss Baxter's edgy weirdness. Ash didn't know the reason for Baxter's absence either, so I asked Kastrina.

'Kastrina, I haven't seen Baxter in a while. Where is he?'

Kastrina looked up from a report she had been reading. For what felt like a long time she stared at me and then said: 'Don't flatter yourself. You need maturity and experience to do that job.'

'I'm not after his job. I just want to know where he is.'

'I don't think Baxter's absence is any of your business.'

'I need to know for professional reasons. Claimants keep asking for him.'

I'd found Kastrina's recent behaviour unsettling. I could look into her eyes and see nothing. There was no frisson of lust, guilt, shame, interest, anything – it was as if all her emotions had been switched off at the mains. In a way it made our working relationship easier – but it was also extremely infuriating.

'Well if you must know he's been sent on compulsory extended sick leave.'

'I'm sorry to hear that.'

'And if you think that Dr Hammer is going to sign you off on full pay, you're got another think coming. Compulsory sick leave is not an option open to new recruits. Even self-obsessed hypochondriacs.'

'That wasn't what I was thinking. I'm perfectly fit, I'll have you know.' I carefully focused my gaze on her face, consciously not looking at any other part of her body. 'Just tell me, how come Baxter's on a long term sickie?'

'Didn't you know,' said Kastrina in a manner that implied it was common knowledge, 'Baxter was taken away.'

'Taken away! What do you mean taken away?'

'It was extremely upsetting for Mr Blunt. Baxter was screaming all sorts of horrible things at him.'

'I don't understand.'

'Baxter was sectioned.'

'Are you sure?'

'Of course I'm sure. Men in white coats; they came and took him away to Barrow Hospital. I had to help them put this canvas jacket on Baxter. To stop him hurting himself, they said.'

I could hardly take in the full implications of what she had said. 'Surely shouting at Mr Blunt doesn't contravene the Mental Health Act. In fact, I would have thought that giving Mr Blunt a bit of the verbals was a cast-iron sign of sanity.'

'Your flippancy is offensive and inappropriate. This is a serious matter.'

'Too right it's serious. You can't just lock up people for behaving strangely. We'd all be out of a job if they could do that. So what actually happened?'

'Isn't it obvious? I'm surprised Baxter hadn't been removed earlier. His fantasies had got out of hand.'

'I liked his fantasies. I thought the freak show act was part of his job.'

'It was becoming increasingly distressing for Mr Blunt. Mr Blunt and Baxter started as trainees together. They went back a long way. Baxter was one of the old school; he saw this as a job for life.'

'So he was crazy even then.'

'Civil Servants were dedicated to their work in those days. And of course Baxter was a bit of a legend for his re-usable envelope. But he couldn't sustain that level of creativity. It was a shame. While Mr Blunt steadily moved up the scale, poor old Baxter, once the golden boy, ambled along as a clerical officer. Baxter must have been on the counter for ten years – by then he was beginning to make lots of mistakes. As you well know it's not good to have a colleague on the brink of 'counter shock' in your team on a Thursday afternoon. So in the end Mr Blunt got Dr Hammer to sort out Baxter's medication and move him to a quieter job on reception. Mr Blunt genuinely cared for Baxter.'

'That must have been a first. He'd probably got a buyer for his kneecaps.'

'You don't understand what a dedicated man Mr Blunt is.'

'But this is appalling. I still don't understand why Baxter was taken away.'

'Sometimes I wonder about you, Max. Didn't you notice how much he'd changed?'

'Not really. He seemed to be a lot saner than most of the people who work here.'

'Baxter never recovered from the pest controllers coming to deal with the rats in the courtyard. He became obsessed by it. For days he talked about a nuclear spill. He wasn't safe on reception. Dr Hammer said he'd suffered a psychotic episode and diagnosed him as paranoid schizophrenic or something serious like that.'

As I talked to Kastrina, it dawned on me that a grain of good had unexpectedly come out of our roadside coupling. I realised that I no longer felt intimidated by her manner.

'Well it's a shame. I always liked Baxter. Even if he was as flaky as a biscuit.'

## ~ FORTY EIGHT ~

'Did you have a good weekend?' I asked Cynthia as I located a file in my box, put it in front of a claimant and pointed with my pen where to sign.

Apart from on PI day, when the adrenalin is pulsing, if files are up to date, and the paperwork is in good order, working on the counter was a doddle. After a few weeks' practice it's easy enough to fall into a rhythm that allows you to sign-on claimants and talk to a colleague working alongside at the next window.

'We went to the beach at Weston to cool down,' Cynthia replied. 'Have you ever been there?'

Yes, I had. Weston super Mare: sounded slightly exotic, slightly Mediterranean. I'd been expecting a warm westerly and azure seas. But the town turned out to be a marketing man's invention. Sure, it had wide promenades and a rusty pier. But twice a day, at the speed of a galloping horse, the sea is sucked out over the horizon leaving miles of olive coloured mud. Not sand – mud. I was in no rush to return.

'Did you see the sea?' I asked.

'I think I saw it, but you can never be sure, can you? We were on the beach and Bill had a rather unfortunate accident.'

'Oh?' I'd heard about Cynthia's husband Bill and his accidents.

'I'd just rubbed sun oil on his back when a cloud of ladybirds descended. The lotion must have attracted them; they just went for him. He was covered by them, head to toe.'

'Ladybirds!? Are you sure?'

'Of course I'm sure. Ladybirds are behaving strangely because of the heat.'

'Really?'

'Yes, they've turned nasty.'

'What do you mean?'

'Well, poor Bill, he couldn't run into the sea because it was about ten miles away. So I wrapped him in a towel and tried to squash them. Unfortunately, that made it worse because they started to bite.'

'Bite? Ladybirds don't bite.'

'They do now. They were like tiny flying piranhas.'

I was having difficulty adjusting to this new image of the ladybird. The metamorphosis from cute red and black spotted blob – the inspiration for my childhood reading books; the name of the little short trousers I'd worn when I was four – to razor-jawed monster shook the very foundation of my beliefs. It was like finding out that Blue Peter presenters were junkies.

'So there's poor Bill being bitten to death by ladybirds – but it gets worse. You've probably noticed this – if you crush a ladybird it releases a horrible smelling yellow fluid as a defence mechanism. It's like acid and it burns.' I didn't know this, but nodded my head in acknowledgement all the same. 'As I tried to brush the ladybirds off Bill, they started excreting this foul stuff all over him. He looked like a sausage covered in mustard. I didn't know what to do. I've never seen anybody in such agony. By now a crowd had gathered around us on the beach. Somebody had run off to get help but what we really needed was some water.'

'A young man with long blonde hair, who seemed to know what he was talking about, said that urine would ease the suffering. I didn't like the sound of that at all. But he said urine killed the pain if you got stung by jellyfish – it's the uric acid in it, apparently. In the end there must have been about twenty men, standing in a circle urinating on my husband. They all seemed eager to help.'

'Didn't Bill mind?'

'He was beyond caring. It seemed to do the trick, however. The doctor reckons he should be out of hospital by the end of the week.'

I stood transfixed; my work autopilot had become disengaged. In my mind I had a picture straight out of a Hell's Angel's initiation ceremony. The scene featured Cynthia's husband writhing in the sand while being pissed on by a group of laughing louts.

'On reflection,' Cynthia said in a thoughtful way, 'I suppose it wasn't a particularly good weekend.'

A man was banging his fist on the counter.

"'Ere, any chance of signing on?' came a voice from the other side of the screen.

'With you in a moment,' I replied, only half-hearing the question.

'What's the bloody hold-up?' came the voice again.

My eyes focused beyond the screen to a line of people snaking across the signing-on hall and out of the door. Forty faces were staring at me; forty people were looking at me, Max Redcliffe, the civil servant who had become so detached from reality that he could drift off into his own thoughts and keep a room full of people waiting.

Ash's words of warning resonated in my head. I had caught the X-ray specs syndrome. It was official; I had become desensitised. I could see this reflected in those staring eyes. They hated me. And I hated myself.

## ~ FORTY NINE ~

At least it was cool downstairs in the Cabbage Patch. I thought I'd do a
half-hour's weeding and then crash out on the sacks. Although weeding
was mind-numbingly boring it did at least give me the opportunity to think.

Earlier that morning I had asked Mr Blunt for an emergency job review
meeting. I needed to suss out Mr Blunt. Exactly what did he know? And how
far would he go to use this information against me? He stared at me with his
goldfish-bowl eyes; he seemed surprised.

'That's an unusual request. It's usually the management who arrange the
JARS, not staff.'

'Mr Blunt I've been thinking about what I learnt on my ARF course.'

'Good.'

'I want to join the Fraud Squad.'

I watched for his reaction. A spasm did indeed quiver across his face –
though what this signified I wasn't sure.

'I'm very busy at the moment' he said, as he checked what appeared to be
an empty diary. 'I can fit you in on the 18th August.' That was in four weeks
time.

'Can't we make it sooner?'

'No.' And he walked away.

I looked around me. My world had become brown, the colour of slurry.
The 70s was a very brown decade; and nowhere was it browner than in the
Civil Service. Brown paint, brown furniture, brown envelopes, brown hessian
sacks – I was surrounded by the colour of stagnation and decay. The drabness
was suffocating. I could even taste it. I had had enough of the brown world
of the dole office. Sometimes I had this dream of a sudden shock of macaw
parrots – with their startling combination of vivid scarlet and electric blue –
flying though the lush emerald green jungle. A brilliant flash of a living

rainbow. I yearned for colour.

Over the last few days I'd secretly been gathering the paperwork in preparation for hot-wiring. Yet I was becoming profoundly uneasy with the idea. Knowing the Hounds of Hell were lazy and ineffectual and I was unlikely to get caught didn't help. I was fighting a voice that told me I was doing wrong. I could hear my Dad. This was stealing, and it went against everything I had ever been taught. I tried to justify it to myself by thinking that everybody was at it, that power corrupts, that this sort of thing just happens... or ...or something like that. If I was to get out of Union Street I had to shut up that nagging voice.

As I pushed the drawer into the cabinet, it jammed. I pulled the drawer out again to see what was obstructing it. Tucked away at the back, was a file that must have fallen out of the tray and become lodged in the drawer space. I could see that it was an old file, the paper was aged and the typeface appeared to be different, old fashioned; it was smaller and less even than I was used to. I put the file on the 'to check' pile and copied the name and address that was written in swirling copperplate handwriting on the front. Archibald Alexander Leach, Hughenden Road, Horfield, Bristol to my list. I carried on with my work – but now I felt unsettled. What was particularly bugging me was how the file came to be there in the first place. It was almost physically impossible for it to have become dislodged from a box. I couldn't understand how it could have happened. And then the name, Archibald Alexander Leach, that had a familiar ring. Archibald Alexander Leach. Who was it? It stirred a memory. Archibald Leach? Archibald Leach? I returned to the pile, and breaking Owen's golden rule, opened the file to check the claimant's occupation. ACTOR. It was then that I knew what I had in my hands. It was Cary Grant's dole claim. The lost file – the Koh-i-Noor of claims. Archie Leach, the most sought after dole file – ever.

An hour later, over a pint at the Bay Horse, I told Ash about my discovery. By now my excitement was almost uncontrollable. I'd eaten three packets of salt and vinegar crisps and even though I didn't smoke I was now eyeing-up Ash's ciggie tin; I needed something to do with my hands.

Ash's reaction to the news was not as I had expected – Ash leant backwards in his seat and roared with laughter.

'You've found what?' he said incredulously.

'Cary Grant's dole claim. Well, Archie Leach's actually, but you remember Owen said it's worth a fortune. You were there when he said it.'

'I know, but he was winding you up.'

'What?' I knew about his other stories but I had never considered that this was a piss-take. 'No, it was for real. People really do collect these things,' I said. 'I'm sure they do.' I added. I was now trying to convince myself as well as Ash. 'No, he was being genuine; what about his collection of Gloucestershire cricketers? It really does exist.'

'Have you seen them?'

'He offered to show me.'

'But have you actually seen them?'

'Well, not as such.'

'I thought it was one of Owen's little fictions – being down in the Cabbage Patch all day does funny things to your mind. In that twilight world you begin to see things differently. He'll be joining Baxter soon.'

'But just supposing it is genuine, what do you reckon I ought to do?'

Ash still didn't look like he was convinced. 'Have a quiet word with him; if this collecting thing is for real, well that's okay; if it's not, well, you've made a complete arse of yourself.'

'But Ash, this could be big bucks, this could be my lucky break,' I said desperately.

'Or you could end up looking like the biggest pillock in Union Street,' replied Ash.


Owen was sitting in his little cabin. To show respect for the old guy I knocked on the thin wooden door.

'Owen, what would you say if I said that I'd found Cary Grant's file?'

I watched Owen's face closely. 'I'd say that you weren't telling the truth because he was called Archibald Leach.'

'Yeah, okay Owen, but what if I'd found Archibald Leach's file then?'

'I'd say that you'd be kidding me.'

'Why would you say that?' Owen was being unexpectedly obtuse.

'I would say that because I don't believe it exists any more – I've been looking for it for thirty years, I should know.'

'But you said that you knew that it did exist.'

'I'm sure it existed once. But that was a long time ago. My belief is that a private collector had it stolen to order.'

'So what do you reckon this is then?' I said as I produced, with a theatrical flourish, a file from behind my back. Owen jumped up as if he'd been sitting on a spike and made a move to grab the file from me, but when he saw the claim more clearly. his hand stopped in mid air. For an instant his mouth gaped open.

'Let me see that,' Owen said in a reverential tone.

Owen was silent, he held the file by the edges and turned it over like a connoisseur handling ancient porcelain.

'Excuse my language, Max, but in answer to your question I'd say bloody hell. That's what I'd say, bloody hell!'

He studied it with the eyes of an expert. 'End papers good, cover slightly foxed, binding slightly frayed – but nothing that can't be mended – and most important of all, the signature is as clear as a bell. Look at this: Previous employment: Actor. Previous employer: Paramount Studios.' Owen snorted with laughter and repeated 'Actor with Paramount Studios! Max, you've made my day. No, you've made my year. All my life I've been looking for this, and here it is. Archibald Leach, Actor with Paramount Studios!' Owen held the claim to his chest and ever so gently hugged it.

'Mind you, I can't say that I'm not disappointed that I didn't find it myself, but the rules are the rules, Max.'

'What rules?'

'Oh you have to abide by the rules – it could be anarchy without the rules. Fortunately for you rule Number One is finders-keepers – oh yes, you found it – it's yours. That's the rules.'

'But that seems so unfair. It's your Cabbage Patch.'

'Well maybe,' said Owen ruefully. 'There's one thing I need to know. Let me ask you this. Where did you find it?'

'That's the funny thing – it was wedged at the back of a drawer – I'm sure it was hidden by somebody – it couldn't have fallen there. Perhaps they'd put it there intentionally, and one day were going to retrieve it.'

'What do I do next?'

'Well, we put it up for auction – there's one every month.'

'What sort of auction?'

'It's a private postal auction – this is an undercover operation. Mind you, you've got to keep quiet about this. Only a select few know about the collector's network. We have to do this quickly – less chance of being caught. There's bound to be gossip; in a way it's good that you've found it because I'd be the prime suspect. The myth of Bristol's lost Cary Grant claim has been around for years.'

'What do you think it'll get?'

'Difficult to say, this is the Rembrandt of claims; there's no catalogue price for something like this. What makes it particularly important is that signature – Cary Grant is sought after, but Archibald Leach is the Holy Grail. A file like that is sure to end up in America.'

'But you must have an idea.'

'Well it's out of my league; I couldn't afford it I can tell you. I'll have to be satisfied just holding it. It's priceless.'

I was hoping for thousands, if not, hundreds of thousands of pounds. I was dreaming of a life of ease and luxury unwinding before me. I was going to travel; I was going to party – and best of all, Astral would be coming to ME, gagging for it.

'But everything has a price,' I pleaded. I needed to know exactly what scale of fortune was heading my way.

'Well, if you pushed me I wouldn't be surprised if it fetched, well let me see...' Owen hesitated, looked at the file and handed it back to me as if he were giving me a gift – 'five hundred pounds.'

I did all I could to hide my despair. I felt as if my brain was being wrung like a sponge. I felt stupid. What was I thinking? No wonder Ash had been giving me funny looks. I felt a grey gloom descend. I am a firm believer that fate gives with one hand and grabs back with the other. This was a lesson I'd learnt from a very early age. I could remember the pure pleasure of finding an enormous shiny half-crown on the pavement only to go home and find that my hamster had been horrifically and mysteriously mangled in its exercise wheel. I was certain that these two incidents were cosmically related.

Until now I had had no idea of the sums of money being talked about. Yet with all this mention of Rembrandts and Holy Grails my thoughts had become grossly ambitious. And then this. A pathetic five hundred pounds. Owen's estimate had left me feeling let down and sick.

'I can see you're shocked,' said Owen. 'A nice little windfall, eh?'

'So you reckon £500?' I said, trying to conceal my disappointment.

'We'll put that as a reserve price and wait and see. This is going to cause a lot of excitement.'

Owen moved towards the door. 'Well, excuse me, but I've got a few messages to dispatch.'

As Owen went into his cabin I could hear him talking to himself: 'Archibald Leach, Actor with Paramount! I never thought I'd see the day.'

I couldn't face going upstairs; I walked to the far end of the room and lay back on the hessian bags. Even down in the Cabbage Patch it seemed to be getting hot. I'd never felt so defeated. I wanted to curl up and die.

## ~ FIFTY ~

Astral looked up from her work and said, 'You ought to be more careful. You left a claim on your desk. Don't worry, I've put it into the computer room.'

It took me a while to understand the significance of this.

'Thanks, where was it?' I said, smiling and trying to hold her gaze for as long as possible.

I was puzzled. After the storming of the counter, I'd paid extra attention to ensure that all my claims were processed correctly. I wanted PI day to go smoothly – I didn't want anything left to chance.

'It was hidden under a load of stuff.'

I thought no more about this until half an hour later when I noticed the papers in my in-tray had been disturbed. A rush of terror shot through me. It was at the bottom of my in-tray that I kept my trial counterfeit file.

I scrabbled through my papers. Euan Minster's fake claim was gone.

'Astral, you know the claim you found,' I asked, trying to control the tremor in my voice, 'tell me again, where exactly was it?'

'At the bottom of your in-tray.'

'And what did you do with it?'

'What do you think I did with it? I told you, I put it in the basket outside the punch room.' She added in an annoying Violet Elizabeth lisping voice, 'Thay thank you!'

'Thank you, Astral.' Shit. Shit. Shit. 'How long ago was this?'

'About an hour ago. What's wrong Max?'

This was the first time that I had found Astral to be anything less that absolutely adorable. For a moment, Astral's charms had temporarily disappeared behind a cloud. Nine months on and the veneer of unrequited love was losing its polish.

'I just wish that people would stop trying to be so bloody helpful.'

'There's no need to be like that.'

Any moment, the details from my hot-wired claim were going to be fed into the computer, claxons would sound, and I would be dragged away to the goldfish bowl and interrogated by the Hounds of Hell. Being charged with fraud was bad enough without the humiliation of a grilling by Bart and Feltch.

There was a problem. Although I had planned my research meticulously, there was one thing that I hadn't yet got round to doing. What I'd forgotten was the very thing that stopped this experiment from being an act of fraud and legitimised it as a piece of 'action research.' And that was to insert the note that said, Congratulations – you've uncovered a bogus claim. I had to get that claim back, and quickly.

I walked down to the computer suite. I could see that there were three piles of files on the table outside the room waiting to be processed. I sorted frantically through them but Euan Minster's claim wasn't there. It was too late, I was screwed.

Even now I could imagine Bart and Feltch putting on their coats and rolling their shoulders in anticipation. Electrodes or a rubber truncheon were preferable to the sneering sarcasm and self-congratulation that I would suffer as I explained to the Hounds of Hell what I had been doing. It's okay, I'm a sociologist. I'm undertaking some ground breaking empirical research. I thought Mr Blunt would be pleased. Of course I was going to tell you about the loophole. I was expecting an incentive award for this. That's insulting – the idea of personally profiting from this venture never entered my mind. Go ahead, involve the police. But don't blame me, if you're accused of time-wasting.

But there was still one last chance. If the file wasn't on the table outside it must either be in the computer room waiting to be input, or it was in the out pile ready to return to the Section. The sirens hadn't sounded yet, so I was banking on the former.

I had the beginning of an idea – what I needed was the right person to help me. For what seemed like an age I stood in the corridor watching people walk past – mostly staff I didn't know from other sections. Then, in the distance, I saw Che approaching, carrying a mug of tea, slouching his way to the Signing-on Hall. I had recently noticed Che studying a book called The Big Book of Mischief. Perhaps this was a good time to see what he'd learnt.

'Hi man.'

'Hi comrade.'

'Che, can I have a word with you?'

'Sure man. What's up?'

I pulled Che into a corner.

'Look Che, you know how that NERD computer is supposed to be so advanced you could chuck water over it and it won't malfunction.'

'Uh, no, I didn't know that. In fact, thinking about it, that surprises me. I thought those things were extremely sensitive to moisture.'

'Yeah, that's exactly what I thought. But Mr Mills said you could throw a bucket of water over the computer and it wouldn't affect it at all. Now I understood Mr Mills to be speaking metaphorically, Ash however – who we all know is a computer obsessive – says he was speaking literally. So we've got this little bet. Which is why I need your help.'

'Look, man,' said Che, looking alarmed, 'if you think I'm going to have anything to do with throwing a bucket of water over that machine you've got another think coming. You seem to have forgotten this afternoon's PI afternoon.'

'Whoa, hang on, you're one step ahead of me here.' I raised my hands, palms outward, in front of his chest, as if I was stopping a horse. 'I'm not talking about a bucket of water. No way. More a mug of tea is what I was thinking of. How about spilling your tea over that wanker Mills's keyboard?'

'You don't understand, Max. Mug or bucket, that's irrelevant. What I'm saying is that we'd have another counter invasion on our hands if that heap of metal went down. Why would I want that? Why would you want that? You didn't fare too well out of the last riot, I seem to remember.'

I ignored that. I hadn't got time. 'Ever heard the expression *agent provocateur*, Che?'

I could see I'd hit a nerve here. I knew by listening to Che and his colleagues in the canteen that their self-respect was currently suffering a dive due to a severe lack of street action. Any action, in fact. I paused before I added. 'Get the under-classes rising and all that. Che, all I'm asking you to do is go in there, have a word with Mills, and in the process spill your tea over his keyboard. If the computer does go down I owe you a pint.' Owe you a pint – that was the clincher.

'Comrade, now you are talking.'

'Okay, let's do it.'

I stood hidden behind the door waiting for the signal for action.

'Mr Mills, I urgently need to ask you something,' I heard Che say.

'What are you doing in here? You know this is a restricted area.'

Then, in a split second there was the muffled sound of foot scraping on carpet – as if Che had tripped – followed by a not particularly convincing 'oops'.

Mr Mills shouted. 'You stupid bloody idiot.' That was the sign I was looking for.

'You've spilt tea over my keyboard,' Mr Mills yelled. 'What the heck do you think you're doing in here?'

I sidled into the room as Mr Mills, who had his back to the door, was holding his keyboard upside down furiously trying to shake the tea out of it. The small green screen of his computer was still illuminated so I assumed that the system hadn't yet crashed.

'This keyboard costs hundreds of pounds. If you've upset Nerdy you'll be in big trouble.'

I quietly went over to the pile of claims and began to shuffle through them. There must have been about 200 and they weren't in alphabetical order.

Mills continued to shout, 'That's exactly why we don't allow clodhoppers like you in here.'

As I thumbed through the files time seemed to freeze-frame. I found myself thinking how different the computer room smelt from the rest of the office; the dry, electrical odour reminded me of my Dad's enormous old valve radio. The box radio was the size of a tea chest; I could picture the yellowing dial with such exotic names. What were they? Stockholm? Helvetia?...

And there it was. I pulled up my t-shirt, shoved Euan Minster's claim down the front of my Wranglers and slipped out of the room. Che followed several seconds later.

'So what's the verdict – did the computer crash? Is Nerdy a quivering wreck?' I asked.

Che was in a state of high excitement, laughing and twitching with adrenalin. 'Did you see that? I threw the whole cup right over his keyboard. Direct action or what? The man went crazy.'

'Did it crash though?'

Che thought for a moment 'You know, I don't think it did. His keyboard was well and truly mashed though. That's another blow for the ruling classes.'

'I'll buy you a pint anyway.' I walked alongside Che as he made his way back to the canteen to get another drink. There was something that I'd wanted to ask him for some time. 'Che, tell me, in the riot a few weeks back, why you didn't join the other side?'

'One of the most difficult decisions I've ever had to make. It was tempting. The problem is that I would have blown my cover. I'm not ready for that yet, I've still got things to do.'

## ~ FIFTY ONE ~

I was working on the counter when Ash slipped me a note saying that Owen wanted to see me.

'It's been sold – Owen wouldn't say how much, but he seemed pleased.'

As soon as my shift ended I hurried downstairs to the Cabbage Patch. Owen looked in ebullient mood.

'Max, I've just had a message through the internal mail – it's been sold at a record price for a film star. Not as high as John Lennon's claim, mind, but pretty good all the same.'

Over the days since I had found the claim, I'd become resigned to the fact that I wasn't going to be a millionaire, and my sexual magnetism was unlikely to be drastically enhanced by my recent good fortune.

'Look Owen, stop the procrastination, how much did it get?'

Owen replied slowly, savouring the figures: 'Seven-hundred-and-fifty-eight-pounds.'

What was I complaining about? £750 was the sort of money I'd been trying to save to go travelling. So, despite my initial despair, seven hundred and fifty eight pounds was certainly a cheering sum to be presented with unexpectedly.

'Phew, seven hundred and fifty eight, that's good.'

'Don't forget there's 15% commission to the auctioneers – you'll end up with, say six hundred and fifty.'

'That's okay, that'll do fine.'

I felt elated. The grey fog had cleared. I could see a future. My good fortune was at last going to allow me to leave the monochrome world of the last ten months.

Of course, there was a little matter that I needed to sort out with Mr Blunt. I wasn't sure about the approach I was going to take. I could break the news straight away or I could let Mr Blunt drone on for half an hour and then announce, 'Well that's tough tits you fat bag of jelly, I'm off to South America.' It would be then that Mr Blunt would make his accusations. But what did he know? And how would he use this information against me? At least I'd be ready for this. Whatever happened, in a few days I'd be out of Union Street.

'So what are you going to do with this windfall?'

'After taking you out for a lunchtime drink, I'm off to a bucket shop to buy a cheap flight to South America.'

## ~ FIFTY TWO ~

I listened to the soporific whirring of the fan. The draft rustled the papers in Mr Blunt's in-tray; the brass bell had been put on top of them to stop them blowing away. I was sitting with my knees almost touching my chin. That bloody chair.

Mr Blunt was going through his usual routine. Even in this heat, when a fine rime of perspiration clung to his smooth forehead, Mr Blunt wore his voluminous jacket.

The black biro that I had been holding slipped from my moist hand and rolled under Mr Blunt's desk. For a while I considered retrieving it – but the close proximity of Mr Blunt's lathering sandalled feet deterred me. The fan whirred. At least it filled the silence.

At last Mr Blunt looked up and spoke.

'So you want to join the Fraud Squad?'

I'd forgotten about my spontaneous request. I tried to think why anybody in their right mind would want to work with Bart and Feltch.

'Yes, I think what they do makes a difference.'

'I'm glad to hear you say that. We'll make a civil servant of you yet, Mr Redcliffe.' I felt as if an icicle had been thrust into my heart. 'But I'm afraid you'll have to join the queue. And there's no guarantee that you'll pass the qualifying test. It's rigorous, very rigorous indeed.' I wondered what the test would involve. Being able to hit the urinal without pissing on your shoes, probably.

'You'll be pleased to know I passed on your name to Regional Headquarters after your bravery last month,' he beamed.

What was this? Mr Blunt being nice? This was alarming. If he carried on like this, telling him to shove his job was going to be more difficult than I'd anticipated.

'I wasn't being brave – I just shouldered a couple of punches.'

'Mr Redcliffe, you are too modest. At last you are responding well to good management.' He paused, and then asked, 'How is your health? Dr Hammer tells me that you didn't appear to take his suggestions seriously.'

'My health is fine. There has been a ridiculous misunderstanding about health.'

'Dr Hammer says that your denial could exacerbate the problem.'

'There is no problem – even my cracked ribs have healed.' I was trying hard not to get narked by this. I knew it was part of Blunt's strategy to undermine my confidence.

'Well, we'll come back to your affliction later. We need to make plans so that you get the support you deserve. Meanwhile, how did you find the ARF1 course?'

'Very useful,' I lied.

'Miss Klebb seemed disappointed with your performance. She said you didn't put into it as much she had hoped.' For a moment I wondered which performance Kastrina had been talking about. 'When Lee Woods came back he was a changed person. It was remarkable, he was a maturer, more confident man.'

'Well, yes, he probably was. But he has little experience of life; he's a bit of a milk drinking mummy's boy. He's coming from a different starting point.'

'You see, Mr Redcliffe,' Mr Blunt was pointing his pen at me and stabbing it in the air 'this is exactly your problem. You think you know it all.' Mr Blunt's façade of conviviality was already crumbling. 'You don't seem to realise how much your inadequacies are holding you back. If only you'd pull yourself together. With unemployment rising there's a career for you here. A recession is heading this way. Do you know that economists predict that in ten years' time there could be two, perhaps three million unemployed? Think of that. That's a lot of Unemployment Benefit to be issued. Think of the opportunities. The Department will be crying out for people with a modicum of talent. In a few years' time you could be a team leader. Having your name mentioned in dispatches to Head Office can only do you good. You've got the ability but, and I'll speak frankly here, you have an arrogant streak. Your career is being held back by your attitude.'

Here we go again. Attitude. It went back a long way. Throughout my childhood I had been lambasted for 'not being serious enough', for 'not concentrating,' for 'being too easily distracted,' and most tiresome of all for 'NOT HAVING THE RIGHT ATTITUDE.'

I can remember it well. I was eleven. I'd accidentally set fire to the scout hut during Bob-a-Job week. I'd lit a bonfire, but it had got out of control. Nothing serious. The flames had charred one of the walls; I beat it out in no time. Despite my protestations of innocence Akela pronounced me a troublemaker, a troublemaker with the wrong attitude. It was a mistake. I was doing my best. 'Dib, Dib, Dib, Dob, Dob, Dob' we chanted. Do Our Best. And what did I get in return? For the next month, at the end of our Wednesday evening session, after the Union Jack was taken down and carefully folded, I had to stay behind to sweep out the hut. There's nothing more frustrating than doing your best and still getting shat upon.

'I'm not sure that it is my attitude. Don't you think it's perverse that our careers' – I hesitated over the word our, I felt uneasy about linking myself with Mr Blunt in this way – 'are built on the misery and misfortune of others. With due respect, you sound like an undertaker rubbing his hands with glee over the prospects of a mass disaster.'

'How dare you say that,' said Mr Blunt angrily, 'your analogy is abhorrent, absolutely abhorrent. What you are intimating emphasises just how far you have got to go before I can sign you off your probationary period, let alone put your name forward for the Fraud Squad.' As he said this he patted my file.

Probationary period! What a load of crap! I could feel a heat welling up inside me. I had had enough of Mr Blunt's pompous self-satisfaction and the way he sat in his chair and peered down at me.

'Excuse me Mr Blunt, but I really do have to stand up.'

'I'd prefer you to remain seated.'

'It's the chair.'

'Are you feeling alright?'

'The chair's a bit low.'

'I've never had that complaint before. Are you having one of your attacks?'

'No, I'm not having one of my attacks. I don't have attacks. The chair is making my back ache.'

'People like a low chair. It's what is called an easy chair. If you sit back, you will find it more relaxing.'

'I don't want to relax.'

'Dr Hammer said that this is your problem. You get tense and then the electrical charges in your brain short circuit and scramble your lobes.'

'I can assure you my brain is not short circuiting.'

'Denial is one of the symptoms.'

This topic of conversation was really beginning to bug me.

It was time for me to get out of Mr Blunt's annoying low-cut chair. But I had to decide where I was going to stand. Should I position myself, court-martial like, in front of Mr Blunt's desk with my arms straight by my side? Perhaps I should perch casually on the desk corner? Or should I, and this was the option that appealed to me most, put both hands on the desk and lean confidently forward pushing my face just inches away from Mr Blunt's wet blubbery features?

Well, no. I slowly raised myself and slouched with my hands deep in my pockets at a respectful distance in front of the desk. At least looking down on his moist head and thinning hair gave me confidence. I could see damp tidemarks of sweat under the armpits of Mr Blunt's jacket. Before I knew what I was saying I heard myself asking,

'What's in that file?'

'That file is confidential and is nothing to do with you.'

'But it's got my name on it.'

'It may have your name on it, but the information belongs to the Ministry.'

'Why can't the Ministry let me see it then?'

'It's Ministry policy not to let staff see their confidential files. There are things in there that I have been told in confidence. Besides, you might be upset by them.'

'What? I looked down at Mr Blunt; I could hardly believe the fatuousness of the man. 'Upset? What sort of things?'

'Let's just say that there is information in there that you wouldn't want other people to know about. It's safe with me though, I can assure you.'

'It's a big file, somebody must have told you a lot of things. And how do you know these things are true – that they're not made up by somebody who has a grudge against me.'

'Does somebody have a grudge against you?'

'Well I don't know. If you'd let me see the file perhaps I could tell you.'

I shifted a step forward. Like coaxing a stick from the jaws of a dog, I knew I had to move carefully. I had to be firm, but not threatening. Too much pressure and Mr Blunt would hold on harder. Come on boy, I was saying to myself. Come on, give it to Max. But Mr Blunt moved the file closer to himself – he didn't seem to be responding as desired. I was now standing with my thighs pressed hard against the desk edge. A grab and I could have that file. The whites of Mr Blunt's magnified eyes were looking up at me. So what do you do to teach a disobedient dog a lesson? I had never had a dog, but I'd seen what the louts in the park do. You take the leather lead, you fold it in half and you raise it above your head....

From where I was now standing I noticed my pen on the floor. I bent down to pick it up.

Maybe I moved too quickly and Mr Blunt misinterpreted my lunge – for there was a violent scraping noise as he pushed his chair backwards and stood up. 'What the hell do you think you're doing?' he yelped.

'Excuse me?' I was as shocked as he was – but for a different reason. 'I was picking up my biro. I dropped it earlier; it was hidden under the chair.'

We were now standing with the table between us. Careful not to make any more sudden movements, I slowly shifted to the side of the desk so that I could get a better look at the file. But Mr Blunt was having none of this. Mr Blunt moved likewise; but first he swooped the file into his hand, and then he sidled round the furniture, using the desk as a barrier. We were poised like kids in a playground; a quick move to the right, a quick move to the left. Catch me if you can.

'I don't know what game you are playing, Mr Redcliffe, but it is a very dangerous one. If you don't sit down now, I will phone Dr Hammer for emergency medication.'

Okay, I thought, I will sit down. I jumped from the side of the desk and sat in Mr Blunt's chair.

'Who do you think you are? Get out of my chair!' Blunt shouted, slamming the file onto the desk with such force that its pages spilled out onto the brown leatherette surface.

Even in the brief moment it took Mr Blunt to pick up the scattered papers, I was able to scan their contents. It took me no more than an instant to realise the meaning of what I'd seen.

In a way I was disappointed. It's dissatisfying to find your adversary isn't as smart as you think. My burgeoning file contained nothing more than computer printouts, scraps of waste paper and printed ephemera – none of which related to me, my career or otherwise. This wasn't information from Interpol – it was pieces of paper picked randomly from Mr Blunt's waste bin. The file was a sham. My file was filled with rubbish. What a sad, pathetic thing to do.

Mr Blunt realised he'd been rumbled and stood by the desk looking deflated. Sweat was running down the sides of his maroon face. For a few seconds there was silence. I felt flat and drained. It wasn't the moment of effervescent glory that I had been looking forward to.

But I had had enough. Of this interview. Of Mr Blunt. And of my time with the Ministry of Work.

'Okay, Blunt, I'm going to make this easy for you. I don't know why, but I am. I quit.'

I knew that Mr Blunt wouldn't try to stop me.

## ~ FIFTY THREE ~

Simon and Garfunkel's America was playing on the juke box. I felt a soft body squeezing next to me as I waited at the bar to order a drink.

'I put this song on for you,' said Astral.

'Thanks.' It wasn't quite the right America, but I didn't want to spoil it.

'We never did get to do the bandaging practice did we?'

'No, I was looking forward to you showing me a few of the techniques. They might still come in useful.' I smiled.

'I'll miss you, Max.'

'I'll miss you too, Astral,' I said, trying hard to show the minimum amount of emotion.

'No, I will.'

'Yeah, sure.'

'I mean it, Max, I will…'

Well that's great. My last day at work and Astral starts to show some affection. Good timing Astral.

'…I know things got off to a shaky start when we first met. Let's face it Max, you acted strangely. Anyhow I've enjoyed working with you. I think you're really nice – for a Londoner.' Her hand was gently resting on my arm.

'I think you're really nice.' My mind was racing again. What does she mean by this? I was back a year ago in the dole queue when I misinterpreted her offer of 'Do you fancy a job?' as 'Do you fancy a fuck?'

Astral continued, 'I've never met anybody like you before. You're different, you're one of the few men I've met who actually listen.'

'Are you drunk?'

'No, Max, I think you're … she was searching for the right word… and then she said it, the word that every man dreads, the word that signifies the evening is over, you're going home by yourself and a good screw has just been wiped off the menu. The word being … sweet.

I hate being sweet. Sweet means, you'll talk and I'll listen. And I'll get a

211

kiss on the cheek at the end of the evening for my endeavours. I want a bit more than that. I want to kiss you, to fall over, to entangle my body with yours, to slip and slide, to lie there happy and peaceful and for us to love each other forever.

But sweet was unexpected. 'Why didn't you say any of this before?' I asked.

'Com'on, Max, you're always staring at me like a big wet dog saying nothing. Sometimes I thought you'd forgotten how to speak. I was waiting for you to make a move.'

'But I did.'

She looked blankly at me for a moment and then smiled. 'Oh, you mean the jam and scones!'

'Maybe it wasn't the best place to take you.'

'No, I liked it. It made me laugh.'

I'd felt so stupid that afternoon at the coffee shop– the memory of it now was making me feel uncomfortable. 'But you told me you were going out with Kayne Bender.' I said.

'Why didn't you warn me about him?'

'I did.'

'You said he was a really nice guy.'

'Did I? I don't remember it.'

I wanted to be clear what Astral meant. 'So you were waiting for me to make a move?'

She ignored my question. 'But then you got off, if I remember rightly, with Kastrina. What was I to think?'

'Oh Astral. That was a mistake – you know that. Haven't I suffered enough?'

'Well, it didn't help. Max, my opinion of you dropped. Then there was Justine.'

'How did you know about Justine?'

'Everybody knows about Justine. But that's not the point. You didn't ask me.'

I was at a loss. I didn't understand 'Astral, why didn't you say...?'

She shrugged. 'I don't know. You were always getting off with somebody else. I had severe doubts about your taste in women.'

'Taste in women! Astral, all I ever wanted was you!'

'Ere skip, while you're at the bar, mine's a pint.' I didn't even have to turn round to know who was interrupting this brief moment of rapture.

'In a funny sort of way,' said Lee, 'I'll be sorry to see you go.'

I was astounded. First Astral, now Lee. This was a plot; they were in it together. They were taking the piss.

'Yeah, well, I'll miss you too, Lee.' In truth, until now I hadn't for a second considered that I'd miss Lee one little bit.

'You're sort of different, with your posh voice, your tea shops and your funny clothes.'

'I haven't got a posh voice.'

'Well you don't speak like you're from round 'ere. You sound more like that Bamber whatshisface on University Challenge.'

'You watch University Challenge?'

'You saying I'm thick or something?'

'I just didn't expect you to.'

'Well I prefer the Krypton Factor. I'm thinking of going on that.' The Krypton Factor was a quiz show in track suits. It featured pub bores rolling around an assault course and then doing one of those back-page comic book quizzes. I knew if I said anything more it would sound snobbish or hurtful. I changed the subject.

'And what's wrong with my clothes? Have you had a look in the mirror recently? What about the stuff you wear? Look at you – you look like a ... footballer. I'm surprised you haven't got a perm.'

Lee gave a shocked look that indicated that he had indeed considered this.

'I think a perm can look good on a man.'

'Well, that's a matter of opinion.'

'I'm not saying there's anything wrong with you, Max. Sometimes it's interesting to hear what you and Ash are speaking about. Mostly you talk a load of old guff, though.'

I was beginning to understand why Lee would miss me. It wasn't for the sake of companionship; it was more out of curiosity. At least he didn't say I was sweet.


I could hear a voice shouting through the noise of the crowd.

'Cheers comrade, send our solidarity to the Freedom Fighters.'

I raised a glass to Che, who was leaving with Bolton Bob and The Other One. Over the last couple of weeks I'd noticed a change of mood in the anarchist camp. Che's credibility had taken a surge since – in his words – he'd trashed the computer room. I'd heard Che say to the comrades 'There's nothing like a spot of Luddite action to raise the spirits.'

I raised a clenched fist and shouted back, 'Thanks, lads – I'll remember your advice about the llamas.' I realised even after all this time I'd never had the opportunity to ask them what it was all about – for the moment the mysteries of the anarchist ideology were to remain a closed book. But they'd already gone. It was 1.55 and they started work again at 2.00pm.

'Well, Lee, you look after Astral. She likes you.'

A big smile cut across Lee's face. 'Does she now.'

'Of course she does. She thinks you're the cat's testicles.'

'There you go – you're talking posh again.'

'Lee, is that how you think posh people talk?'

'I ain't never heard that expression before.'

'Maybe not. Anyhow Lee, here's your pint of Scratch. Cheers!'

My resolution from many months ago to be nice to Lee had been broken as soon as I had made it. This was the first time that I had ended a conversation with Lee without telling him to piss off.

'I'm trying to say goodbye to Astral. Be a good fellow and fuck off.'

Well, maybe not.


'And,' Astral added, 'sometimes I quite fancy you.'

Now this was unexpected.

'What?

'Shhh. You heard'

To my surprise Astral moved her hand down my back and slid the tops of her fingers into the back pocket of my Wranglers….'And we never did get to do the bandage practice,' said Astral gently pummelling her fingers.

I didn't get it. Was she telling me that I had stood a chance? Why now? When I'm about to travel to the other side of the world. How had I got it all so very wrong? Why had I been worried about making a fool of myself? I'd been such a prat not to make a move.


When I joined the scrum at the bar to get in last orders, something familiar happened. A hand was put across my eyes and a voice whispered, 'guess who?' Judging by the whiff of the stable and the large breasts pushed into my back I was in no doubt who it was.

'Couldn't handle it eh?' she breathed into my ear. 'You college-boy quitter,' she taunted.

I then felt a hand snake round my waist and glide into my pocket. I was wondering just what was going on. How come I was in demand all of a sudden? Until now I'd never made the connection. Menial low status jobs are a turn-off. Nobody really shags the milkman; a government minister, however loathsome, is another matter. Had I become emasculated during my time at Union Street? If I had, I was glad to see that the process was reversible.

'Get off, Kastrina.'

'How did you know it was me?' she asked, sounding annoyed.

'Who else could it be?'

'I just wanted to say goodbye.'

'Well be a good girl and say goodbye like everybody else. To my face, not my pants.'

It was well past two o'clock when Astral came over to say goodbye. As I held out my arms to give her a hug, I involuntarily scanned the room over her shoulder to see if Lee was watching.

'Bring me something back from your travels?' she whispered.

I was choked. 'I will.'

I held her tight. She smelt like new mown hay. It was as if we were back at the Christmas party.

'Come back soon, Max.'

'Yeah.' I couldn't speak.

'I've got to go.' She was already late.

Perhaps the Ministry of Work wasn't such a bad place after all. Maybe I could cancel my flight.

## ~ FIFTY FOUR ~

'Okay man, before you disappear off to South America I want to ask you something.'

The team had gone back to work. Ash, however, as my mentor, felt duty bound to stay behind to keep me company.

In my mind I was still replaying my conversation with Astral and wondering why I was in such a hurry to leave.

'You know Ash, they're not a bad bunch of people really,' I said.

I still had Paul Simon's words spinning in my head. 'Cathy I'm lost' – I said though I knew she was sleeping.'

'They're a bunch of bastards.' Ash replied.

'Come on, they've all got something good about them.'

'You are pissed. What's Kastrina got that's good about her. Apart from her tits. Or Feltch and Bart. They're evil fuckwits, man. And you know it.'

'What about Lee, he's all right.' I wanted to tell Ash about Astral, but I knew he'd come out with his 'she's too good for a sorry-arse like you' put-down.

'Max, you have really lost the plot. Lee's the biggest arsehole of the lot.'

'Oh come on, they all mean well in their own right.'

'Forget them. Move on. Anyway, I want to know about your secret.'

'My secret?'

'The one that Mr Blunt knows about. You know, Max, I told you mine; about how I'm on the run from the Railway Police. I want to hear yours.'

'Ah yes. Things have been happening so fast in the last few days that I haven't had a chance to give you some very important news. Something that affects both you and me – big time.'

'Affects me? Big time?'

'Big fucking time. Sure. Very much so, and it sort of ties in with my secret.'

'So what is your secret?'

It's to do with when I did my Jack Kerouac thing in the States a couple of years ago.'

'The time that guy gave you a head job in the desert.'

'He offered, but I didn't accept.' I said firmly. Sometimes I wished I hadn't told Ash about this incident. 'Now do you want to hear this or not? This is important.'

'Go ahead.'

'Anyhow,' I said, coming back to the original subject 'the night before I flew to New York I stayed with my friends Boz and Susie in Greenford.

Well, Boz and I were lying on the floor listening to Jimi and admiring the artex ceiling. That artex is brilliant stuff – you can stare at it for hours. We were seeing animals and all sorts in the swirling patterns. Endless free entertainment, I tell you. Anyhow, Susie gets the frights. She starts pacing around, freaking out that we're going to get busted, that she'll get sacked. She was sure the flat was being staked-out and that somebody was going through the bins. Paranoia whoa! She was really losing it. "Being busted for dope, " she said, "isn't exactly a good career move when you're a probation officer." "It would add credibility to your career," I suggested. "Not with the people who pay my wages. " I tried to calm her down, but she yelled that "I was a no-hope, weak, lazy, good for nothing soap-dodging hippie." I thought the soap dodging-part was a bit out of order, actually.'

'So I said, "Look Susie, man, cool it. Get me a plastic bag and I'll take the evidence with me." I emptied the ashtray and put the bag of butt-ends in my trench-coat pocket. "OK, happy?" Well she wasn't, but that was all I could do. Bad scene.'

'As far as I was concerned it was all quickly forgotten. The next morning Boz gave me a lift to the airport and I was on my way. I was feeling really good as I checked in my bags – you know that exciting edgy exhilaration you get when you're off on your travels. The world's yours, plans are flexible and it's just up to you.

'Things, however, started to go downhill as I went through emigration. As I handed the man my passport he leant forward in a friendly way and asked: "Do you know how much money you're allowed to take out of the country? "

I wasn't expecting a question like this. What was going on? Was he asking for help with his crossword or something?

"No idea. What is this? A general knowledge quiz? " I joked.

'This wasn't the answer he was wanting.'

"I think we'd better have a little chat," the official said in his pleasant-enough home counties voice. "Would you come this way please? "

'We walked towards a door marked interview room. Another man, who had appeared behind me, followed us in. I wasn't particularly worried – who has ever heard of somebody being stopped leaving the country?'

"I have to warn you that under the Exchange Control Act the maximum amount of currency you are allowed to take out of the United Kingdom over a period of 12 months is £300. Can you please show me the contents of your wallet."

'£300!! Fat chance. All I'd got was £90.00 in Travellers Cheques. As I reached into my coat to pull out my wallet, my fingers touched – ever so slightly, but it was definitely there – the thin soft skin of a polythene bag. I could feel the colour drain out of my face.

"Mr Redcliffe, are you all right?" There was a roaring noise in my head, I felt faint.

"Yes," I shouted, over the spinning whine in my ears.

The man looked through my wallet. Please, please, please, ask me any question. Any question. Even questions on football. But don't ask me to empty my pockets.

"Well, everything seems to be in order there. No problem."

Thank you God. Thank you God.

"I think," came a voice from behind, "we ought to see what else Mr Redcliffe has in his pockets."

'Oh Shit!'

'So what happened?' asked Ash.

'It's almost too embarrassing to talk about. The customs men thought it was hilarious. A plastic bag full of roaches – being smuggled OUT of the country. Well, in short I missed my flight and was booked to appear at Uxbridge Court the next day. They thought I was such an idiot they didn't put me in custody, they even gave me back my passport. I could hear them laughing at me as I closed the door.

'But you did get to the States?'

'Well yes, I did. In retrospect I can't believe it. Like you, I ignored my appearance at the court. I couldn't take it seriously. I'd been so stupid; it didn't seem real. I turned up at the airport the next day and said I had missed the flight, and was there any chance of going today. To my surprise they said yes. And that was it. I was on the next flight. The whole thing seemed like a dream. Maybe they hadn't had time to process the paper work; or it was a different shift. I'd still got my visa, so how were they to know what had happened the day before. Shit, I don't know how I got to be on that plane, but I did. Anyhow, what I'm saying is… that I've been wanted by the fuzz ever since.'

'Join the club, man.'

'But here comes the interesting bit. When I had my little set-to with Mr Blunt the other day and we were running round the desk playing 'catch me if you can,' he dropped my file. My papers scattered everywhere. I was able to have a good look at them. My file appeared to contain nothing more than a random pile of scrap paper, notes and old computer printouts. At first, I couldn't understand it. There was nothing of relevance about me, or my past, in that file. I then realised that this ever-growing file had been a sham – it was a fake.'

'So you're saying our files are just a load of crap.'

'You got it. You see, Blunt just pretends that he knows something about you. We all have dreams, and we all have secrets. Even Mother Theresa has done something she's not proud of. The more innocent the person, the more ashamed they are of their indiscretions. But Blunt knows nothing. It's part of his plan; he doesn't want us to leave. With these targets he keeps on telling us about, he needs all the staff he can get. The problem for him is that nobody in their right mind wants to work at Union Street. So he has to use veiled threats and innuendo to make people stay.'

Of course Mr Blunt was unknowingly aided and abetted in his mission by Baxter. He capitalised on Baxter's paranoiac world where everybody is being watched and everything you've ever done is recorded. Baxter, with his crazy ideas, unwittingly encouraged us to believe that Mr Blunt knew all about our past. It must have been with a heavy heart that he got rid of Baxter. But eventually Baxter had got too weird, even for Blunt's plans.

I could feel a wide smile on my face. I had that exhilarating end-of-term feeling. 'Ash, the bloater knows jack-all. We're free.' I sat back and spread my arms along the top of the velour sofa. For the first time in ten months I felt I had a future; I could run, I could breathe, I could see colours, I had a life ahead of me.

Ash put the lid back on his tin. He was acting calmly – or else he was in shock.

'I'll miss you,' Ash said

'Ash, don't you understand? The scut knows jack all. About you or me. He knows nothing about the Fat Controller. Don't let him get away with it.'

'Sure, I'm just taking this news in. This sudden vision of freedom does your head in.'

I could understand what Ash was thinking. After all the warnings he had given me about getting sucked into the system it didn't seem right that he was the one left behind. There's nothing worse than seeing a mate leave – and in the process realising that you're the one who's stuck. I'm sure he was pleased for me, but I bet he couldn't help feeling that the leaving party should have been his.

'Ash, I'll miss you too. Are you going to be okay?'

'Sure I'm going to be okay. You know me, I've got a plan.'

'Yeah, of course. Don't forget the X ray specs syndrome,' I said.

'I'm out of here way before that happens.'

'Make sure you are. I don't want to have to come back and get you.'

'You won't have to do that, man, I can assure you.'

## ~ FIFTY FIVE ~

I could imagine the conversation:

MR BLUNT: Remind me Miss Klebb how long has he been with us?

KASTRINA: Ten months – nearly a year.

MR BLUNT: Nearly a year. I didn't expect him to stay for that long. They rarely do.

KASTRINA: I felt he was beginning to outstay his welcome.

MR BLUNT: You're right. After six months his cynicism was beginning to poison the system. And he'd started doing silly things

KASTRINA: He was certainly getting to Lee. I could see that Lee was becoming quite unsettled. I think we're getting rid of him just in time.

MR BLUNT: There's nothing like a counter riot to help staff re-evaluate their career.

For a couple of seconds neither of them speak. Yet there is a silent conversation going on – they both understand exactly what each other is saying.

KASTRINA: Yes, the storming of the counter worked out far better than I had expected.

MR BLUNT: Are we anticipating anyone else leaving in the near future?

KASTRINA: Ashley Hill will be next.

MR BLUNT: About time. He's well overdue. If he doesn't show signs of resigning soon, you might have to help him on his way as well.

KASTRINA: I give him a couple of months – at the most. Did you hear that Redcliffe found the Archie Leach file?

Mr Blunt flaps his hand as if he is brushing some crumbs away.

MR BLUNT: Everybody knows that. I understand he got a good price too. I thought I had hidden it well. But obviously not.'

Kastrina leaves.

Mr Blunt views his in-tray and allows himself the luxury of a moment's reflection. The news is good. The unemployment figures are still edging up and are predicted to reach the 2 million mark by 1980. He feels proud to be working in one of the government's most dynamic departments.

Of course he is still annoyed by Redcliffe's attack. But it's one of those things a manager has to put up with. It's happened before and more than likely it will happen again  He needs these people.

He is concerned about Baxter. Over the years the unceasing abuse on the counter had slowly worn him down. For a while, after he'd been moved to an easier job on reception, Baxter appeared to be back to his old self. But there had been murmurings and complaints about Baxter's increasingly bizarre behaviour. The whispering, the notes to staff, the fantasies came to a head when the pest control people arrived to deal with the rats in the courtyard. Eventually it got to a stage where Baxter's hallucinations could no longer be tolerated and he had to go. It was unsettling for everybody when Dr Hammer called in the men from the hospital. Mr Blunt was sorry about that.

He reaches for the last piece of paper in his in-tray. An application form. He scans it for ten seconds and throws it on his desk in disgust. Another sybaritic student. He stares at the grey wall for a moment and then pulls the form towards him and writes on the top of the paper. 'No interview required. Start A.S.A.P.'

## ~ FIFTY SIX ~

As I walked along the street I thought about Astral. I yearned to climb with her to the realms of beyond. I wanted her as a soul mate. I wanted us to read the same books – the Beats, the good Doctor, Tim Robbins and Nabokov – and listen to Bob Dylan and Loose Windscreen, and laugh at the same jokes. She was truly a goddess. I thought about all this, but most of all I thought about her fantastic body and the mind-blowing sex we would have together.

I glanced back at the Dole office. It was my first experience of a proper job. Is that what all work is like, I wondered.

I wanted to get home and pack. Large thunderclouds were building up in the west; the weather was stifling – the air seemed heavy and lacking in oxygen. As I walked past the police station I heard a yell from across the road. The shout came from Otto Grolier who was waving a quart bottle of cider at me.

"ere, want a drink?'

I held no animosity towards Grolier. Indeed, as Ash had pointed out, it was doubtful if he even remembered kicking me.

'No thanks mate, I'm leaving.' I shouted.

For the first time in months I could feel the weight lifting. I didn't want to work at Union Street anymore. Nor, and this hit me from nowhere, did I ever want to sign-on again. I'd had it with free loading. I'd been sleepwalking. 'Hit Me with a Flower' was self-justifying naivety. And Tina Turner could bog off. Who did she think she was? I wasn't sure about Ash's grand plan – that would come later. I knew however that it was time to start making my own luck. It was as if I'd suddenly woken up and thought – yeah, I want some of that.

I didn't know what I'd do after South America. I did know that I needed to move on and do something with my life. After I'd come back for Astral.

Grolier waved and staggered on his way. I don't know if he'd even heard what I said. But I wondered at my words – and punched the air. Yes, I really am leaving.

## ~ FIFTY SEVEN ~

The plane climbed over the Staines reservoirs. I pressed my cheek against the window and picked out the features in the landscape I knew so well. Running parallel to the M4 I spotted the A40 and the swirl of suburbia that made Ruislip. For a second I swore I could even see the tiny thread of a road that would have been Cherry Tree Avenue.

It was a perfect September morning: mellow, clear and bright. On the ground the air was warm, but tinged with a pinch of autumn. It was 7.30 am and the long shadows of the early hours accentuated the flow of the landscape.

The hot summer – the driest on record – had come to an end the evening I finished work. Thunder rolled around the Avon valley as I packed my bags, and then the clouds opened and roof-hammering rain fell throughout the night.

The dustbowl countryside had quickly recovered and was now a deep grass green, intermittently broken by yellow fields of recently harvested corn. Clumps of trees glowed with an autumnal radiance. I could follow the thin roads from town to town, and imagined thousands of people dragging themselves from their beds, preparing for their day of brown drudgery. I felt lucky and excited. I had nothing incriminating in my pockets this time. I thought I could recognise the sweep of Chesil Beach, tinged with white breakers. And then the land disappeared. For hours, all I could see was a flat slate grey sea – vast and empty. A lonely tanker cut its way across the wide ocean. I thought about Justine and wondered if she had ever got beyond St Malo. I dozed; I dreamt of Owen opening the envelope containing £100 along with a note – ' Buy yourself some fresh chocolate'; I dreamt of Astral and our farewell kiss ...I thought about her parting words 'come back soon Max,' It wasn't that easy to ditch the fantasy girlfriend after all. But I was already moving on, I was thinking ahead, not back. Maybe Ash was right, perhaps 'getting the knowledge' was the key. But I didn't want to think about that right now.

I felt good, I felt free. It was like the vast summers that seemed to stretch for eternity when I'd been a student. Those long empty days offered so much promise and freedom. Sure, I was nervous, I had little idea what to expect when I stepped onto the tarmac at Georgetown Airport on the banks of the Demerara River. Years later I would reflect how easy it had been to leave Union Street. Why had it taken me so long? Well, money for a start. But was that really what was holding me back? Is this what happens? The rut gets deeper and the fear of doing something new gets stronger. And yet in the end it was that simple. When you're young and have no commitments, it is your duty, you owe it to yourself, to get up off your arse and explore the world.

It must have been eight hours later when the ocean changed colour, to dark blue, to emerald – to the colour of a peacock's neck. And then pure white sand. A string of islands, so beautiful, so perfect.

At Port of Spain – Trinidad – the air smelt of wood smoke and cinnamon. In the airport lounge, little bigger than a garden shed, I drank my first Carib Beer while I waited for my connecting flight to Guyana. In the bar I got chatting to a nervous hippie who had visited Jonestown. 'It's a scary shithole, man. Crazy, crazy people. The dark heart of South America. Jim Jones, the guy who runs the place, is a head case,' he warned. What was it that Cynthia had said?

It was night now; I was tired. Once I got to Guyana I had little idea what I was going to do. But I didn't care – the Caribbean warmth made me relaxed...

I flew over the Orinoco River in the dark. At Georgetown, as I climbed from the plane and stepped onto the runway, I could feel I was on another continent. The night was loud with the sound of tree frogs croaking like squeaky doors. An aroma of peat and vegetation permeated the moist air; you could sense that the Amazon jungle was not far away.

On the runway, at my feet, I noticed the biggest moth I'd ever seen. I bent down to take a closer look. Its wingspan must have been the size of a small bird. It was black and yellow, with a skull motif on its abdomen – a Death's Head Hawkmoth; a harbinger of bad luck. I wanted to pick it up and admire it, but remembered the anarchists warning about entomological activities.

Then the orange light of dawn began to spread across a wide tropical sky. I had escaped – to my lost world.

## ~ AFTERWORD ~

### BRISTOL 2001

'*So who was that?*' asked Grace as she pushed a strand of rich raven hair behind her left ear.

'*That man was one of my claimants – you know, from when your Mum and I worked at the Dole Office here in Bristol.*'

'*Oh.*'

'*It's strange, but I was glad to see him. Even now I wonder what happened to some of them. They were living on the edge of an abyss, so near the brink. For a moment I felt united by a strange bond. Even if we have nothing to say to each other, it's good to know some survive.*'

'* It was a funny time. Looking back on it I am grateful for it. And at least I met your Mum.*'

Grace stopped listening and stared at the menu intently. *There's nothing more nauseating than the details of parental romance.*

I changed the subject. '*Seeing him took me back twenty-five years. You wouldn't believe how different it was in the 1970s. It was before Thatcher. Before Punk. Before Rap. Before Hip Hop. Before Drum and Bass.*'

'*Dad, you are so embarrassing!*'

'*Okay. Before Microsoft. Bill Gates was still at Harvard.*'

'*Before Mobile phones?*'

'*Yeah, definitely before mobile phones. Before IKEA even. Well, in England anyway.*'

Grace looked at me with pity, as if my life had only been half lived. '*I'm glad I wasn't around then,*' she said.

'*You know what I mean. The little things were the big things in those days.*'

'*And what happened when you went to South America?*' Grace knew the answer, but she always seemed to like hearing the story. '*Didn't something awful happen at Jonestown?*'

'Well, in the end I never got to Jonestown. I had this churning stomach upset – Montezuma's revenge. I was incapacitated for days. It meant that I never got to my intended destination. It was the best thing that could have happened to me. You see, the Jonestown community was lead by a messianic nutter and some funny things were happening there. The Jonestown settlers all ended up killing themselves. They drank cyanide; they put it in the Kool-Aid. Men, women and children, they lay down and died with their arms around each other – mass suicide, hundreds dead.'

'Oh my God!' exclaimed Grace 'that's dreadful.'

'I probably wouldn't be here now if I hadn't got the screaming abdabs.'

'Dad! We're in a restaurant!'

Grace was respectfully silent for a moment and then asked what has really been on her on mind all this time.

'But Dad, why did you take a drink from that awful bottle?'

'I know it sounds stupid but sometimes a little gesture like that's important. It was the acknowledgement of some small bond. Everybody craves respect, however far they've fallen. But, God, it was disgusting – Bootleg Baileys they call it – ethanol and condensed milk. The ethanol probably comes out of the back door of the hospital. You've got to be rock bottom, really rock bottom to drink that stuff.'

'You might at least have wiped the top of the bottle.'

'Anyway, I'm here to hear about you,' I said, changing the conversation. I'd had my fill of thinking about the past; they were different times. That was then. This is now.

I cut through the flaky crust of my venison and ale pie. 'How's University? What are you up to?'

~ WHERE ARE THEY NOW? ~

Twenty-five years on and it took some time to track down the whereabouts of colleagues and claimants.

Here's what I found:

**Owen:** retired in 1978. He died six months later from a dust related lung disease.

**Ash:** I am still in contact with Ash. Three months after I flew to South America, he left the Ministry of Work and got a Training Opportunities Grant to train as a Computer Systems Analyst. He was right about the symbiotic relationship between man and machine. (And I was wrong about root vegetables.) After making bin loads of money he has recently retired – at the age of 50 – from full-time work. He now divides his time between his cottage in North Wales and his home in the idyllic Chew Valley, near Bristol, where he has a small business making wrought iron garden furniture.

**Astral:** when I returned from my travels she wasn't there. I should have known. Apparently she retrained as a reflexologist. I have no idea where she is now – though I sometimes wonder. Even after all these years.

**Eric Blunt MBE:** did indeed climb his golden staircase and held the rank of Principal Officer in the regional office in Plymouth when he retired in 1999. In the millennium year he was awarded the MBE for his services to the unemployed.

**Che:** lectures in social sciences at one of the new 'portacabin' Universities. I get a Christmas card from him every year.

**Lee Woods:** was appointed manager of Westbury-on-Trym Job Centre in 1991. He is married with two children. He continues to support Bristol Rovers.

**Kastrina:** following several official complaints about her behaviour towards claimants she was moved to Human Resources – where she continues to work as a senior manager.

**Kinsale twins:** after a brief period of fame in the 1980s as guitar makers to the stars, life has now settled down. One of them, who knows which, continues to build musical instruments of great beauty. The other works as a dental technician from a shed in his backyard.

**Baxter Malone:** was assimilated back into the community in the late 1980s. For a while he lived in a bed and breakfast in Weston-super-Mare. I don't know where he is now.

**Justine:** hey, we got it together! Soon after I returned from South America we shacked up. She had come back from her travels not long after I left Bristol. She had made it as far as Spain. Our relationship lasted a stormy seven years during which time we had two children. She now manages a pub in Clifton; one of the few pubs in Bristol that still sells real draught cider. She also has a unique collection of 'World Ciders' including bottles from South Africa, Kazakhstan and Patagonia – complete with apple worm. Don't mention this book to her. She says she was 'cruelly misrepresented – it wasn't like that.'

**Otto Grolier:** continues to work his patch at the top of Park Street. If you see him, buy him a sandwich and say hello from me.

The whereabouts of the other Ministry of Work staff and claimants are unknown.

**Max Redcliffe:** And me? On my return from South America I got my hair cut and enrolled on a post-graduate course that majored in social anthropology. Justine and I had little money but they were good times.

1976 had been the threshold of a new age. Mr Blunt was right about unemployment. By the 1980s numbers had rocketed from one million to three million. And then mysteriously they started to decline. And where were those jobs being created? As Ash had predicted, computers were the future – though they didn't get rid of the crap jobs. The Thatcherite philosophy of the 1980s and 1990s killed the loafer lifestyle I had lived as a student and after.

I still ask myself whether I would have gone ahead with the fraud if I hadn't uncovered Cary Grant's claim? Was it another fantasy – the sort of lifeline you grab onto when you're plummeting into a dark hole? I'm glad I didn't have to wait around to find out.

I now work as a social anthropologist specialising in South American civilisations. Thankfully, Union Street was my only experience of working for the civil service. Though I have occasionally been contracted to work as a freelancer for the Department Of Development Overseas (DODO). You may see my name on the credits of TV travel programmes.

# ~ ACKNOWLEDGEMENTS ~

This is for slackers everywhere. Save your energy for that moment, whenever it is. You'll know when it comes – and you'll be ready for it.

Along the way I've had support from many people. *'Where's My Money?'* started from a germ of an idea at one of Claire Williamson's Imagination Stations. It was nursed along in Annie's Salon – with the help and encouragement of Annie McGann, Rich Garford, Trevor Coombes and Christina Zaba. Catherine Mason asked me some interesting and stimulating questions. Hilary Arundale provided editorial advice and on-going long distance support. Pete Harper entertained me with a nice turn of phrase and also provided me with the story about the kneecaps. Andy Borthwick guided me through a life changing time in Guyana. Gill Marles did the typographic wizardry.

Thanks to Jill Moss and Mike Houghton for the use of Stepiau for what I thought was the final sprint, but turned out to be the halfway mark. Also to Alan and Jennie Brown for their Normandy retreat Le Mee with its memorable view from the rubbish tip of Mont St Michel. Challis, as always, who gave me the courage. Wish you could be here now, Chris.

Support was also supplied by Liz Reece, Ruth Ennals, Alex Shearer, Lesley Woodward, Keith Scott of Islington Central Reference Library (www.askalibrarian), Mike Mills, Exeter Central Library. Also thanks to shed builder Steve McAllister for providing shelter from the storm.

I have fond memories of sitting in our study for many hours with Matt and Hannah – them playing on the computer, me writing. They were the best company I could have had, even when I had to tell them to turn the volume down. And finally – all my love to Maggie for endless support, ideas, encouragement and space.

*Chantry Cottage, Aldbourne, 11 August 2007.*